YOUR LOVIN

*Mr Logan's Daughters have been so good to me.
They asked if they could call me Rose and I said
of course my dears. Joan has already invited me
to her large Norfolk farmhouse for Christmas.
She was shocked to hear I was all on my own
last year and wants to make it up to me.
Kathleen is quite the most beautiful girl and
always so well turned out. She has promised to
lengthen those lounge curtains I've been so
worried about. She said she was surprised you've
never offered to alter them for me Caroline but I
told her you've never been clever with a needle
like she is. Well we can't all be good at the same
things in life can we? I just count myself
fortunate to have two such wonderful new
Daughters . . .*

Caroline's relationship with her mother had
always been stormy but that summer her own
daughter, Juliette, turned sixteen and she learned
a lot about family life . . .

Your Loving Mother
DEANNA MACLAREN

SPHERE BOOKS LIMITED
30/32 Gray's Inn Road, London WC1X 8JL

First published in Great Britain by
Sphere Books Ltd 1983
Copyright © 1983 by Deanna Maclaren

For my mother,
with love and heartfelt thanks
for not inspiring me to write this book.

The poem on page 40 was written by
Stephanie Fawbert (aged 15).

TRADE
MARK

Set in Plantin

Printed and bound in Great Britain by
Hunt Barnard Printing Ltd., Aylesbury, Bucks.

1

... don't worry about me I shall be all right on my own this Christmas. I have made myself a small pudding just big enough for one. I put some brandy in it. Not that I usually have liquor in the house. I only keep it for trifles and Funerals. I am not accepting your invitation as it would be too perilous a journey through the snows of Winter. Although Xmas is traditionally a time for Families to be together I know you have a lot of friends who will ask you out and I don't want to be in the way. It's too cold for me to venture out much now. At my age (sixty-four next Birthday!) I can't take any risks. I don't go further than the post office near the cemetery to collect my Widow's Pension. I don't get much but enclosed is £5 for you to buy my Granddaughter a little something. Please give my Best Regards to Leonard. Will sign off now as it is time for my Tablets. (Nerves still bad. Dr Stewart is worried about me but I tell him how you always say I'll live to be a hundred.

I am, as always, Your Loving Mother.

Laughing, Len skims the blue Basildon Bond back to his wife across the glass-topped dressing table. 'The usual seasonal message of joy and optimism. It's being so cheerful that keeps your mother going.'

'Don't sit on the quilt, Leo,' murmurs Caroline absently. 'You'll crush the down. We'll have to go up and see her in the New Year.'

Damn. He shouldn't have taken the piss out of the old girl's letter. Len pads across to the wardrobe. 'All right. But I don't see why she can't come down for Christmas. All she has to do is park herself on the inter-city from Edinburgh and I'll meet her with the car at King's Cross. No sweat. The way she writes you'd think we were forcing her to cross Siberia by mule. Have you seen my silver cuff links?'

'Third drawer down.' Caroline winds a strand of long dark hair onto a heated roller. 'You know what she's like. She enjoys being miserable. It gives her immense pleasure making me feel guilty at the thought of the brave grey-haired widow basting a pathetic single turkey portion with her hot, lonely tears.'

Len hurls a pile of socks onto the carpet. 'They're not here. And what's all this about her nerves? She's not cracking up, is she?'

'Of course not. When we were up there in the summer I had a word with Dr Stewart. He assured me that mother's fighting fit. The pills he gives her are just placebos. Swallowing handfuls of them each day gives her something to do ... they *are* there, Leo. You haven't looked.'

'I *have* looked, damnit.'

Calmly, Caroline moves to the wardrobe and throws the silver cuff links onto the bed. 'What do you want these for anyway? Surely you're not going to wear a suit? You know Miles always dresses casually.'

'All day at work I'm togged up in a filthy printer's apron. When I go out in the evening I like to wear something decent. I shall feel more at ease in a suit.' Len regards his wife, carefully smoothing what looks like beige Polyfilla on to her cheeks. 'What about you, then? With all your new-fangled Women's Lib talk, why are you daubing on war paint?'

'Because I admit I lack both the bone structure and the confidence to go without. Besides, Annabel will be aglow with all the latest make-up from Harrods' beauty counter.'

'Make-up? Embalming fluid more like.'

'That's unfair. She's the same age as me. And at least I won't look out of place, as you will in that suit!'

'Even if I decked up in Miles's fancy silk lounging pyjamas she'd still make me feel like something the cat sicked up.'

'That's absurd. Annabel is one of our oldest friends.'

'One of *your* oldest friends.'

Right from the word go, Len reflects as he takes his shower, he and Caroline have never hit it off with regard to their friends.

'What a laugh,' Len remarked, years ago, studying the guest list for their first party. 'All your lot are called Samantha, Giles and Nigel, and all mine are Bert, Bill and Coral.'

'Who's Coral?'

'Just a girl at work.'

'You've fucked her.'

'Course I haven't.' Course he had. Tasty little piece she'd been, too. 'Don't tell me you're jealous?'

Caroline went for him then, all wild eyes and tearing claws. He pulled down her pants and he had her over the back of the sofa. She screamed blue murder. But she didn't tell him to stop.

Just for devilment, Len did not cross Coral's name off the guest list. He hoped Caroline would lose her rag again so they could enjoy an action replay over the sofa. But his new young wife appeared to have forgotten about Coral – until she turned up at the party.

He couldn't help feeling sorry for the girl. Coral had shellacked her brittle blonde hair and come in a low-cut dress that resembled crumpled carbon paper. Caroline treated her like something new at the zoo.

'Nigel, do come and meet Coral!' she shrieked. 'She's an old friend of Leo's. Darling, did you make that lovely dress yourself? I thought so. How clever of you to get such a close fit.'

Bitch, thought Len. Coral had a rotten time, got legless on vodka, and was taken home and screwed by one Nigel or another – probably both. Coral got her own back by giving him a rough ride at the works the following Monday.

'Well, hello there, *Leo*!' she crooned. 'From the look of your lioness on Saturday I'd say we'll soon be congratulating you on the arrival of a sweet little cub. And how long is it since you two set up a den together ... a month?'

Caroline always insisted on calling him Leo. 'Darling, I can't possibly tell my parents I'm going to marry a Len. Besides, Leo sounds noble and masterful.'

Caroline's mother disagreed. When compelled to acknowledge his existence, she would refer to him as Leonard – as if, he thought bitterly, he were some poncy hairdresser.

Len turns the shower to cold, then grabs a towel. To hell with the lot of them. I've done all right. I earn a good screw. I've got an XJ6, a comfortable pad and a classy looking wife with long legs and big knockers. And I'm fitter than most of

3

the weeds my teenage daughter hangs out with. Not bad for a bloke who's pushing forty.

He rubs the towel over the steamy mirror and examines the six foot length of his body. Len considers he's in excellent shape, thanks to a daily jog through the woods and an occasional work-out at the gym. Miles once offered to put him up for the Guildford golf club, but Len scotched that one.

'I work in the print, Miles. It's noisy and dirty but at least it's honest money in my hand at the end of the week. I don't need to arse lick for business contacts.'

Easing on his grey suit, Len watches Caroline zipping up a dress made of some soft red material with a hole in the front that reveals a generous slice of cleavage. For a moment Len is tempted. But sixteen years of marriage have thrown up too many barriers. Caroline is no longer the type of woman to tolerate being jumped on over the back of a sofa. Besides, he reasons, studying her more closely, she's corralled herself in a pantie girdle.

He compromises: 'You look nice, love.'

'Thanks. So do you.'

They smile at one another, like wary politicians photographed at a peace conference, both quietly confident that the truce will never last.

'What did you buy Annabel and Miles for Christmas?' asks Len, swinging the four-year-old Jaguar past the stone griffins guarding the Laceys' drive.

'A carriage clock to replace the one the au pair dropped in the dishwasher. And I made some mince pies for Annabel to hand round at her carol singers' party next week. She's an excellent cook, but hopeless at pastry. Which reminds me. If she serves up boeuf bourgignon, don't say, "This is a cracking stew, Annabel," like you did last time.'

'It was a compliment. I'm a connoisseur of stews. I make good ones myself.'

'There is more to a succulent casserole than sousing frying steak and curried beans with a bottle of Guinness.'

Len parks the car under the lantern by the oak front door of the converted coach house. He grins as he visualises the scene next week when the local children arrive to sing their carols. Annabel fondly regards the occasion as perpetuating a charming feudal tradition, whereby the lady of the manor extends largesse to poor village children who cluster round her, wide-eyed with gratitude. Conveniently, she prefers to ignore the fact that all the working class residents have long ago been driven out of the village by commuting trendies earning only marginally less bread than international lawyer Miles Lacey.

Len's daughter Juliette once donned a disguising anorak and joined the five carol singers. She reported that they stood ranged on either side of the inglenook, looking dutifully waiflike as they warbled 'Silent Night' through their mufflers. Annabel and her twin daughters, arrayed in long evening dresses, smiled gracious encouragement from the Chesterfield while Miles dipped into his velvet smoking jacket and handed each of the singers a 10p piece.

The Laceys, Len notes, are sporting three Christmas trees this year. The tallest dominates the extensive front lawn, spangled with enough lights to cause a power blackout in Guildford. Not that an electricity cut would phase Miles. Naturally, he has his own generator. By the patio doors in the sitting room glimmers a golden tree, laden with packages which bear witness to the versatility of Harrods' gift wrapping department.

The third tree, glistening with artificial frost, comes into view as Annabel invites them into the candlelit conservatory for dinner. Through the arched windows, Len counts twelve silver water lilies shimmering on the rippling water of the floodlit swimming pool.

Caroline clears her throat. Her dark brows are semaphoring a frantic message: *Stop gawping, Leo! Don't lean back against that tree or the silver frost will shower onto your jacket and Annabel will think you've got dandruff. Say something sociable. And forget the winter wonderland crack. You did that to death last year when Annabel invited an interior designer to do up the conservatory as an ice palace.*

Hastily, Len turns to Annabel and admires her dress. She is in her middle thirties, skewer thin, with red-gold hair expensively frizzed to resemble crinkle-cut potato chips.

Her dress, however, Len regards as a bit of all right. Plain black, and slit to the thigh. Just the sort of gear that would suit Caroline.

'I'm glad you like it,' Annabel murmurs, in her hot-buttered voice. 'But it's really such a desperately old rag. I should have given it to Oxfam years ago.' She pats her concave stomach and whispers to her husband as he dissects the crown roast, 'Just a tiny portion for me, darling. You know what they say: what goes in stays on.'

Len cheerfully accepts an enormous plateful of lamb and reflects on the misery of being a fashionable, wealthy woman. From his limited experience of the breed he knows they'll carelessly spend a mint on clothes, hair-dos, perfume and jewellery. But because of their figures, the one thing they daren't squander their husband's loot on is a good blow-out.

Miles sits down, and pushes up the sleeves of his truffle-coloured cashmere sweater. 'Take your jacket off, old boy. Make yourself at home.'

'I'm fine. Really.' Len helps himself to broccoli and earns a glare from Caroline for not offering it to Annabel first.

'Which way did you come?' asks Miles, carefully pouring three-quarter measures of Château Cheval Blanc into the crystal glasses.

'The usual route. Over the Hog's Back and right at the turn off,' replies Len, noting with satisfaction that Miles's thinning, newly permed hair is showing streaks of grey. 'But I got a bit bogged down in all the late night shopping traffic coming from Guildford.'

Miles nods. 'You'd have done better to detour along that B road. I'll show you on the map after dinner.'

'You mean that road that leads past the Green Man? Didn't you say you had a very good supper there recently, Caro?'

'Where?'

'The Green Man. On that B road near the Hog's Back.' Caroline looks glazed.

'You remember! You said you were coming back from Annabel's and stopped off at the pub for a leak.'

'I never said leak!'

6

'Quite right,' grins Miles. 'Ladies don't leak. They tinkle.'

'*Anyway*, you told me you dived in there and had some of their home-made chicken pie. I'm sure it was the Green Man.'

'What does it matter?' says Caroline irritably. 'It was just a pub. I can't recall now where it was or what I ate.' She turns to Annabel. 'How are the girls?'

'I didn't know the Green Man served hot food,' remarks Miles.

'They're fine. I've offloaded them onto their grand-mother tonight, and she's going to their end-of-term concert tomorrow. But of course they'll be moving on to secondary school in September, and then we're seriously considering taking them out of state education.' Annabel slices the fat from her lamb and piles it onto her sideplate.

'I think they've been taken over by new people. Caroline said the staff were very pleasant, and the food was great. Don't know about the beer, though. It used to be right swill there.'

'I thought the local grammar school had an excellent reputation.'

'I'm sure I remember reading in the local rag that the Green Man is a free house now. With any luck they'll be doing real ale.'

'It was superb in the days of the Eleven Plus. But the whole system has changed now. If they're lucky, the girls could be sent to the grammar school, but they might just as easily get dumped into that appalling comprehensive near the housing estate.'

'I think you'd have to go a long way to beat Badger's.'

'But don't you have any control, any influence at all over where they're sent?'

'I had a few jars of Holdens the other day while I was waiting for the car to be repaired. Bloody magnificent. Second strongest beer in Britain, you know. You have to hand it to this real ale – it makes you really reel.'

'Oh yes, you can write to the education authority setting out your reasons why you believe your children should attend a particular school. But as Miles pointed out to the

7

headmaster, everything depends on how articulately and persuasively you phrase your arguments. The whole thing has turned into an intelligence test for the parents, rather than the children.'

'Merc giving you trouble, then?'

'Frankly, with your financial resources, Annabel, I'm surprised you didn't send the girls to private school right from the start.'

'Oh, the Mercedes is fine. It was Annabel's little Renault I had to take in. She seems to imagine she'll wear out the clutch if she uses it too much.'

'You certainly believe in wearing out all the old jokes,' counters Annabel.

But Miles, too, is adroit at listening to two conversations at once. 'If the children were boys,' he tells Caroline, 'I suppose I would have put their names down for private schooling. But a good education isn't really as essential for girls, is it?'

Miles winks at Len as Caroline, bridling, rises to the bait and launches into her equal-rights-for-women lecture.

Len long ago accepted that he'd married a groupie. But being Caroline, there was no question of her joining the normal village societies like the W.I. or Young Home-makers.

'I can do without demonstrations on how to knit a balaclava helmet from left over spaghetti,' she scorned. 'I want to be useful and active in improving our community environment.'

When Juliette was a baby Caroline marched with a deputation to encourage the manager of Sainsbury's to set up a crèche. Later on, she sat down in the high street to goad the council into providing a zebra crossing. After that came the PTA, the Prisoners' Aid Association, and now Women's Lib.

The Butch Bunch, as Len refers to them, invade his front room on the third Thursday of every month. Len usually clears off to the pub and plays darts. Not that he feels threatened by all this liberation crap – it's just another fad of Caroline's which will pass, like all the rest. Len's main gripe about the bra-burning brigade is that as Caroline considers it demeaning to act the role of hostess and provide light refreshments for her guests, there is never any cake for him to eat up when he comes home from the pub.

'Magic cake this, Annabel. Chocolate. My favourite. All right if I help myself to another slice?'

'Gâteau, Leo,' breathes Caroline icily. 'It's chocolate *gâteau*.'

No one else is having seconds. They sit and watch him eat each mouthful of the creamy confection, Annabel toying politely with a teaspoonful of lemon sorbet to keep him company.

As he swallows the last crumb, Annabel rises and motions her guests into the oak-beamed sitting room. Miles stokes up the fire, taking logs from the rush basket specially woven for him by a marvellous little man in Norfolk.

'Such a character. You wouldn't believe. Can't imagine how he makes a living at those prices. Now, what'll you have, old man? Cognac, port, scotch ... ?'

Len is thirsting for a beer. 'Scotch will be fine.'

Annabel passes him coffee in what looks like a gilded eggcup. Len finds it impossible to slip his finger through the fragile fluted handle.

Christmas presents are exchanged. There is a Gucci handbag for Caroline, a leather-bound road atlas for Len, and a pretty Liberty print waistcoat to take home for Juliette.

Annabel kicks off her black suede sandals, and wriggles her toes into the Casa Pupo rug. Anaesthetised by the scotch, Len listens hazily as she confesses that yes, the new computerised cooker (which he knows cost as much as her small Renault) is fearfully efficient, but in her heart of hearts she'd feel much more at home with one of those simple Swedish log stoves.

Len inches his leather chair away from the roaring fire. Beneath the wool jacket his shirt is sticking to his back. His tie is throttling him.

Mile is talking of the threatened rise in mortgage rates. He speaks with the smug awe of one to whom such matters are blessedly academic – as if they were discussing Russian peasants having a hard time because of the poor grain harvest.

'It'll affect me pretty badly,' he says cheerfully, refilling

9

Len's glass. 'What with the mortgages on the yacht and our place in Wales as well.'

'It was a little weaver's cottage,' smiles Annabel nostalgically. 'Completely ruined, of course. Would you believe, the previous owners had installed central heating and electric log fires. My workmen had an awful job ripping it all out.'

'Fortunately, our mortgage is pretty low now,' says Len. 'In another five years we'll have paid it off completely.'

Miles shakes his head. 'False economy, old lad. You should sell up and invest in a bigger property. I don't mind telling you, I made a packet when we sold that old oast house of ours in Kent.'

Annabel's eyes are huge with indignation. 'House prices are ridiculous these days. There's a man in the village with a similar house to this, and he's just had it valued at £100,000. I mean, it's insane. I said to Miles, if he can get that price for a place that hasn't even got a swimming pool, then whatever is our house worth? It's wicked. Honestly, I think this whole property racket has got quite out of hand.'

Miles smothers a yawn. 'Thank God I've got the boat to escape to at weekends. Did I tell you I'm thinking of changing it for a Eurobanker 38?'

Len rallies. 'The trouble with weekend sailing is that it doesn't give you enough exercise to work off all those expense account lunches. You should take up jogging, Miles.'

'No need, old chap. I'm naturally fit. Time enough to panic about coronaries when I reach your age.'

Annabel stretches full length on the sofa. 'Leo's quite right, Miles. The only exercise you get is sitting on that damn floating gin palace hacking up phlegm from those disgusting cigars you smoke.'

The scotch bottle is empty by the time Annabel leads them upstairs to the guest suite. It comes complete with solarium and sunken bath. Len permits himself, at last, to loosen his tie as he puts through a call to his daughter.

'Hi there, gorgeous. Did I wake you up? I thought I'd better let you know that we're staying the night as I've had one too many to drive. Have you had a good evening?'

10

'So so. I finished writing up my physical notes and then I watched the late movie on the box.'

'I thought you had a Village Players rehearsal.'

'I dropped out. They're all a load of slime. When will you be home?'

'The plan is to have a late breakfast here, and come back about midday. Will you be in?'

'Very funny. You know my Saturday morning routine. But I'll try and crawl out of bed in time to make you a nice strong cup of tea. I should think you'll need it after Annabel's dishwater Earl Grey.'

Len grins. She's OK, is Juliette. Mates of his are burdened by diabolical teenage offspring, forever slamming doors and bursting pimples over the bathroom mirror. Fortunately, the adolescent rebellion bit seems to have passed Juliette by. Although she's inherited Caroline's striking good looks, she's exhibiting none of the wayward, wilful ways of her mother at that age. Thank God. Juliette has occasional boyfriends, of course, but in general she's more concerned with passing her O Levels. Sensible kid.

Caroline is already tucked up in one of the single beds. Len undresses and slides in beside his wife. He can tell she isn't really in the mood, but he presses on anyway. At dawn, he takes her again, persisting until the cry of her climax shatters the early morning silence of the house.

Everyone except Len is listless and hungover at breakfast. Len tucks into bacon and eggs, but it doesn't taste right without fried bread. As there's no toast on offer, he attempts to mop up the juices with a croissant, but it crumbles in his fingers and flakes into the egg yolk. The cardboard coloured mess looks like the fibrous paint he's just decorated his downstairs cloakroom with. Len gives up and lays down his fork. No doubt Annabel's devoted Philippino maids will spend a rewarding afternoon making with the Silver Dip.

Caroline and Annabel sit silent and haggard over their untouched grapefruit, gazing with bloodshot, unseeing eyes out on the garden. The breakfast room overlooks a miniature Japanese watergarden. It makes Len yearn for long wild grass bulging with molehills.

Miles, ever the valiantly genial host, enquires how Leo's

allotment is coming along. It has long been a sore point with Len that Caroline will not permit him to grow vegetables in the garden.

'I hear,' Miles says gamely, surreptitiously dropping aspirins into his orange juice, 'that last year was a washout for leeks?'

It is clearly time for the guests to depart. At the door, Caroline kisses Annabel's dry cheek and murmurs, 'You must come over and see us in the New Year.'

'We'll fix a date once we've got Christmas out of the way,' agrees Len. 'Though I shall be away for a few days, up in Edinburgh.'

'Actually,' says Caroline flintily, 'Juliette and I will be coming too. It is *my* mother we're visiting, you know.'

'I *meant* all of us.'

'Then why make it sound as though if we're lucky Juliette and I will be allowed to trail behind with the luggage balanced on our heads.'

Len can't imagine what he's done wrong this morning. But he knows for sure he'll find out on the drive home. Caroline turns to wave at the smiling couple propping one another up in the porch. As he turns the Jaguar onto the road she snaps:

'What did you mean by making that remark about Annabel's dress?'

'What remark?'

'*What a stunning dress, Annabel. Why don't you get one like it, Caro?* Have you any idea how much that *old rag* cost?'

'For Christ's sake! Don't tell me you've been sitting there sulking all this time over a casual remark I made *last night*! Why brood over it? Why didn't you mention it when we went to bed?'

'Oh, isn't that typical! I daren't say anything last night because you were sloshed and you'd have started shouting. Then this morning you start groping me at dawn – '

'Well it's always best with the dew on it – '

'Which means I can't get back to sleep and I'm exhausted and incapable of coherent speech until midday.'

'Gordon Bennet! Didn't I tell you before we left yesterday that you looked smashing in that red dress?

Didn't I? Anyway, I don't know why you're so hung up over the Laceys' money. They're not that well off. He's up to his puffy eyes in debt and I happen to know he's been on the verge of bankruptcy more than once.'

'The Laceys' idea of bankruptcy is not being able to take the girls to St Moritz *and* to Nice.'

'I still maintain it's all show. Look at the way the plastic marble round the sunken bath was peeling off.'

Len puts his foot down over the Hog's Back. Reckless on such a hazy, gloomy winter's day, but he is anxious to get home and fall asleep over the afternoon sport on TV. In the valley below, lights glimmer enticingly through the mist. It always comes as a disappointment to Len realising that it isn't a glittering, cosmopolitan city down there, only the barrack town of Aldershot.

'Don't go so fast, Leo. God, I loathe motor cars.'

This was another of Caroline's past campaigns: *Ban the Car – Bikes Are Better.*

'Why didn't you ride your bloody bike to Annabel's, then?'

'Because it's too bloody far.'

'And to think, when I first met you, you used to give me regal little waves from the back of Daddy's Daimler.'

'We've all progressed, physically and spiritually, along different paths since then.'

'We certainly have. What was Daddy's opinion, by the way, of the suspension of the Black Maria they flung him into?'

'You really are a shit, poking fun at the dead. For God's sake don't make cracks like that when we go to Mother's. You know she's paralysed with shame that Daddy died in prison.'

'I still don't see why she had to take herself off to Edinburgh after he was arrested. Did she live there as a kid or something?'

'No. Her ancestors were Scots but she was born in Chelsea.'

'Snobby.'

'Very.'

*

Rose would have given herself to a black man rather than admit she'd grown up in Fulham. A few years ago, she went back there and spent the day wandering round her old haunts. It wasn't a sentimental journey. She did it more in the spirit of an ex-prisoner of war who, in peacetime, is driven by the obsession to view once more the horrors of her internment camp.

She expected to find that Fulham had blossomed into a desirable, even exclusive area like neighbouring Chelsea. But Artillery Road remained depressingly as she remembered it. In Chelsea, similar terraced houses had been developed into what the colour supplements called bijou homes, with bay trees set in tubs against the newly whitewashed brick. There was nothing fresh or leafy about Artillery Road. Just a row of grimy, cramped houses, separated by dank passages permeated with the smells from the lean-to lavatories in the back yards.

Even the meat factory was still there. The Artillery Road gang had played and fought in its disused rear entrance. The girls trailed through the dust in their mothers' old dresses, and smeared their faces with rust from the gates as make-believe rouge. The boys built matchwood barricades against an invasion from the Petrol Road mob.

Guy Fawkes night was best. They'd make a huge bonfire in the middle of the road, letting it burn until the tarmac began to flame. The challenge was to get the fire engine clanging down their street before the Petrol Road gang managed to ignite their tarmac. All the boys got a tanning from their fathers for that, but they said it was worth it.

Rose never knew her father. He was run over by a tram soon after she was born. Her mother died when she was five. All Rose could remember about her was the soft, lilting quality of her voice.

She was cared for by her father's sister, Flo, who had four children of her own and a husband who drank. When he ran short, the day before payday, Flo had to take the big brown teapot down to the Homing Pigeon and get it filled with ale. He always promised he'd give her the 1/6d back, but he never did. In a rare sober afternoon, he made Rose a magnificent wooden hoop, which he painted red. Rose hired it out to the gang for a farthing an hour.

All her earliest memories were of feeling unwanted and unwelcome. Flo's children called her spiteful, complaining that she pulled their hair and told tales. Rose was forever in trouble, and in tears. But at least it was better than being ignored.

Once, she ran away and hid in a derelict basement all night. But no one came looking for her, so she crept back home. Flo lathered her backside with a strap and sent her to bed without any supper. Rose heard them all down in the kitchen, talking about her. What a trial she was. How she'd come to a sticky end. Defiantly, Rose slid her hand under the lumpy mattress and retrieved her bag of acid drops. She always tried to have a secret supply of sweets available, as Flo made quite a habit of packing her off to bed hungry. Rose earned the money taking the neighbours' sheets up to the bagwash every week.

In the summer, each street held a party for the kids. Artillery Road looked unbelievably gay, then, with streamers looped from house to house, and trestle tables covered with red paper, laden with festive food. When she was thirteen, Rose leaned against the table and then found her dress had stuck to the paper. Everyone tittered and whispered. Flo dragged her home, soaked her bloodstained dress and knickers in cold water, and told her the most terrifying things about what men did to girls.

The following year, Flo declared she was too old to attend the street party.

'You're leaving school and going into service. I've got you a job in a respectable house, so you make sure you behave yourself. If you get yourself sacked, or in the family way, I won't have you back here. D'you understand?'

Rose nodded, and went upstairs to pack her cardboard suitcase. Flo needn't have worried. Rose had no intention of returning to Artillery Road for a long, long time. Not until she was rich. Well dressed. Married. And safe.

2

Mrs Scott-Peters lives in a tall, narrow house in one of Edinburgh's more select suburbs. She has no friends and is merely on nodding terms with her neighbours, which is exactly as Mrs Scott-Peters wants it. As a child, she recalls, the entire street was forever in and out of the house, borrowing cups of sugar and nosing into your business. Mrs Scott-Peters is having none of that. This is a respectable area, where people keep themselves to themselves. It's the right and proper way to be.

Of course, there is no denying that it's a trial not having a man to lean on. People have no idea what a strain it is, suddenly finding yourself on your own after thirty-nine years of Married Life.

Caroline is fond of sending letters in spiky handwriting, urging her to *get out more, Mother. Make some friends, ask your neighbours in for coffee.*

Caroline is determined not to understand, broods Mrs Scott-Peters, sprinkling salt on the icy front path. She won't see that I don't need strangers interfering in my life. What I crave is Lester back, and everything the way it was before that ... that misunderstanding about the council funds. I want to be a wife again. Not a widow.

If Lester were here, he'd have got rid of the damp in the back bedroom and had the central heating mended. The repair man would never have dared speak to Lester the way he did to me.

On the morning of her daughter's visit, Mrs Scott-Peters walks up the hill to the call box and phones the central heating firm again. They are engaged. She feels tearful with frustration and exhaustion. She has cleaned the house from top to bottom, renewed the hot water bottles in the spare beds and prepared a beef stew for their dinner tonight. She'll make the dumplings later on. Leonard will be pleased. All men like dumplings.

16

After lunch, she had intended to re-polish the hall floor, but she discovers that the grocer has forgotten to send round the suet with the rest of the order. She struggles into her fur coat, hat, scarf, gloves, socks and boots. It is half a mile to the grocer's, uphill in a razoring wind. By the time she returns, the grey December light is already fading. Caroline said they'd be here by four.

She is longing for a cuppa, but reluctant to clutter up the lounge with tea things before Caroline arrives. It's a nice room, she decides, as she finishes the ironing. She's glad she chose the wine-coloured covers for the suite. Dark red and grey was always Lester's favourite scheme. Tasteful, he said. Mrs Scott-Peters liked those colours because they never showed the dirt.

Of course, it was shameful the way they'd taken most of her beautiful antiques when Lester went ... got into that bit of bother. The bailiffs had tried to be kind, she appreciated that. But she'd nearly died that morning, watching them troop in and out of the old house in Surrey, carrying out the silver, the rosewood dining table, the crystal. All her best things. The neighbours' net curtains had been twitching like ghosts with convulsions. Still, the bailiffs had let her keep her rugs, and the nice glass fronted cabinets she displayed all her ornaments in.

Mrs Scott-Peters folded the pressed tea towels over the airing horse and treated herself to a chocolate digestive. When she was younger and slimmer she'd eat a packet of chocolate fingers at a sitting. Now, fearful that Caroline will nag her about her weight, she only allows herself the very occasional half-covered digestive.

Not that I'm really fat, she informs her reflection in the mirror over the bookcase. It's just that not being very tall gives me a dumpy appearance. And I shouldn't have let that girl at the hairdressers perm my hair so tight. All those curls make my face look puffy.

She dabs on fresh powder and a smear of lipstick. The clock on the mantelpiece says half past four. Caroline is late. Mrs Scott-Peters plumps the cushions and sweeps up biscuit crumbs from the carpet.

Will they want a proper tea when they arrive, or just cake?

17

If they ask for sandwiches I might not have enough bread, she panics, nibbling another biscuit. I wish I'd ordered two extra loaves. And does Leonard prefer white or brown? I should have got one of each.

Too late now. They're here. Caroline and Leonard all done up in sheepskins. He must be doing all right then. Coats like that cost the earth. Juliette is wearing a fun fur jacket, flying open in the wind, with a thin flowered waistcoat underneath. Strange how the young never appear to feel the cold.

Mrs Scott-Peters experiences a surge of relief as she watches Caroline striding briskly up the path. It will be good to have her family round her again. Someone of her own to talk to.

Len has to stop the car three times on the journey, while Juliette is sick. Caroline calmly provides green Marks and Spencer plastic bags for the purpose, which are then handed to the chauffeur for disposal. He flings one over a hedge near Grantham, another into a Yorkshire ditch and the third is drowned in a Border stream.

'Really, Leo,' Caroline protests. 'It's ecologically irresponsible to foul up the countryside like that.'

Len recalls that last summer Caroline plastered the Jag window with *Take Home Your Rubbish* stickers. 'What do you suggest, then? That we march up your mother's garden path ceremoniously bearing green bags of puke?'

'Oh, shut up,' moans Juliette.

Caroline turns round and says mildly, 'You're not making things any better for yourself, reading in the back of a moving car.'

'I'm not reading, I'm revising.' Juliette dabs her mouth with a tissue. 'I've got to learn three Keats sonnets before the start of term.'

Len feels sorry for the kid, huddled pale-faced in a corner, muttering on about Grecian urns. It seems like only yesterday that she was a bright-eyed child in ankle socks, making him laugh with her outrageous subjects for I-Spy. It occurs to Len that they all smiled more readily when Juliette was younger.

18

'Not much further now, kiddo. When we get there, Caro, you take her straight indoors and I'll see to the luggage.'

'Jammy for you,' murmurs Caroline. 'I shall be bracing myself against the verbal avalanche waiting to engulf me at the door. Why are you late, my blood pressure's worse, the woman in the post office was rude to me, I suffer from the cold more than anyone but of course you do feel things more when you're on your own.'

'You're fifty minutes late. I've been looking out for you since a quarter to four. Hello, Juliette, how peaky you're looking. Give your Granny a kiss, that's right. I'm sorry about my hair, I had it done but the girl made it go all frizzy, it didn't even get crushed under my hat when I had to go out in the cold this afternoon. The grocer wasn't at all apologetic about putting me to all that trouble over the suet and then I couldn't have a cup of tea because I was expecting you.'

'Really, mother, there was nothing to stop you having some tea.'

'I wanted to wait for you. I didn't know you were going to be this long. Now don't stand there cluttering up the porch. I want to greet my son-in-law.'

Len bends and kisses Mrs Scott-Peters awkwardly on the smear of powder near her left ear. Warily, he follows the women into the long narrow hall. Death Row he calls it, with the lethally polished lino covered by rugs designed to send him skidding into the china cabinet beside the stairs.

He heaves the luggage upstairs and returns to find his family grouped round the front room gas fire. Mrs Scott-Peters is making tea, sending forth a torrent of information from the kitchen about the grocer, the damp in the back bedroom, the faulty central heating, the cold, the weather in 1947, and her Nerves.

As Len enters, Caroline rolls her eyes towards the bookcase. The books have been removed and replaced by silver-framed photographs of Caroline's father. Not recent pictures, Len notes, but snaps that appear to have been taken during his courtship and early marriage.

Tall, dark-haired and lean, Lester Scott-Peters lounges in well-cut flannels against an open topped MG, smiling with all the menacing charm one associates with the young George Raft. A far cry from the pasty-faced man who died of pneumonia in Ford jail. Carefully arranged round the photographs are Lester's cigarette case, his silver pen, black leather wallet, six pairs of gold cuff links and a pot of African violets.

'I suppose,' Len says doubtfully, 'it's her way of remembering him.'

'It's obscene,' hisses Caroline. 'Like a shrine. She'll be lighting candles and hurling incense around next.'

Mrs Scott-Peters carries in the tea tray and instructs Juliette to move next to her mother on the sofa, so Leonard can have the best seat next to the fire.

Reluctantly, Len crosses to the low chair, which is finely balanced on three prongs. As he sits down, his knees almost hit his chin, sending the chair swivelling sharply round. Len lurches from side to side, shifting his weight in a desperate attempt to control the neurotic Dervish. But the slightest movement is enough to set it awhirl once more, making Len feel like a child trapped in the Whip at the fair.

'That's right. Make yourself comfortable. You must be tired after all that driving,' smiles Mrs Scott-Peters. She pours his tea first, sugars and stirs it for him.

Bloody ironic, reflects Len. When he'd first met Caroline's mother, she treated him worse than a toe-rag. That was in the days when he'd been impressed by Daddy's Daimler, and the big house up on the hill.

Lester Scott-Peters was one of the local Mr Bigs. He was a company director and treasurer of the local council. His wife had taken one look at Len, and although she hadn't exactly said he was from the wrong side of the tracks, she managed to imply that he left a nasty smell which no amount of lavender air freshener could ever remove.

Naively, Len had imagined the Scott-Peters to be vaguely upper crust. All the outward trappings pointed that way. The double-barrelled name, the antiques, the crystal, the monogrammed silver. And the daughter, Caroline, had such style. Len would never forget that afternoon when she turned up in his works yard with a silver fox jacket round her shoulders and the information that she was in the club. Oh, she was a cool, classy cookie all right.

After the wedding, Mrs Scott-Peters had been forced to change her attitude. After all, it would never do to let the neighbours know that dearest Caroline had fallen for a bit of rough. No, open hostility was out of the question now. Instead, she adopted a patronising air, as if he were a bright scholarship boy they all had a duty to encourage.

She had a tendency to carol at her blue-rinsed buddies: 'Leonard has such a fascinating job. He's in the media, you know. And he's so clever, he also finds time to dabble in electronics.'

It would be left to Len to explain that in fact he was an apprentice compositor, earning a bit on the side as an amateur electrician. He turned down Lester's offer of a job, took his City and Guilds and from then on had managed to provide Caroline and Juliette with the best of everything. Yet throughout his marriage, his mother-in-law had regarded him as she would a mongrel puppy that had been given a home, but nevertheless had to be watched in case it crapped on the carpet.

So what have I done, Len wonders, as Mrs Scott-Peters cuts him a second large slice of Battenburg cake, to deserve this sudden gushing elevation into the bosom of the family?

Len tunes in to the end of Mrs Scott-Peters's exhaustive account of what the doctor said and what she said to the doctor. Caroline escapes upstairs muttering that she must get the unpacking done.

The first item out of the case will be the scotch, suspects Len. They have only been in Edinburgh an hour, but already he is feeling ragged. He doubts if one bottle of hooch is going to be enough to see them through until Monday.

Twenty minutes later, a flushed Caroline discovers her mother setting up the ironing board.

'Whatever are you doing, mother?'

'Getting the dinner ready. This lace cloth is for the table. I meant to iron it this afternoon but I was so worried because you were late.'

'Don't let's fuss with a cloth, Juliette can lay the table for you, and I'll peel some vegetables.'

'No, I'd better set the table. Juliette won't know where I keep the best cutlery.'

'I'll find everything. Don't worry.' Len senses that

Juliette is grateful to have something to do.

'Now you put the casserole on, mother, and give me a peeler. Leo, we'll need another chair in the dining room.'

'I haven't got one. We'll have to use the old piano stool. It's in the cupboard under the stairs. I meant to get batteries for the torch but when I got to the shop I couldn't remember what sort it took and the girl was most unhelpful, not to say rude. If your father – '

'No sweat, love. I can manage. By the way, Caro, did you bring my thick green sweater?'

'I can't remember. Did you leave it out for me to pack?'

'No. I just assumed you'd put it in.'

'Well I don't know if I did or not. I am a human being, Leo, not a mind-reading computerised packing machine.'

Len heads for the scotch. He lies on the mustard candlewick bedspread and drinks straight from the bottle. The whisky tastes faintly of lipstick. Downstairs, the women's voices are rising:

'Do you want me to use the raffia or melamine mats?'

'Melamine. Mother, you've got that casserole turned up far too high. You'll burn it.'

'Would you mind out of the way, Caroline. I can't get to the knife drawer.'

'Have you got a dish for these potatoes? They're nearly done.'

'I put the blue Wedgwood to warm in the oven. What's happened to it?'

'I put the peas in it.'

'But I was going to put the peas straight into the casserole.'

'Surely you've got another dish the potatoes can go in?'

'Yes, but it's got a chip in it. I like to use my best things when you come. Lady Evelyn gave me the Wedgwood. Rose, she said – '

'Never mind all that. We're not royalty, you know. Did you salt the sprouts?'

'Yes ... no ... '

'Too late now. I've poured the water away. Right, we're set. I'll carry the casserole and you bring the veg. Juliette, for heaven's sake, we'll need at least another three place mats for these hot dishes.'

22

'You said melamine, and there aren't any more.'

'Really, Juliette! For a girl who's taking eight O Levels you're sometimes not very bright. It's a pity they don't set you all an exam in common sense. And don't just stand there sulking! Get the raffia ones out! And hurry up, my fingers are burning! Le ... o! dinner!'

Len edges warily into the dining room. It never fails to amaze him that preparations for a simple meal should so swiftly degenerate into open warfare. Juliette is chewing her dark hair, resentfully slapping raffia mats onto the table. Caroline is wearing her martyred, *Do I have to organise everything, and everyone, all by myself ALL the time*, expression. Mrs Scott-Peters looks hunted, and petulant.

They sit down. Caroline immediately leaps to her feet again and pulls out her chair. 'Leo, you've given mother the piano stool. It's cutting into her legs.'

'I'm all right.'

'Nonsense. Swop with me.'

'Really, I like sitting on a stool.'

'Don't be silly. You look like a bird of prey perched up there.'

With the exchange completed, Mrs Scott-Peters peers into the casserole. 'Oh dear. I've forgotten the dumplings.'

'It doesn't matter.'

'Yes it does. I'll just go and do them. It won't take long.'

'Sit down, mother. We don't need dumplings.'

'It won't taste the same without them. And I wanted to make dumplings for Leonard.'

'For heaven's sake, mother. Leo doesn't *like* dumplings. *None* of us like dumplings.'

'What do you mean you don't like them? I ordered the suet specially. I went out in the cold all the way up the hill to the grocer's for it. If I'd known –'

Caroline slams the lid back on the casserole. 'All right. *I'll* go and do the dumplings. You just sit there.'

Mrs Scott-Peters stifles a sob. 'What's the point when you don't like them? You used to like them. They used to be your favourite. You should have told me you'd gone off them. It's very difficult for me when I don't see you very often. I can't be expected to know ... '

Forty more hours to go, calculates Len. He knows now for

23

sure that one bottle of scotch is never going to be enough.

'Please, Leo, not while we're here. You know I can't do it with mother in the next room.'

Len removes his hand from his wife's breast, and turns over. Funny how women develop so many scruples as they get older. She never worried about her parents being able to hear when he first met her.

Len was asked up to the big house to fix some bedroom wall lights. Miss Scott-Peters sat on her white counterpane and watched him work. When he'd finished, she sauntered across the pale carpet, shoved her hand into his overalls and grabbed his balls. Cool as you like. Len backed off, fast.

A few weeks later, he ran into her again, in the Queen's Head. She was perched on a bar stool, drinking gin and orange with her well-heeled art college friends. His mate saw her smile at him, and bet Len he wouldn't dare ask the bird for a date. They ended up going to the flicks.

Five minutes into *Gypsy* she was at him again. Yet when he drove her home in his van, she turned frosty, and told him to keep his hands to himself. He preferred her like that. He didn't want her acting like a prize slag. He could get one of those any day. But Caroline was something special. He wanted to respect her.

Len was chuffed when he took her to meet his mates in the Public at the Queen's Head, and she put on that snooty face, and cut glass accent. That was when he fancied her most.

It was crazy. He wanted her to slap him down. Yet some perverse instinct goaded him to keep at her. In the end they'd had it away in the moonlight, down by the river. Len assumed Caroline agreed to go the whole hog there because she found the river more romantic than his grubby old van. He'd lusted after her like mad, but when she gave in he remembered feeling disappointed in her. Stupid, really.

He was flabbergasted when she went and put herself up the spout.

'We'll get married on your birthday in November,' she announced calmly. 'I'll only be just over three months gone, then. It won't show. My family will hit the roof, of course, but I can handle them.'

24

She had, too. Lester even insisted on giving them the deposit for a house. 'I've found you a nice little place, ten miles away in a little Surrey village called Maybrook. Three beds, on a decent sized corner site, with woods on one side and a small bungalow on the other, so you'll not be overlooked. And at the bottom of your garden is a large meadow. It's held in trust by the Church, on condition they never build on it. That's a bonus for you. Means you'll always have a pleasant outlook from the back.'

Len fought strenuously against the move to 5 Roman Lane. But pressure from the Scott-Peters forced him to cave in.

'It's for the sake of the baby,' Caroline argued. 'And don't call it 5 Roman Lane. I intend to rename the house Lavender Cottage.'

'I don't like accepting charity from your father. I'd rather we started off in a small flat that's honestly ours. I want my son to know reality from the word go.'

'Son? I favour a daughter myself.'

And so it turned out. The choice of names was Caroline's, too.

Juliette Victoria Lambert breaks loose on Sunday, alleging a burning desire to inspect Edinburgh Castle. Len had hoped to slope off to the pub, but his mother-in-law has other plans for him.

Dutifully, he borrows a ladder from neighbouring Mr Logan, and mends the broken guttering causing the damp in the back bedroom. He shows Mrs Scott-Peters how to bleed the radiators so the central heating will work properly. He changes the plug on her hair dryer, and fixes new washers on the kitchen taps, enduring all the while the widow's girlish laughter as she flutters helplessly around him.

Len feels unnerved. This new me-silly-little-woman, you-big-strong-man pose sits as uncomfortably on her as an ill-fitting wig. What's her game?

Monday breakfast is fraught. Juliette, anxious about the long car journey ahead, spills Rice Krispies all over the floor. Len doesn't notice, blunders in and treads them into the carpet. Mrs Scott-Peters swallows three of her pills with

25

her weak tea and whispers that the mess really doesn't matter.

'I'll clear it up later. It will give me something to do when you've all gone.' She sighs. 'Goodness knows when we'll all be together again.'

Caroline, consumed with guilt at leaving her mother alone, assumes an attitude of brisk efficiency.

'Leo, are you sure you haven't left any socks under the bed? Juliette, have you taken your car sickness tablets?'

'Would she like to have a bucket in the back with her, just in case? I've got a spare plastic one under the sink.'

'No, stay where you are, mother. The tablets should do the trick.'

As Len loads the luggage into the car, Mrs Scott-Peters shifts from foot to foot in the porch, desperately dreaming up delaying tactics.

'Have you enough food for when you get home? What about the bread? I've got an extra loaf – '

'There's masses of stuff in our freezer, thanks all the same, mother. Look, I'm sorry we can't stay any longer. But Juliette's term starts tomorrow ... '

Her mother's eyes fill with tears.

Wretchedly, Caroline blurts: 'Why not come down and see us in the spring? When the weather's better. A week in Surrey would do you a power of good.'

'A week's no use,' grunts Mrs Scott-Peters. 'I'll come for a fortnight.'

'Bloody *hell*,' mutters Juliette, hurling Keats onto the back seat.

No one speaks until they have cleared Edinburgh. Len is not sorry to see the back of the place. It's one of those cities, he decides, that looks grand from the air. But viewed from ground level, with that massive castle and five storey grey-stone houses looming over you, Edinburgh is just plain depressing.

'All things considered, it didn't go off too badly,' Len asserts. 'Duty done and all that. To give the old girl her due, she did seem to be making an effort to get along with me.'

Caroline laughs shrilly. 'Of course. Didn't you realise you've been promoted to head of the family? I'm afraid she

26

now regards you as a surrogate husband. Someone to lean on and do odd jobs for her. At one point I thought she was almost trying to flirt with you.'

Juliette giggles.

'Nevertheless,' persists Len, 'she was making an effort. Look at the way she positively dragged me in front of the telly to watch Match of the Day with her.'

Caroline shakes her head. 'Mother is so infuriatingly perverse. On Saturday nights when Daddy was alive, she'd sit there in sullen silence when the football was on. But now he's gone, she makes a ritual of watching it every week. And that damn shrine, with his photos and personal things laid out like holy relics. She's getting morbid. It gives me the creeps.'

'I think you did the right thing inviting her down for a visit. A change of scene will cheer her up. I must admit, I do feel a bit of a bastard driving away and leaving her there in that gloomy house. I've told you before, Caro, we may have to consider inviting her to live with us.'

'No! My mother and I could never co-exist under one roof. It was bad enough before I was married. In any case, we'd go bankrupt trying to feed her. Did you see the monstrous way she stuffs food away? No wonder she's beginning to look like Humpty Dumpty.'

'She's also got two bottles of Sanatogen and some Clove Tonic wine at the back of the sideboard,' puts in Juliette. 'I noticed them when I was setting the table.'

'And then there's the half bottle of cherry brandy stashed behind the Domestos under the stairs,' adds Len.

Caroline shrugs. 'Well, if she is a secret boozer, good luck to her. I've always thought it unfair that old ladies are supposed to faint with horror if you offer them more than half a glass of sherry.'

'But what an insane situation,' laughs Juliette. 'There's you and daddy swigging scotch in the bedroom, and Granny glugging brandy under the stairs ... '

'She always was secretive,' muses Caroline. 'When my father was alive she had a passion for Mars bars. But she knew he'd nag her about getting fat so she used to hide in the broom cupboard and scoff them there.'

27

'Odd how people change,' remarks Len. 'I was riffling through some of those old snaps of her and Lester. There's one taken in some sort of formal garden, when she was only a few years older than Juliette, I guess. And she looks surprisingly slim and pretty. Really quite elegant. What would she have been doing then?'

'The smart clothes were probably gifts from her employer,' guesses Caroline. 'Before she was married, mother worked as a lady's companion, remember.'

Within three years of going into service, Rose had established herself as Lady Evelyn Lyall's personal maid. She achieved this position simply because none of the other maids in the Chelsea house were prepared to keep their mouths shut about Lady Evelyn's little weakness.

Lady Evelyn breakfasted on a strong cocktail, prepared and smuggled up to her by the faithful Rose. She tippled away at the sherry through the morning and generally passed out after lunch. If anyone rang, Rose said her ladyship was resting. At five, she would run a bath for her mistress, and bring her aspirins and black coffee. On a good day this, plus a large Bloody Mary, were sufficient to revive Lady Evelyn in time to slip into her Fortuny and join her husband and guests for dinner.

Rose greatly admired Sir Desmond Lyall. Tall, distinguished, well mannered, he at all times treated his wife as if she merely suffered from a poor constitution, not a chronic thirst for alcohol.

Rose was careful never to let him down. When Lady Evelyn collapsed in a drunken stupor in Harrods, it was Rose who whisked her home in a taxi . . . Rose who headed off curious newspaper reporters and telephoned Sir Desmond at his club with the information that Lady Evelyn was overtired, and might benefit from a little holiday. Scotland, perhaps? Rose had always longed to travel. She enjoyed enormously the ensuing trip to Edinburgh.

Lady Evelyn drank because she suspected her husband of being unfaithful to her. Rose had no way of knowing if this were true, but it suited her to foster her ladyship's fears.

'Tragic, the young Countess losing her husband so

suddenly, my lady. But she seemed more cheerful at dinner last night. Sir Desmond is so gallant, isn't he? He really brought a sparkle to her poor, sad eyes.'

In return for her loyalty, the Lyalls were generous to Rose. She had her own attic room, overlooking Eaton Square. This was luxury to Rose, who had grown up sharing a sagging double bed with Flo's two daughters. In addition, she received clothes, chocolates, twenty-five shillings a week and, Lady Evelyn's condition permitting, Sunday afternoons and every other Wednesday off.

'Behave yourself, and don't go dragging no followers back to that posh house,' Flo had warned her when she left Fulham.

The advice was quite superfluous. Rose had no intention of fooling about with riff-raff like the milk boy. Her virtue was the one asset she possessed, and she was determined to hang on to it. When she gave herself, it would be in wedlock. And when she married, it would be to better herself. She appreciated that the right man would take some finding. But she was young. She could wait.

Meanwhile, Rose devoted her spare time to exploring the more exclusive areas of London, observing how the rich lived and played. And not once did she write to Flo, or return to the terraced house in Fulham.

3

'Mind you don't sprain your wrists swishing those dildos,' grins Len, slipping a set of darts into his pocket.

'Modern dildos don't swish. They vibrate,' Caroline informs him absently, busy setting out four of her second-best wine glasses on the coffee table.

It irritates her that Leo regards her Consciousness Raising group as just a bunch of aspiring lesbians who meet solely for the purpose of carping about their husbands. She watches him back the car out of the garage, marvelling at his egocentric assumption that women have one inexhaustibly fascinating topic of conversation: their men.

The women arrive promptly at eight, considerately leaving their boots in the hall so as not to soil the sitting room Wilton. They take it in turns to bring some wine. Frances, a tense brunette who is deputy head of Juliette's school, usually offers a Peter Dominic *Village*. Elfin-faced Babs, only a few years older than Juliette, will rummage in her multi-coloured straw bag and produce a flask of mead made by her boyfriend. This evening, Wendy unwraps a bottle of Sainsbury's Table Red. Fair haired, swathed in a pretty Laura Ashley smock, Wendy resembles a pregnant version of the glowingly healthy girl in the old Ovaltine advertisements.

A fifth member of the group has fallen from grace. 'I am sick to death,' Babs asserts, tossing back her cloud of Pre-Raphaelite red hair, 'of ringing Sue up to ask if she wants a lift here on my moped, and hearing her bleat that Adrian is bringing friends home unexpectedly and she's got to cook. Or Adrian has arranged to go out, and they can't rustle up a sitter. Or Adrian *might* be going out. Sod bloody Adrian. Then if I do persuade her to come, Himself sits there glowering, saying What About My Dinner and What Time Will You Be Back? And even if I do hustle her bodily out of the door I have the uneasy feeling he's going to give her hell when she gets home.'

'Sue's got no one to blame but herself if she insists on wearing the welcome mat round her face,' asserts Caroline.

'After all, we're only asking Sue for one evening a month,' says Frances, holding her wine up to the light. 'But when I meet Adrian in town he glares at me as if I were an urban guerrilla hell bent on abducting his precious wife.'

When the group started, six months ago, they intended to meet fortnightly. But this has proved impossible. Frances, ambitious and bucking for a headship, is involved in endless conferences, courses and PTA meetings. Babs, who works on the local travelling library, locks herself away in her bedsit in the evenings, allegedly to read for her A.L.A. exams. Judging by Bab's smugly bleary eyes, Caroline suspects the course of study centres more around Masters and Johnson than Dewey. As for Wendy, despite her pregnancy she still devotes most of her spare time to sorting stock for the Oxfam shop she organises.

They take a pride in appearing busy, committed members of society. Caroline tells herself it is ridiculous to feel inferior because she does not work, even part time, outside the home. Nevertheless, when the other three were justifying not being able to meet more often than once a month, she was appalled to hear herself murmuring defensively:

'Oh I absolutely agree. Personally I find there's *so* much to do in the garden at this time of year.'

She invited Annabel to one meeting. But after that, Annabel cried off, protesting that they were all far too intelligent for her. Although the women laughingly demur at this judgement, Caroline senses that they are not displeased. They are faithful readers of the *Guardian*, and grateful for their monthly feminist fix from *Spare Rib*. Babs raids her library and passes round the latest doctrines from Greer, Millet and Jong, who Frances's lecturer husband jocularly refers to as the High Priestesses of the Movement.

Tonight, with the women sprawled on Caroline's comfortable Parker Knoll suite, the topic under discussion is Women's Health. An article in *Spare Rib* urges the use of natural sponges instead of tampons. The group is loud in its condemnation of the scandalous profits made by tampon manufacturers, though Babs is dubious about inserting natural sponges in case they squeak.

Frances frowns. Although the group scorns the notion of appointing an official chairwoman, it is normally Frances who takes the lead in preventing the discussion from degenerating into frivolity. Smoothing her tailored Jaeger dress over her bony knees, Frances reads aloud from a new health handbook.

'The chapters on breast examination and cystitis are very sensible and reassuring,' she informs them, 'but as this book is geared for the American market, it does go overboard on the togetherness aspect. During menstruation, for example, we are encouraged to gather in a sisterly group and remove the blood from one another, using a sort of vacuum cleaner.'

Listening to the self-conscious laughter, Caroline realises what it is that disappoints her about the group. We are too cosily middle-class and unadventurous. We kid ourselves that by banding together, we're in the vanguard of the international fight for women's emancipation. But in truth we all still possess a dismally suburban, net-curtain mentality.

Admittedly, the first few meetings had evoked a heady euphoria in Caroline. Feeling increasingly isolated in her cloistered village environment, she had clutched gratefully at the lifeline offered by the group. It was such a relief encountering women who, like her, were totally uninterested in kitchen conversation and toddlers' tales.

But what do we actually do? she muses. What do we achieve? We sit by the fire, drinking wine, talking about ourselves.

Why aren't we out renewing the campaign for a crèche at the local supermarket?

Because the manager will say the cost of providing toilet, first aid and supervisory facilities is prohibitive.

Why aren't we demanding a refuge for battered women?

Because the authorities will allege that in a nice respectable neighbourhood like this there are no battered women. And even if there are a few, it's the women's own fault for going out to work, becoming aggressive and not

32

taking proper care of their men.

Why aren't we drafting a questionnaire to determine Maybrook women's attitude towards equality?

We tried it. First we couldn't decide on the wording of the questions. Then Frances balked at using the school duplicator in case it prejudiced her chances of promotion. And since all the others work in the evenings it would have meant me distributing the questionnaire single handed, so we dropped the idea.

Why didn't we join the Anti-Abortion march in London?

Because it was raining ... the car wouldn't start ... Frances's boys had flu ... Babs had her period ... Wendy had to clean up the house because her mother was coming ... Adrian wanted his dinner ...

The ironical thing is that Leo regards me as a staunch crusader. He doesn't realise that although I've joined countless action groups, I've never at heart belonged to any of them. It's never been me who's initiated a campaign. I've merely drifted into it, gone along with the current project and wandered off when I got bored.

The women have noticed her silence. Wendy, china blue eyes round with concern, asks gently, 'How did the visit to your mother's go?'

Caroline is aware that she could talk non-stop for days about her difficult mother and find her group in total sympathy. They all have a mother problem.

Bab's mother disapproves of her live-in boyfriend, and is prone to make embarrassing dawn swoops on her daughter's bedsit. Wendy feels frustrated because her mother refuses to believe that 'little Wend' will be able to cope with a new born baby. She is preparing to commandeer the spare bedroom and help/interfere. Frances's mother lives with her, in a granny flat. If Frances arrives home later than 10 pm, mother has a 'turn' which requires her to be nursed through the night and cossetted for days afterwards.

Discussing their mothers had formed one of the first strong bonds between the members of the group. With their fathers, the women have an easy going, affectionate relationship. Yet they all feel racked with guilt about their mothers.

Guilt at not visiting her more often. 'But when I do she

treats me like a child. Even when I'm fifty she still won't accept that I'm grown up.'

At not being the perfect daughter mother dreams of. 'I do try to please her. But she's always picking.'

At feeling no affection for her. 'But she was always so indifferent to me. She loved my sister best.'

At the resentment engendered by her mother's growing dependence on her. 'She brought me up to be independent. Now I am, she doesn't just want to change the rules. She's moved the court as well.'

Tonight, Caroline refrains from burdening her friends once again with the saga of her mother. Instead she comments wryly,

'When I was in Edinburgh, we happened to watch that advert for floor detergent. You know, the one where two frantic women are rushing to get their respective floors clean in time to pick up little Johnny from school. Both my mother and I said, in unison, *How ridiculous!* Great, I thought, mother is getting the message at last. Then she went on, *As if anyone would still be cleaning their floors at three in the afternoon.*'

Wendy nods. 'I asked my mother if she would mind not giving my young niece dustpan and brush sets for her birthday. I thought mum would explode. But instead she said I was quite right. It's not till they are older, is it, that girls learn the satisfaction in cleaning things properly?'

'My ma was horrified when she dropped in and found me swabbing out the loo in my white satin trousers,' says Babs. 'She's threatening to buy me a nice sensible cotton overall.'

Wendy leans forward eagerly. 'That reminds me. One of the theatre girls gave a lovely crushed velvet skirt to my Oxfam shop. It's just your style, Babs.'

Frances reacts as if she has just heard the end-of-lesson bell. The women's health book is tidied away in her large leather bag. Homework must be set, and the blackboard rubbed clean.

'What about the topic for next month?' she asks crisply. 'Shall we discuss sexist advertisements?'

No! Caroline longs to scream. I don't want to talk about sexist ads, sponge tampons, mothers or crushed velvet skirts. Do none of you realise that for the past year I've been desperately worried because I seem to have gone off sex?

Caroline shows the women out, then returns to the sitting room and pours herself a large scotch. She lies full length on the sofa, toasting her toes before the glowing embers of the fire.

How could I admit that to the group? We've always carefully skirted the subject of sex. Perhaps because any confession of dissatisfaction would imply too blatant a criticism of our partners. And we are all too damn decent to expose our men as lousy lovers.

Even so, Caroline has often been tempted to explode the sex bomb at a group meeting. What daunts her are the individual personalities of the women themselves.

Radiantly pregnant Wendy the Fair appears to enjoy such a cosy (the bitchy would say smug) relationship with Tim, her social worker husband. He is a chunky, amiable, unfailingly kind man. Caroline imagines Wendy arriving home to find him waiting in the gingham curtained kitchen with cocoa and hot dripping toast. Tim will have devoted his evening to polishing the stripped pine doors with beeswax.

Caroline can hear the pair discussing every aspect of their day, laughing together, sympathetic, supportive. Unlike Leo, Tim reacts favourably to the women's group, and has offered to teach them car maintenance.

She watches Tim slip an arm round Wendy's shoulder, and help her up the stairs of their little terraced house. They look in on the half finished nursery, where Wendy spent the afternoon sticking up a frieze of feminist-approved fairy tales. (Cinderella is definitely vetoed, what with all that dreary sweeping, and the indignity of being rescued by a man.)

And here are Tim and Wendy snug between the flowered flannelette sheets. He holds her securely in his arms until she falls asleep.

Leo hates Caroline cuddling up to him in bed. He complains she makes him hot.

No, decides Caroline, if I admit to Wendy that I no longer fancy Leo she'll feel sorry for me. She'll tell Tim. And then they'll both ooze concern and quiet understanding, and

35

recommend a compassionate Marriage Guidance Counsellor. Quite unbearable.

Neither can Caroline face confiding in young Babs. She and her art student lover are still at the stage Caroline remembers enjoying with Leo sixteen years ago – where a series of furious arguments lead to passionate lovemaking, followed by a time of almost sentimental tenderness for one another. To Babs, sex is obviously like a constant, pleasurable itch. She would find Caroline's lack of libido totally incomprehensible.

Caroline lights a cigarette. So that leaves Frances. In theory she should be my best bet, as she's nearest to me in age. Yet when I look at Frances, with her angular face and severe, razor cropped hair, it's impossible to imagine her stripped of her Jaeger and lying soft, warm and willing in bed.

Babs did, in fact, once trespass on the deputy headmistress's marital bedroom. After a particularly violent row with her lover, she sought refuge for the night with Frances and Elliot. The back door wasn't locked and Babs discovered them, so she reported to Caroline, sitting up in twin beds wearing matching French cane pyjamas. Frances was practising yoga facial exercises, which required her to snarl like a tiger. Elliot was providing spiritual support, reading aloud passages from Rilke.

There is nothing at all sensuous about Frances, Caroline realises. If I mention my sex problem to her, Frances will only look impatient and imply that she grew out of all that sort of thing long ago, in the same way one gives up bubble gum, or stamp collecting.

Caroline is unable to decide whether it is sex that bores her, or just lovemaking with Leo. How aghast dear Truth-is-All Wendy would be if I confessed to my talent at faking orgasms. But what else can I do? Leo would keep on at me all morning if I didn't put a stop to his efforts by threshing about and groaning ecstatically.

And surely no married woman still feels that thrilled anticipation after seventeen years with the same man? (Be honest. Sixteen years. Absurd the way Leo insists on adding a year onto our anniversary so Juliette won't discover she

36

was conceived out of wedlock.)

Caroline stretches, and slips a cushion against the small of her back. Why can't I just admit that all I'm trying to do is justify starting an affair with Adrian? By this time tomorrow I shall have been to bed with him. I shall know for sure, then, whether or not I'm frigid.

She did not make a conscious, deliberate decision to start an affair. Like everything else in Caroline's life, it was just something she slid into.

Driving back from Annabel's one evening, she stopped off at the Green Man for a drink, and fell into conversation with a youngish, fair-haired man at the bar. Her initial amusement at being chatted up congealed into embarrassment when she learned that the man was Adrian Gage, ogre husband of the lapsed member of her women's group.

To her surprise, he was not the King Kong clone she had envisaged. He talked entertainingly about current books, films and plays and possessed an air of latent energy that instantly appealed to her. She felt, as she watched him order her third scotch, that he was controlling a strong physical force, which if unleashed ... She found her eyes drawn to the bulge in his well cut slacks. Swiftly, she finished her drink and fled. But not before she had agreed to lunch with him the following week, at the same pub.

Relieved to discover so early on that he was Sue Gage's husband, Caroline told him her name was Bianca. She also took the precaution of being deliberately vague about where she lived. Fortunately the Gages moved in completely different circles from hers, and Sue never came to the group now, so there was little danger of them all meeting up socially.

Driving to her assignation with Adrian the following week, Caroline developed a migraine. Examining herself in the car mirror, she realised it was hopeless. Her head felt as if it were being ground through a mincer. She looked a wreck. The pain had reached her eyes, dragging the surrounding skin into pinched, ugly lines. For the first time Caroline realised how much she was growing to resemble her mother.

Angrily, she shoved the mirror away and stumbled from

the car to a phone box. Adrian must not be allowed to see her like this. Anyway, the thought of smelling pub shepherds pie made her want to heave.

Trembling and cold, she dialled his office.

'Moston and Gage, Estate Agents,' barked the receptionist.

Caroline pushed in a coin. It stuck. The pips sounded and the line went dead. Swearing, she tried again. Black spots were beginning to dance before her eyes. She rested her throbbing head against the cool glass of the box.

'Moston and Gage!'

God woman, there's no need to shout. Don't you realise that to a migraine sufferer any sound above a whisper is like having the entire London Symphony Orchestra in your head, giving forth with the 1812.

Again the 5p piece jammed. Almost in tears, Caroline dialled once more, inserting 10p this time.

She was through. 'Who's calling?' rasped the receptionist.

Caroline baulked at confessing that it was a personal call. She anticipated the woman's knowing tone, the snide aside to the office junior that it was just another bored housewife on her way to get laid by the boss.

'Just connect me with Mr Gage, please,' she said firmly.

'But I have instructions to make a note of all Mr Gage's callers, madam.'

'Look, if Mr Gage wants you to know who I am I'm sure he'll be the first to tell you.'

Suddenly, Adrian was on the line. Caroline felt like a schoolgirl ringing the headmaster to explain why she'd have to miss an important exam.

'My poor Bianca,' Adrian said with deep concern. 'Migraines are misery, I know.'

Caroline imagined him crossing her name from his diary and flicking through his address book for an available reserve.

'You must take yourself home, draw the curtains and flake. I shall be in the Green Man at the same time next week if you can make it. Then perhaps we can go somewhere afterwards, and do something interesting.'

So that's the score. Caroline pours herself another scotch. This is to be no junior league coy flirtation. Adrian Gage demands action. In the pub, he met a lady called Bianca. A woman of the world. He wanted her. If she goes to lunch with him tomorrow, he will assume Bianca lusts after him, too.

'You stink of whisky.'

Juliette has quietly entered the darkened room, and is leaning over the back of the sofa.

The sheepskin on Juliette's coat tickles Caroline's face. 'I didn't hear you come in.' What I mean is, I didn't even realise you'd gone out. Oh Caroline, what an irresponsible parent you are.

Juliette throws off the coat and flops in front of the fire. 'I was round at Gail's. We've been set a huge essay project on the role of the Nurse in *Romeo and Juliet*. So we're each doing half to save time.'

'That sounds sensible.'

Sensible. That's my Juliette. Sensible, prosaic and yes, dull. Admittedly, most teenage girls look lumpy and uninteresting in bulky navy skirts and crumpled white blouses. But Juliette makes not the slightest effort even to keep herself clean. Her long black hair hangs like matted hessian. Her face and fingers are smeared with ink.

What on earth do I know about her, this fifteen-year-old who is my daughter? When I was her age I was randy as hell, playing truant from school and infuriating my mother by putting blonde streaks in my hair.

But Juliette appears to enjoy school. She certainly has hardly any other topic of conversation. At least with me. God knows what she finds to giggle about for hours with Gail. And when she's not enmeshed with Louis XIV or Keats, she's learning her lines for the latest Village Players production, or out collecting for Oxfam. I suppose I should be grateful she's so solidly normal, and not into drugs, married men or anorexia nervosa. She doesn't flounce about, slam doors or maintain sullen silences ... like I did. But I had some cause, with a mother like mine. At least Juliette won't feel driven to marry at the earliest opportunity just to get away from me.

'I'm going to have a poem in the school mag,' says Juliette. 'Shall I read it to you?'

Groaning inwardly, Caroline exclaims, 'Yes of course! I'd love to hear it.'

'It might sound a bit strange to you, because it's in blank verse. That means – '

'I do know what blank verse is.'

'Oh. Righto, here we go then.' Juliette lies on her stomach, her loosened school tie trailing in the coal-dusted hearth as she reads:

> 'She walks into the room;
> People turn, look round
> At her dress of red sequins
> Reaching
> Down to the ground.
> Her black hair is smoothed back;
> Large jewels from her ears
> Dangle and quiver
> Like newly shed tears.
> Her slender, smooth nails
> Click
> On the glass of bubbling champagne.
> She drifts past,
> Her dark eyes, thoughtful,
> Dwell on each face,
> Shy deep within,
> Wanting to know
> What impression she's made.
> Then,
> She goes;
> Leaves,
> Glides away without a trace,
> Except for the sparkling glass of champagne
> Standing there,
> Untouched.'

'That's really very good, Juliette. Where did you get the idea from? I mean, are you describing someone specific, or is that how you'd like to be yourself?'

Juliette wriggles on the fireside rug. 'Oh, I don't know, mum. I just dashed it off one evening. There's no deep, inner significance or anything.'

'Perhaps it'll win the magazine prize.'

'No. Penelope Horner, the Head Girl is sure to get that. I write stuff that everyone reads and enjoys. No one actually wades to the end of Penelope's turgid account of *Winter in Weybridge* – but because it's considered literary, it'll win a prize.'

Caroline lights a cigarette. Red sequinned dresses ... dangly earrings ... champagne. I had no idea Juliette harboured such fantasies. I wonder what she'd say if she knew I was planning to commit adultery tomorrow. Come to that, just what is the extent of Juliette's personal sexual experience?

Unnerving mother-daughter chats have been avoided, as the matter was handled most responsibly by Juliette's school. Caroline merely signed a form giving permission for her daughter to watch sex education films, about which Juliette said not a word at home.

Juliette has boyfriends, of course. Downy faced sixth-formers from school, and long-limbed lads from the tennis club. But Juliette treats them all with the same off-hand friendliness. She always courteously introduces them to Leo and me, and is rarely late home. A smart move, Caroline realises, as Leo is definitely the type to hurl himself into the role of carpet pacing Victorian father if the need arises.

'Shall I make us some coffee?' asks Juliette.

'Not for me, thanks. I'm off to bed. It's your father's away darts match tonight, and you know what a stew he's likely to be in if his team lost. I intend to be soundly asleep when he gets in.'

And I want to be fresh for Adrian tomorrow. As Caroline climbs the stairs she smiles, appreciating that Juliette must imagine her mother to be too old for sex. All girls of that age think their mothers are past it. I did about mine.

Lester Peters was the handy man called to Eaton Square to mend some broken shelves. One afternoon he poked his head round the kitchen door and told Rose that Lady Evelyn had just fallen downstairs.

'She's all right. Just a little dazed and confused,' he said. 'I expect she was feeling overtired, and missed her footing.'

Rose gave him a level look. His blue eyes were bland. 'That'll be it,' she replied. 'I'll take Lady Evelyn to her room.'

Over the following months, Rose kept an eye on Lester. He was definitely promising. He was at the house most weeks, making himself useful. His work was neat. He was careful not to throw his weight around with the butler. But most important, he didn't blab about anything he saw or heard.

Like the morning Lady Evelyn was rushed to a private clinic with cut hands after she smashed the whisky decanter. Or the time when Sir Desmond locked up the liquor cabinet, and Rose discovered her ladyship ransacking the larder for cooking sherry.

Throughout every commotion, lean, lanky Lester resolutely got on with his work. Rose approved. She admired a man who knew when to look the other way.

Having determined that he was unmarried, and alone in the world, Rose allowed him to accompany her on Sunday afternoon walks. He didn't intend to be an odd job man all his life, he told her.

'The thing about a posh area like this is that the nobs are desperate for ordinary blokes to come and fix things for them. I mean, around Eaton Square you can buy caviare, antiques, fancy clothes, no bother. But where do you go for screws, hammers, practical stuff? What I'm planning is to open my own hardware shop, with a repair business on the side.'

'How will you get the money to start?'

'I'm working on that,' grinned Lester.

Rose was impressed. Admittedly, Lester was secretive, his mouth was too thin and his long silences frightened her. But he was a go-ahead type. He would do.

A year later, Lester went into business on his own account. Rose never enquired where the capital for the shop had come from. And Lester never volunteered the information. Once he had set up on his own, Rose allowed him to kiss her. But no more. Not even when he bought a red MG and took her for spins to Windsor.

They were married at Chelsea Registry Office when Rose was twenty-three. Lester had given her a choice:

'We can have a slap up white wedding, Rose, with all the trimmings ... '

The expression made Rose feel like an oven-ready turkey.

' ... And there'll be enough left over for a downpayment on a house. Or I could use the cash to start another shop. I've been offered some premises cheap in South Kensington. Reckon I could really clean up.'

Oh, how Rose yearned for a house of her own. But she had always possessed the patience to wait for what she wanted.

'Expand,' she said. 'We'll live above the Chelsea shop for the time being. Then I can still work part time for Lady Evelyn.'

Her ladyship was overwhelmed with gratitude that dearest Rose would not be leaving her. She insisted on paying for Rose's going away outfit, and the honeymoon in Eastbourne.

Rose was adamant about Eastbourne. 'We'll start as we mean to go on,' she told Lester. 'Decent and respectable. And we'll stay at a proper hotel, not a tatty boarding house.'

'Aren't you inviting any of your family to the wedding?' he asked.

'No.' She didn't want that common Fulham crowd swigging brown ale at the reception. Besides, it was August and they'd all be away hop picking.

Lester insisted on accompanying Rose to choose their bits of furniture. 'We'll get the best we can afford,' he declared. 'That way it will always have a second hand value.'

They went to a sale, and came home with a tapestry covered sprung suite for £14. 19s. 6d. and an oak dining set which cost only sixteen guineas. Rose had to admit Lester possessed a sharp eye for a bargain.

Rose and her new husband enjoyed a week of blazing sunshine in Eastbourne. Day after day they lay in the long grass on top of the cliffs. On their last morning, Rose sat hugging her blue polka dot sundress round her knees, looking out at the clouds rolling in from the sea.

'They say they're war clouds, Lester. What will we do?'

'Get rich,' he said.

'But you'll have to go in the army.'

'Not me. Didn't I ever tell you about my dicky chest?'

'There's a lot of things you never tell me, Lester.'

He slid his hand underneath her skirt and snapped open her suspender. 'Come here. Have I ever told you how much I fancy those three little freckles at the top of your thigh?'

Rose moved her leg away. 'But Lester, if you don't join up, people will send you white feathers. I don't want everyone calling you a coward, and not speaking to us.'

He laughed. 'Don't fret yourself. I shall be a pillar of the Home Guard. Tireless in my efforts to rescue mothers and babies from blazing rubble. But one thing they're not doing, Peg o' my heart, is taking me away from you.'

Rose glanced round, satisfying herself that no one could see them. Then she lay back with him in the long grass, pulling down the straps of her sundress.

4

'Wow, Mollie! I'm really sorry you didn't win our Radio 2 Singalongaphone competition. But it's been great talking to you. And now – '

'Actually, we've met before you know, Dave. I was standing right at the front when you came to open our local supermarket in 1974.'

'No kidding! Wow! Well as an old friend I'm counting on you to ring in again, Mollie. So long for now – '

'Oh, I certainly shall, Dave. I'm quite an experienced broadcaster, actually. I was on the Peter Murray Carry On Singing competition.'

'You were? Fantastic! Well thanks – '

'I didn't win then, either. But I sang *Some Enchanted Evening* all the way through.'

'Wow! That must have sounded really great. I'm truly sorry I missed it.'

'I just want to thank you most sincerely for having me on your show, Dave. I'm really thrilled.'

'The pleasure was all mine, Mollie. Goodbye – '

'If I could just make a few dedications? To my dear husband Bob, listening at work, with many thanks for twenty wonderful years of marriage. And my two darling sons, Jason and Ryan, and Auntie Edie, who's taping this next door, Gran, Connie and all my friends and relations in Leicester, not forgetting . . . '

'Stupid bitch.' Caroline jabs off the radio and squirts Leo's shaving cream round what Annabel's beauty magazines coyly term the bikini area.

God, how I hate all this thick, fast growing hair. All being the apposite word, she reflects, carefully drawing the razor round her thigh. All those wasted hours spent shaving, plucking, waxing, creaming, even conditioning. Blondes have a far cushier time of it. What a disaster, though, when I tried bleaching it. Orange, it went. *The burning bush, ho, ho* quipped Leo. Still, at least the razor will tidy it up a bit, even if I do have to suffer the stubble tomorrow. I only hope Adrian appreciates all the trouble I'm going to on his behalf.

It is years since Caroline deliberately prepared her body for a man ... bathing, smoothing, painting, perfuming ... selecting clothes which will slide off easily. She chooses her prettiest front opening bra, silk cami-knickers and a flame red wool dress which zips up the back.

With her glossy hair brushed out, Caroline takes the handmirror to the bedroom window to check that her lipstick is on her mouth, not her teeth. In the lawn below, crocuses are pushing through, beguiled by the unexpectedly warm February sun into believing that winter has finally fled.

Appalled, Caroline stares into the mirror. Sod that sunshine! The cruel bright light is showing up all her lines, making her skin look grained, coarse ...

'Old,' whispers Caroline. 'I look old!'

Hastily, she steps away from the window, and studies herself in the full length wardrobe mirror. That's a little better. Her hair looks good styled like this, curling softly onto the polo neck of the Jean Muir. To afford the dress, she'd fed the family on mince for a month. But it was worth it. The fine wool hugs her full breasts, then swirls to a few inches below her knees, revealing long slim legs and elegant strappy shoes.

Before she leaves, Caroline examines her face once more. This time in the oval glass of the mirror in the hall. She smiles. Yes, that's how she remembers herself. Thick dark lashes fringing violet-blue eyes. A wide, sensitive mouth. And blessedly clear skin. Encouraged, she sprays on Arpège, ignoring the cold voice of reason pointing out that the hall is not only gloomy, but the mirror needs resilvering.

She times her arrival so as to be ten minutes late at the Green Man. Adrian's white Cortina is already there. Caroline strolls slowly across the car park, swinging her handbag by its long leather strap, conscious that he is watching her from the window.

Rounding the corner towards the saloon bar door, she is

dismayed to find Adrian waiting on one of the outside bench seats. He is wearing a dark blue blazer, and grey slacks. A local map is spread across the elm table.

Is he circling possible lovers' lanes, wonders Caroline. She hopes he has had the foresight to bring a rug.

He rises. 'Hello there, Bianca! You've brought the good weather with you. Much too nice a day to sit in a stuffy pub and eat, don't you think?'

Instinctively, Caroline's hand flies to her face. Those wretched wrinkles. That hateful sun. Damn! She had been counting on the flattery of the dim lighting in the pub.

It is on the tip of her tongue to allege that direct sun disagrees with her ... makes her eyes water ... her lips blister. But such a protest is hardly in keeping with her image of today. The Biancas of this world are confident creatures, svelte, brilliant women eagerly seizing life and moulding it to their will. They do not possess rheumy eyes, cracked lips and the desire to cringe in dark corners.

As Adrian fetches the drinks, Caroline recalls those teenage pub crawls with Leo, in the days when she had gloried in the sun. Then, she had lifted her head to welcome it, aware of Leo's admiration as the red lights glistened in her hair. Yet now here she is, seventeen years on, tense with anxiety in case the grey is showing through the black rinse. Wishing she'd had the sense to wear sunglasses. But in February?

'The ploughmans are quite a speciality here,' says Adrian, setting down a loaded tray. 'So I took the liberty of ordering you one. Hope that's all right.'

It is not all right. Caroline is allergic to cheese. It gives her migraine. She visualises the crusty French bread stuck solidly to each cheek of her bottom. However, Biancas who are out to get laid do not carp on about headaches or diets.

Caroline bites boldly into the sharp Cheddar and murmurs, 'So how have you been, Adrian?' Terrific, Bianca. Sensational conversational opening. Such zap. Such originality.

'Thinking of you,' he smiles, staring straight into her eyes.

Caroline tells herself he is not mentally counting the tread marks, aghast at the bags, comparing her with wifey Sue who is a dewy ten years younger. Speedily, she gulps down half a glass of red wine, trying to will herself into a suitably sophisticated mood.

Adrian tops her up from the carafe, chatting easily about his job.

'The woman had asked me to come and give an evaluation on her three-bed semi. She trailed round with me, accompanied by a right sissy of a son – the sort who's only really happy clinging to mummy's skirts. In fact, that's just what he was doing, rubbing his hand up and down her legs. Evidently a lot of kids do it – security, reassurance, all that crap. Anyway, the woman bends down to pick up a stray toy, and at the same time asks me what my fees are. Well, the kid must have had his sweaty fingers curled round the top of her. tights, because as she leaned over, down slid her tights and pants!'

Caroline lights a cigarette and affects a gay laugh. 'What did you do?'

'I couldn't resist it. I said, *I'm sorry, Madam, we don't accept payment in kind.*'

He pushes across the tin ashtray. 'Fortunately, this afternoon should present no similar dramas. I've just got to check on some vacant furnished flats we're due to re-let.'

Caroline manages a cool smile of which Bianca would have been proud. She wonders how much Sue knows of Adrina's flat inspections. And to think Sue is gormless enough to give up her own evenings out because Adrian insists that she cook dinner for him and his cronies.

But at least the seduction is to be satisfactorily stage-managed. Furnished flats come complete with beds. There will be no fumbling across the gear lever, or rolling in long grass with ants and nettles orchestrating a stinging accompaniment.

Adrian is studying her through half closed eyes. 'I have decided,' he says slowly, 'that you have the most perfect, kissable mouth.'

Oh God. He means he expects me to give him a blow job. Well I can't. I won't. Somehow, before we get to the bed bit, he'll have to be told.

Caroline wipes her clammy hands on a paper napkin. The

48

subject of oral sex is a constant source of disagreement between herself and Leo.

'What's wrong with it? Most wives get a real thrill from sucking their husband's cock.'

'I'm not *most wives*. I'm me. I've never enjoyed it. I don't like you doing it to me, and I don't want to do it to you.'

'There seem to be an increasing number of things you don't like doing nowadays.'

'What the hell is that supposed to mean?'

'Oh ... forget it. Go to sleep.'

Obviously, he is implying that our sex life isn't much fun any more. My fault. He can't understand how his teenage raver has turned into a middle-aged mum.

Oh, leave it out, Caroline! Thirty-five isn't old. It isn't even middle-aged. For heavens sake, you are a good looking, sexy woman. You must have something going for you to attract Adrian, a man five years younger than yourself.

She watches him order a second carafe of wine, and slip his arm round her shoulders, across the back of the bench. To her relief, the sun has gone in.

'Mmm, I always feel so wickedly languorous after red wine, don't you Bianca?'

'Oh yes! White wine never seems to have quite the same delicious effect, does it?'

Suppose I catch something? What if I do agree to go down on him and I get oral gonorrhoea? Or crabs? Can you get crabs in the mouth? Do they latch onto the men's moustaches? Come to that, most woman have fine hair on their top lips. Can crabs –

Give it a rest, Caroline! Sparkle. Make with the charm, the sultry looks, the throaty laughs. When you were younger, the old razzle dazzle was second nature to you.

Caroline takes a deep breath. Amazed, she hears herself ask, 'Have you any children Adrian?' *What?*

'Children? Oh. Er, yes. Just the one, Luke. He's three and a half.'

'They're really into everything at that age, aren't they?' Strewth, you'll be asking to see a snapshot next.

'Fortunately, we've got quite a big garden, so the little terror can run wild in there.'

'Oh, are you a keen gardener?'

'To be honest, I do quite pride myself on my compost.'
'Really? I never seem to have much success with mine.'
Farewell, Bianca.
'Ah, well I'll let you into a little secret. Urine.'
'Indeed?'
'Urine, you see, contains some sort of activating ingredient which makes for really rich compost.'
It begins to rain. They both rise hastily, glancing at watches, uttering little cries of surprise at the lateness of the hour.
'It's been lovely, Adrian.'
'Yes, we must do it again sometime.'
'I'll give you a ring.'
'I'll look forward to that.'

Caroline drives home at reckless speed. Of all the naive, adolescent behaviour, she berates herself. Even Juliette could have handled the situation with more style, less gangling naivety. She tears along the Hog's Back, gaining a grim satisfaction in overtaking every car all the way back to Maybrook.

Over the slam of the garage door she hears the phone ringing. The front door key appears to be warped. She fights with the lock, bursts breathlessly into the hall and snatches up the receiver. As the pips sound, Caroline notices Juliette's crumpled velour hat lying on the floor.

'Juliette! Why the hell didn't you answer the phone?'

Her daughter's voice floats down, self righteously, from above. 'We were let out early today to *revise*.'

'Hi? Is that Caroline Lambert?'

Caroline frowns. Who does she know with such a pronounced American accent? 'Yes, speaking. I didn't quite catch – '

'The name's Dallow. I'm calling from a phone box in Bayswater. Maybe you recall that through the International Women's Sisterhood you most kindly agreed to put me up for a while.'

'Oh ... yes *of course*.'

Caroline has completely forgotten. At her women's group a few months back, they agreed that it would be valuable to establish contact with feminists from other countries.

'I'm really looking forward to meeting you, Dallow. When would you like to come?' Dallow *who*? Or was it Ms Dallow?

'As a matter of fact I'm on my way now.'

'*Lovely*.' Recoiling from her own hysterical tone, Caroline consciously lowers her voice. 'Tell me what train you're catching and I'll meet you in the car.'

'Don't trouble yourself, Caroline. I'll just pitch up later.' The pips sound. 'Ciao.'

Caroline races up to Juliette's room. 'Darling, come and give me a hand. A girl – woman – called Dallow is on her way and the spare room's full of junk.'

Juliette is sprawled face down on her Indian bedspread, surrounded by French texts, notebooks and felt-tip pens leaking onto a pile of jam sandwiches.

'Dallow who?'

'I don't know. My only information is that she's American, and connected with the International Women's Sisterhood.'

Juliette carefully slips a crust into the French grammar to mark her place. 'In that case, she'll either be a glowing Californian blonde in sawn off jeans, or a dynamic frizzy haired Jewish New Yorker.'

'Either way, she'll need somewhere to sleep. Can you take four steaks from the freezer, then fetch the almond sheets from the airing cupboard, and matching guest towels. In the meantime I'll start clearing up.'

The spare room smells, not unpleasantly, of geranium cuttings which line the windowsill and a pine chest of drawers. The dressing table is heaped with hexagonal pieces of material which for the past five years Caroline has been intending to sew into a quilt. On the bed is a tangle of leotards, tights, leg warmers, pumps and tap shoes, the legacy of Caroline's flits through local dancing classes.

She began, two winters ago, with keep fit. Rolling around the dusty village hall to the accompaniment of *Campdown Races* falteringly picked out on an out-of-tune piano. Seeking more excitement, Caroline progressed to Music and Movement, circling 'smoothly, gracefully, ladies,' round the Evening Institute to the strains of *Wheel Cha-Cha-Cha*.

Then tap dancing, ('Ain't We Got Fun') bringing back

memories of a little girl in a white dress, rejoicing at her only opportunity to put on red shoes. 'They are to be used only for your class, Caroline. To be seen wearing red shoes in the street is distinctly common.'

Best of all were the private disco dancing sessions organised by Zoe, a glamorous young redhead with a gold chain round her ankle. In Zoe's large oak panelled dining room, mercifully bare of mirrors, Caroline and her friends bopped energetically to a tape of *Saturday Night Fever*. Desperately, they tried to emulate the movements of lithe, winter tanned Zoe. But Caroline suspected that she and the others were displaying as much natural rhythm as a flock of beheaded chickens.

The classes ended abruptly when Zoe was offered a cabaret engagement in Frankfurt. Overnight she became a local celebrity. Under the geraniums on the pine chest is a page from the *Maybrook Gazette* containing a picture of Zoe in a slit skirt, waving from the steps of an airliner. *On the Way Up* reads the caption.

Unaccountably aggravated by the photograph, Caroline scoops up the geraniums and shreds the newspaper into the bin. An hour later the room is fragrant with the scent of lavender bags tucked under pillows. A water jug, glass, boutique tissues and current copies of *Spare Rib* lie on the bedside table. As Caroline is tucking a spare light bulb into the dressing table drawer, the door bell rings. She hurls the vacuum cleaner, duster and spray polish into the airing cupboard and runs downstairs.

'Hi!' smiles Dallow.

She is wearing red velvet jeans and an orange anorak. Beneath a canary yellow rainhat, curls hang limply to her broad shoulders. The hair is grey. Dallow, Caroline calculates, must be at least fifty years old.

'I hitched a lift right down the freeway,' says Dallow, following Caroline into the sitting room.

Her bright clothes jar against Caroline's carefully co-ordinated green and beige colour scheme. Or is it, Caroline wonders, that the room is all wrong? Does it look dull, unadventurous and provincial to a person accustomed to thumbing lifts down motorways?

'It's lovely you're here so early. To be honest, Juliette and I have only just finished getting your room ready.'

'Oh, you shouldn't have troubled yourself.' Dallow heaves her rucksack onto the carpet. 'I carry a sleeping bag. Say, what an amazing room. Are these all antiques?'

'No, they're reproduction yew,' explains Juliette. 'My mother says there's less danger of woodworm than in the genuine article.'

Thanks, Juliette. Your support is truly appreciated. 'It's not too early for a drink, is it Dallow? Or would you prefer coffee?' Have a drink. Please. I need one.

Dallow rummages in her rucksack and pulls out some sachets. 'I never touch alcohol. But I'd love some herbal tea.'

'Let me make it,' offers Juliette sweetly. 'I'm sure you and mother must have heaps to talk about.'

Dallow strips off the dripping orange anorak, and drapes it across the bookcase.

'Make yourself at home,' says Caroline, drawing the sofa nearer the fire.

Dallow sits cross legged on the floor, her back resting against Leo's favourite armchair. She cups her hands, one on top of the other, in her lap.

Caroline busies herself piling logs onto the fire. She wishes Juliette would hurry up with the tea. Dallow's serene smile is setting her nerves on edge.

'Er ... which part of America are you from, Dallow?'

'Maryland originally. But I've spent the last fifteen years on the move. Been round the world twice, in fact. Have you travelled much, Caroline?'

'I ... I know Yugoslavia pretty well.'

The Lamberts holiday at the same Dalmatian coast resort every year. After trial and error Leo has found Yugoslavia to be the one country where men don't automatically start turning cartwheels around his bikinied wife. In the early years of their marriage they visited Sicily. Leo nearly started a mafia war when he discovered one of the beach boys lying at the bottom of a flight of steps, peering lustfully up Caroline's skirt.

Dallow slips off her sandals. 'Sure. I camped out in the

53

Julian Alps for eighteen months. Of all languages, Serbo Croat is the most expressive, don't you find?'

'Oh, here's Juliette with the tea.' Caroline looks longingly towards the drinks cupboard. 'We'll eat early tonight. You must be ravenous after your journey, Dallow. I hope steak will be all right?'

'I'm not into the meat scene,' says Dallow, inhaling her herbal brew. She pats her rucksack. 'Carry everything I need in here. Blackstrap molasses, muesli, dried apricots. Don't worry yourself. I'll just squat here and mix up my own bowl of nutrients. It's what I'm accustomed to.'

With an effort, Caroline stills a mother-hen protest about the value of healthy greens and fresh fruit.

'One thing I would be glad of, if you have it, Caroline, is some fresh made mayonnaise.'

Juliette giggles. 'Mayonnaise and muesli?'

'Oh, it's not to eat. I smooth it onto my skin. Far more effective than expensive face creams and purer, too.'

Lost for words, mother and daughter regard their guest's prune-like complexion. The incredulous silence is broken by the scrape of Leo's key in the lock. Caroline flies to the front door.

'You're early!' she accuses.

'Sorry. I didn't know I had to make a special appointment to come home.' He hands her his raincoat. 'Actually, there's a distribution balls up at the works, so everything's ground to a halt. By the way, a button's come off my mac.'

'I'll do it for you. Listen, we've got a visitor. A woman called Dallow. She's American, connected with the Sisterhood. Try and be polite to her, Leo.'

'Dallow who?'

'I don't know.'

'What's she like?'

'Very interesting, really. She's lived in Yugo – '

'I mean, is she a looker?'

'No. She's hardly in what you'd call the first flush of youth.'

'Oh. How long's she staying?'

'I don't know. She hasn't said.'

'Well can't you find out? Ask her.'

'It would be so rude. Don't you remember the awful way mother used to prowl round people she didn't like, saying *Would you like a cup of tea before you go.*'

'Yes I do remember. Vividly.' Leo pauses at the living room door. 'What are you all tarted up for?'

Caroline realises she is still wearing the flame coloured dress she put on for Adrian. Her lips and nails are painted to match. God, whatever must Dallow think of her?

She murmurs vaguely, 'I had lunch with Annabel,' and urges him into the sitting room to meet Dallow.

Leo steps across the rucksack, glares at the anorak shrouding the bookcase, and perches on the arm of the sofa. Caroline pours him a beer, and a large scotch for herself. As she escapes to the kitchen to prepare dinner, she hears Leo enquire in a tone of heavy sociability:

'Well, now you've made your way here to darkest Surrey, Dallow, I hope you won't be rushing off too soon?'

'I'll just play it by ear, Leo. I never like to schedule my time. I'm more a creature of moods, you know?'

Juliette dodges dinner, announcing that she'll grab a hamburger round at Gail's. There is a film about Louis XIV they want to watch on television.

Caroline realises that it would be the height of bad manners to allow Dallow to squat on the floor eating muesli by herself. The sisterly solution is to bring a bowl and join her guest. So Leo sits in solitary state at the polished table, chomping his way through steak and chips, while the two women kneel on the fireside rug, sharing Dallow's meagre provisions. Between mouthfuls of rolled oats, Dallow tells them about the sorry plight of her women friends in Bedouin encampments.

Half way through the meal, the telephone rings in the hall. Leo answers it.

'It's for you, Caro. Frances.'

'I can't speak to her now, Leo. Tell her I'll call – '

Leo sits down. 'You ought to talk to her. She sounds pretty cut up about something.'

Caroline is reluctant to leave her husband alone with Dallow. He is bound to provoke an argument. On the other hand, she doesn't want to put herself in a bad light with

Dallow by refusing the upset Frances womanly support.

Caroline hurries out into the hall, determined to hustle Frances through her crisis. It's probably something quite minor. A staff room dispute, or one of her sons setting fire to the sofa again.

'Caroline? It's mother. She's ... she's dead.'

'Oh no! Frances, I'm so sorry. How did it happen? Was it one of her turns?'

From the sitting room, Caroline hears Leo asserts, 'I don't care what you say. Yoga is crap.'

' ... at least one a week, so I didn't pay too much attention. Just put her to bed as usual with some arrowroot. Then when I took her tea in this morning, there she was on the floor ... '

'I can meditate perfectly well without contorting myself into the lotus position. I jog five miles every day. I dig my allotment. You'd do better to let the fresh air blow through your head instead of sitting in fetid rooms tying yourself in knots.'

' ... never realised there was so much hassle involved after a death, Caroline. First you have to phone all the relatives to give them the bad news. Then you ring them back with details of the funeral. They all live a great distance away, so they just assume I can put them up for the night. So far I've got twelve people coming and I'm at my wits' end over blankets ... '

'Camping out on the Yugoslavian Alps or with a tribe of Bedouins is not what I mean by the healthy outdoor life. That's not self expression. It's plain self indulgence. I often feel I'd like to drop out myself. But with a wife and child, and a mortgage round my neck ... '

'And the catering is a nightmare. Honestly, I was near to tears in Sainsbury's this afternoon, trying to remember if Auntie Hilda is the one who always chokes on chicken bones, and is Uncle Arthur allergic to ham?'

'No I certainly hadn't realised you were a mother. You're seriously telling me you've left two children in the hands of a commune while you gallivant off round the world ... ?'

'And why was I buying ham anyway?' Frances demands shrilly. 'I hate ham. Why do people always serve it up at

56

funerals? Why can't I give them pâté and quiche instead?'

'I'm sure after the trauma of the day they'll be grateful for anything,' murmurs Caroline. Black spots heralding migraine are beginning to haze her aching eyes. She remembers that all she has eaten today is Cheddar for lunch and that sawdust muesli with Dallow. Alarmed by the ominous silence in the living room, Caroline cuts through France's tirade on racketeering undertakers and promises to phone in the morning.

She finds Dallow alone, peacefully lighting up a joint. Leo is in the kitchen, demolishing an apricot tart.

'I must say, Caro, you've got some bloody peculiar friends. Thank God there's football on the telly tonight. I can't take much more of that weirdo. Why doesn't she wear a bra? Her tits have spread under that jumper like stale eggs across a frying pan.'

'Women in the Sisterhood aren't obsessed with their appearance,' says Caroline, uneasily aware of her flowered Maidenform beneath the expensive wool dress.

'And what's this girlish sitting cross-legged on the floor bit? Have you noticed the way she keeps grabbing her bare foot – her feet are filthy by the way – and shoving it deeper and deeper into her crotch? I mean, what's she doing? Masturbating? Because I tell you straight, Caro, I won't have it in my house on my front room floor.'

'Look, I'm sorry you can't get past her to your chair. I'll try and get her to move.'

'And all that greasy grey hair hanging round her shoulders. How old is she anyway?'

The back door opens to admit Juliette and Gail.

'Gail's colour telly is on the blink. It's boring watching the black and white portable, so we're going to see the film on our set,' explains Juliette, sliding her transistor radio onto the breakfast bar.

You mean you've brought Gail back to inspect Mummy's freakish friend, thinks Caroline.

'I don't know about that,' says Leo. 'If the film clashes with my football ... '

'But it's for our exam, Mr Lambert,' protests Gail breathlessly. 'We *have* to watch.'

Smoky eyes, fringed by tobacco coloured lashes, stare beguilingly up at Leo. Caroline follows her husband's gaze to Gail's starched school blouse, with the top three buttons casually undone.

She sighs. 'Must you have that radio on so loud, Juliette?'

'I just thought you might be interested,' says Juliette, with maddening patience, 'in the fact that the next person on the Jed Jarvis phone-in show is going to be Granny. Your mother.'

'What?'

'They announced it just before this record came on, Mrs Lambert. Listen!'

'And now I'm delighted to say hello to Mrs Rose Scott-Peters from Edinburgh. Are you there, Rose?'

'Hello?'

'Am I speaking to Rose Scott-Peters?'

'Hello?'

'This is Jed Jarvis, Rose.'

'Are we on the radio now?'

'Indeed we are. Broadcasting coast to coast on Radio 2. But you don't sound like a bonnie Scot, Rose.'

'No, I spent all my married life in Surrey. I moved up here when my husband passed on. Now I'm all on my own.'

'Alone but not lonely, I hope?'

'Well I was all by myself over Christmas, Jed.'

'Oh, that's just terrible. Have you no children?'

'I do have a daughter, but she's always so busy. I'm supposed to be going to visit her in the spring but I still don't know if she wants me to come or not.'

'I'll tell you what we'll do, Rose. We'll play this next record specially for your daughter. That's for Mrs Rose Scott-Peter's daughter, living in ... where does she live, Rose?'

'Lavender Cottage, Maybrook, Surrey.'

'So if you're listening in Lavender Cottage, Maybrook, er – '

'Caroline. Caroline Lambert.'

'Caroline Lambert, I hope you're tuned in. How about dropping your poor old mum a line or two and getting that visit fixed up, eh?'

'The cow!' screams Caroline. 'The lying, twisted bitch!'

'What lovely healthy lungs!' beamed the nurse.

'It's a girl.' Lester's voice was flat. 'Can't you stop her making that racket?'

Rose was lying in a private room paid for by Lady Evelyn. She held the baby close to her bedjacket, to muffle the insistent crying. 'I can have a boy next time, Lester.'

Clearly this was not the moment to confess that there wasn't going to be a next time. Rose wasn't enduring another agonising twenty-two hour labour with only a 50-50 chance of giving him his precious son. She'd got what she wanted: one child, to secure her marriage, her future. Overnight, she had turned Lester from a guy with an eye for the girls into a respectable family man. There was no danger now of him abandoning her for someone younger and prettier.

Not that I don't keep myself nice, she congratulated herself. Even Lady Evelyn admired that afternoon dress I made from blackout material, with the bodice ribboned in blue. Lucky ribbon isn't on ration. I'll use some to decorate the baby's bonnets.

Rose planned to call her daughter Maureen. But Lester registered her as Caroline Louise. 'Maureen sounds bog-Irish. Caroline has a much more stylish ring to it.'

Once Caroline was weaned, Rose went back to work, proudly wheeling the baby there in the pram which had once borne Lady Evelyn's daughter. In Eaton Square, you wouldn't have known there was a war on. The Lyalls never seemed short of coupons, and Rose made a point of getting on well with the cook. There was always a tasty bit of steak, oranges, or fresh eggs for her to take home every day.

But after a few weeks, Rose was forced to give in her notice. Caroline, a highly-strung, anxious baby, cried incessantly. She upset the rest of the staff and, worse, irritated Lady Evelyn's delicate nerves.

'I'm afraid we'll have to let you go, Rose,' Sir Desmond said sorrowfully, pressing a white £5 note into her hand. 'But do come back and see us from time to time, won't you? Let us know how you're getting on.'

'For Christ's sake,' shouted Lester. 'Keep the bleeding kid quiet, can't you?'

They were still living above the shop in Chelsea. Caroline screamed in the night, keeping Lester awake, and during the day her howling drove him to distraction when he was trying to serve customers.

In desperation, Rose took the baby for long walks beside the river. She felt raw with exhaustion. Lester, determined to father a son, was at her every night. Rose had never derived much pleasure from lovemaking, but since Caroline's birth she found the whole experience not only distasteful but painful too.

The health visitor said this was nothing to worry about.

'Tell the brute to keep to his own side of the bed for a month or so. You'll soon be back to normal. Now, any other problems?'

'Yes ... I find ... I don't have any real feeling of affection for my daughter. I can't seem to love her.'

'Nonsense.' The health visitor's voice was like a cushion. Soft, enveloping, suffocating. 'All mummies love their babies. You love yours, too, deep down. It's only natural.'

Rose tried to believe her. Though how could she know what love was, when no one had ever shown her any? She certainly derived a glow of satisfaction from the knowledge that Caroline was hers. Was the pleasure of possession the same as love? Rose had no way of telling.

'I can't take much more of this,' Lester said that night, as Caroline's yells drowned the sound of the All-Clear. 'We'll have to sell up and move. Get a house somewhere away from my job.' He had in mind a small town just into Surrey, he said. It would be safer there. Fewer air raids. A healthier place to bring up kids.

Rose went to bed happy for the first time in months. They were moving. They would have a proper home. She would be a decent, respectable housewife. Just like everyone else.

As Lester pulled up her nightdress, Rose willed Caroline to cry, to give her an excuse for escaping his embrace. But perversely, the child slept peacefully. While Lester went to work on her, Rose lay rigid, hoping that by keeping her muscles tense, she could prevent the sperm from wriggling

60

through. As her husband whispered endearments, Rose thought about the discarded white lace curtains she'd removed from Lady Evelyn's bedroom. She'd dip them in cold tea, to turn them a fashionable beige shade, and hang them in the nursery of her new house.

The following day, she took the £5 Sir Desmond had given her, and went to get herself fitted with a contraceptive cap. If she was careful, Rose reasoned, there was no need ever for Lester to know.

5

'Just imagine you're shitting out an enormous grapefruit,' Dallow advises the pregnant Wendy. 'I brought forth my first child in a cave on the side of a Yugoslavian mountain. The peasants clasped me to their bosoms. It was the most exhilarating experience.'

Dallow smiles as Frances enters, patting the fireside rug as an invitation to the deputy headmistress to join her on the floor. Frances's eyes frost in disbelief and she subsides, straight-backed onto the Parker Knoll.

Juliette hugs her knees. This is even better than she anticipated. She can't wait to tell Gail.

'You've never shown the remotest interest in my women's group before,' Caroline accused Juliette that morning. 'No doubt Gail has also suddenly developed an urge to have her consciousness raised.'

'No, Gail's not coming.' Gail, unfortunately, couldn't dodge a Village Players dress rehearsal. 'Look, if you don't want me to be there, just say so. I should have thought you would have been glad of some support, that's all.'

Rarely is Juliette given the pleasure of seeing her mother so discomposed. She has always regarded Caroline as such a dauntingly self assured woman. Caroline would have dominated her daughter completely had not Juliette, in subconscious defence over the years, thrown up her own barrier. It is erected from O Level work which Caroline does not understand ... secret fears and desires exchanged only with Gail ... and strong, strange longings which Juliette shares with no one. Cohering the structure is a patchy veneer of brittle confidence and gritty good humour.

Safe behind her barricade, Juliette watched admiringly as within only three days Dallow contrived to ruffle Caroline's cool exterior. Over breakfast, Dallow wedged herself on the floor between the washing machine and the fridge and, with a mouthful of dried prunes, expounded on the scores of women's associations with which she had been involved.

' ... fascinating Marxist group in Paris. And at the National Socialist Feminist Conference I stood up and ... '

Caroline, concentrating on tying up bacon rinds for the birds, said nervously, 'You do realise, Dallow, that we're just an ordinary bunch of local women. We're not high powered, you know, or political in any way ... '

Dallow slithered her right foot hard into her crotch. She gazed at Caroline politely, expectantly, helping her not at all.

'I mean,' Caroline floundered on, 'I would have thought you'd feel more at home with one of the big London groups.'

'No way.' Dallow spread her hands dismissively. 'I was in Hampstead last week, and could I relate to the group there? To be fair, they were committed and very active. But it was all, "I'll ask Germaine to sign our petition ... No, don't bother, I'm seeing her tonight. I'll ask her. And Vanessa too ... I thought Nessa was in Rome? ... She is, but she's promised to call me this evening ... OK, I'll ring Jill, then, and get her to give us a mention in her *Guardian* piece. She owes me a favour ... But aren't we preaching to the converted by using the *Guardian?* Don't all faint but I had lunch last week with the editor of *Woman's Own* and she was very sympathetic."'

Juliette grinned, hoping her imitation was as devastating when she regaled Gail with it all during mid-morning break.

'It's mighty fine of you to call a special meeting just for me, Caroline,' went on Dallow. 'What I really thirst for is contact with an honest-to-God grass roots group. Like yours. I long to embrace the women who are closer to the basic concepts of feminism. My true sisters of the earth, who understand the primitive pleasure of tasting their own menstrual blood. Now what time does the action start?'

Juliette senses her mother's relief at the arrival of the last member of the group. After Wendy admitting she's due to have her baby not in a cave, but hygienically in hospital, and Frances shocking Dallow with her old-fashioned belief

63

in the three Rs, it is a consolation being able to produce someone mildly unconventional.

'This is Babs, Dallow.' Caroline gives a lighthearted little laugh. 'She's not as drearily domesticated as the rest of us. In fact she has an extremely volatile relationship with the art student she lives with. Life's a perpetual drama for you, isn't it Babs?'

Taking her cue, Babs tosses her red hair, injecting a devil-take-the-hindmost sparkle into her eyes.

Dallow is staring dreamily into the fire. 'I once lived with a Bantu on a reservation. Highly illegal, naturally.' She grasps Babs's hands and declares intensely, 'Of course, after six months you realise you're never going to view anything in quite the same light again, don't you?'

Juliette is disappointed to learn that Dallow is straight. She was hoping for revelations of lesbianism. Neither Juliette nor Gail have ever met a practising lesbian, and they enjoy long, hilarious conversations in Gail's bedroom about what women actually *do* to one another.

Babs gulps, 'You, er, live and travel alone, now, Dallow?'

'I do indeed.' Her heel grinds into the crotch of the red velvet trousers. 'When I was thirty-five I made a conscious commitment and became celibate.'

The women busy themselves lifting or putting down glasses, their faces set in expressions of glazed awe.

Ace, grins Juliette. This will really make them feel like hayseeds.

At last Frances says, in what Juliette recognises as her Now-We're-All-Grown-Up-People-Who-See-Nothing-to-Laugh-at-in-the-Functions-of-the-Human-Body voice, 'Could you elaborate on that for us, Dallow? How you came to make this decision, and how easy it has been to implement?' *Celibacy as a Way of Life. Discuss.*

'I'd be glad to.' Dallow gazes meaningfully up at the ceiling.

Juliette observes her mother twitchily smoking a cigarette, wondering if Dallow is deliberately drawing attention to the champagne stain up there.

'Thirty-five is, of course, a watershed in any woman's life. Because it marks roughly the half way point. As it happened, on my thirty-fifth birthday, I had just come to the end of a meaningful, but totally exhausting relationship with a man.'

Juliette starts counting. For God's sake, just how many men has this old crone gone through in her time?

Dallow twines a lock of grey hair round her finger. 'We had trekked together across the South African Karoo. When the day came for us to part – for his destiny lay east, and mine west – I stood in the burning sun and watched him ride out of sight. Then I flung off my clothes and hurled myself into a water hole. My man and I had battled through wind and rain and scorching heat. At night we had abandoned ourselves to love. Never had my body felt so used. And abused.'

Frances tugs her gaberdine skirt firmly over her knees.

'The water was like a balm. Healing, soothing, refreshing. As I lay there, I knew I wanted my body to feel like that forever. Cleansed, pure, untouched. I had experienced every conceivable physical sensation. Now I would give my body the gift of peace. There and then I embraced the celibate way of life.'

Babs blurts, 'But don't you ever feel randy?'

'It passes,' smiles Dallow indulgently. 'Oh, I know celibate is a boo word. It stinks of dried up spinsters with shrunken vaginas. But speaking personally, I have no need now of sex. Life itself is my orgasm.'

Wendy is looking anxious and concerned. 'I'm sure if I adopted your philosophy, Dallow, I would miss the companionship and support of my husband.' Her tone is reverent. 'I suppose you could say he's my best friend.'

'Scotch anyone?' rasps Caroline.

Juliette wriggles with delight as Frances hesitates, then refuses. Deputy Heads cannot be seen swigging whisky in front of fifth year students.

'What you have to remember, Wendy,' says Dallow, 'is that I had fulfilled my creative span. I had allowed myself the indulgence of bringing forth two children.'

'Having kids is hardly an indulgence, surely?' queries Babs.

Dallow stretches, arching her back. 'But don't we all agree that from a truly feminist point of view, all babies are pollution? Isn't baby a boo word?'

Juliette, who has been sitting tightly cross-legged for the past fifteen minutes, reluctantly makes a dash for the downstairs cloakroom. When she returns, she is infuriated to hear Frances resolutely steering the conversation into more familiar waters.

'By the way, Caroline, I heard your mother of all people on the radio the other day.'

'I didn't know you listened to pop phone-in programmes, Frances,' comments Juliette, ignoring her mother's *shut up, you've had too much wine*, stare.

During the pause, Juliette makes a mental note to mimic for Gail Frances's swift changes of expression. Clearly, her immediate instinct, coupled with years of professional training, urges her to adopt her dismissive Deputy Head voice. Yet because Juliette is her friend's daughter, she cannot in all politeness be snubbed too abruptly. Worse, this is a women's group meeting, and Juliette, as a fledgling sister, cannot be put down at all. In fact, she has to be positively encouraged.

Frances injects some warmth into her tone. 'I regard it as part of my job to tune in to a pop station occasionally. Just to keep up to date on what my pupils are listening to, and being influenced by.'

'It was all a pack of lies,' mutters Caroline indignantly. 'I *have* written to her, ages ago, confirming the spring visit. And I invited her down for Christmas, but she refused to come.'

'Amongst the Bantu,' murmurs Dallow sagely, 'all the old women – '

'When your mother comes to stay, Caroline,' interrupts Wendy, 'bring her round to me for tea. It will be a nice little outing for her.'

'Drop in for a cup of tea any time you like,' invited Rose's new neighbour in the small suburban town of Melford. 'I've got cousins in America, so I never go short. You're always welcome.'

'I won't, thanks all the same,' replied Rose stiffly. 'No offence, but I prefer to keep myself to myself.'

'Well! Suit yourself, I'm sure!' The back door slammed, sending pebble dash raining down onto the crazy paved path.

Rose was unrepentant. Start as you mean to go on, she advised herself. She had no intention of emulating Flo. That tiny house in Fulham had been swarming with Artillery Road folk all hours of the day and night. Let them get one foot in the door and you'd never be able to call the place your own again.

The Peters' new home was only a semi, and rented at that. But for the first time in her life, Rose felt truly respectable.

No one in Melford knew she'd been in service. Or that she'd grown up in a tatty Fulham backstreet. No one need ever know. Lester travelled into London each day by car, and Rose unbent sufficiently to let it be known in Glebe Close that as her poor husband possessed a damaged lung, he had not been passed for Army service.

Rose sang as she scrubbed her floors, cleaned her windows, and ran up parachute silk bedspreads. She rarely sat down, or rested. She was so grateful to have her own little house, and in such a nice neighbourhood, too.

Mind you, she had to admit she missed all the little luxuries provided by Lady Evelyn. The cast-off couture dresses, the sugar, and chocolates. Rose realised she was making it hard on herself by not cultivating the friendship of her neighbours. It meant they refused to tell her when the corner shop had oranges in. And the woman next door never offered a share of her American food parcels. If they were unlucky and got bombed out, Rose knew she had forfeited all the local camaraderie, the rallying round with offers of beds, hot drinks, meals and comfort.

'We don't care, do we Caroline?' she crooned as she pushed her daughter round the park. 'We don't need anyone else.'

Caroline had stopped crying the moment the removal van drove away from Glebe Close. She was an amazingly transformed child, with a smiling, sunny disposition that not even the worst air raids could shake.

Lester was delighted. 'There you are. I told you she'd change once I got her out of London. She likes it here. We'll get a swing. And I'll make a sandpit at the end of the garden. Our boy will enjoy messing around in that.' He squeezed Rose's waist as she stood over the gas stove. 'No sign, yet, of anything?'

Rose carefully strained the peas. 'I'm afraid not, dear.'

Rose made it a rule that whenever Lester was in residence, so was her cap. Just to make sure. What fools men were. What stupid, gullible fools.

'Plenty of time yet,' said Lester. 'Handy having the park so near. When we have a son I'll take him there to play football. Be a laugh, though, if he's brainy enough to go to a posh school and ends up playing rugger.'

Ballet classes, decided Rose. As soon as Caroline is old enough, I'll put her name down, somewhere select. She'll meet some nice girls there. I don't want her mixing with common rubbish . . . anyone likely to fill her head with weird ideas.

'Actually, I rather liked Dallow,' Juliette confesses to Gail as they settle themselves on the school library radiator during mid-morning break. She bites into a Marmite sandwich. 'She said I had a mother of pearl aura.'

Gail is impressed. 'Did she say anything about me?'

'No. But I should think with your colouring, your aura would have a goldy tinge about it.'

'Like a sunrise?' suggests Gail hopefully.

'Probably.' Juliette can afford to be generous. After all, Dallow had not found Gail worthy of any comment. Whereas she, Juliette Victoria Lambert, is shrouded in the unfathomable mystery of mother of pearl.

I shall never forget this, vows Juliette fiercely. Sitting here with Gail, looking out across the hockey pitch. I shall remember that red ball of sun in the bleak grey sky. The stark bare trees. The peeling white paint on the goalposts. The glowing noses and watery eyes of the first years who aren't allowed to stay indoors during break. In a few minutes, the bell will ring, and it will all change. A part of my life will have gone, will be over forever. But this one moment I will recall, with distant affection for the girl I once was.

Juliette yearns to have something worthwhile to feel nostalgic about. To recollect, through misty eyes, a poignant tune, a bitter-sweet kiss, a tragic parting.

But at fifteen going on sixteen, she mourns, what have I to look back on? The hockey tournament. Being sick in the car going up to Granny's. Making stink bombs in the lab. My life is crammed with examination work and preparations for my future. I have no past. Only aspirations.

'Do you remember,' she asks Gail, 'in your very first year at infants school, when they warmed our little bottles of milk on the radiator? How the heat gave it that sweet, almost sickly taste?'

'I wouldn't know.' Gail stands up and brushes crumbs from her navy skirt. 'I always poured mine down the loo. And I never drink milk now because it's fattening. God, I've got to do something about my thighs. They're like pumpkins. Perhaps I'll try Fallow Dallow's muesli diet.'

'She's gone now, you know. There was a note on the kitchen table this morning. Said she'd been offered a lift up to Scotland.' Juliette sighs. 'I'm fed up with being sensible Juliette Lambert, handing in my essays on time and leading the second eleven to victory at hockey. I'd much rather be a creature of moods like Dallow.'

'What's she going to do in Scotland?'

'Evidently there's some self sufficiency outfit up there who sit and commune with the kale to make it grow better. Dallow has gone to lend them her celibate support.'

'I thought you said celibate was a *boo* word?'

'Actually, I was thinking of incorporating that into my Keats essay. You know . . . Keats's quality as a romantic poet is greatly enhanced by his apt choice of certain boo words like nightingale, urn and ripening breast.'

The two girls collapse into giggles and link arms as they walk down the corridor towards their chemistry class. 'I wonder what your mother will get up to now?' Gail ponders.

'Get up to?'

'Mmm. Let's face it, she's always rather enjoyed being the avant garde lady of the village. Stomping round last year with petitions for Prisoners' Wives, and now she's set herself up as a raging women's libber. It's all a far cry from jam and collage at the W.I. I mean, all my mum ever does is win flower arranging contests. But then along comes Dallow, who's so far out she's ready to fall off, and she totally eclipses your ma. Now that Dallow's hit the road, I wonder what Mrs Lambert will do to make us all sit up and take notice of her again.'

Juliette squirms at this analysis of her mother. 'You're fantasising. I don't think mum was at all influenced by Dallow.'

'You wait and see.'

On a blustery March evening, Juliette phones Gail.

'You were right. My mother's just turned herself into a candidate for the funny farm.'

'What's happened?'

'We are to return to a more Basic Form of Life. She has put most of the furniture into store. The central heating has been turned off and she's had an ugly wood-burning stove installed in the living room. We are to be vegetarians, and eat on cushions, staring at the wall where the telly used to be before she gave it to Oxfam.'

'But why didn't your father stop her?'

'He saw all the upheaval and just thought she was spring cleaning. And you know I never pay any attention to her antics. By the time dad and I came to, she'd effected a bloodless coup. The new regime had begun.'

'I bet your father hit the roof.'

'Actually, he's taken it all on the chin so far. He told me in confidence that mum is just going through a difficult time, and we must try to be patient and tolerant. So last night we all sat round with our bowls of roughage, having a sane, mature discussion about the situation.'

'And?'

'All we discovered is that it's impossible to have any sort of conversation whatsoever if you're eating celery, nuts, apples and carrots because the sound of all that frantic crunching drowns out everything else.'

'So what's going on now?'

'Oh, sane mature discussion has been jettisoned. Mum and dad are downstairs having a good old-fashioned row.'

'It's that Dallow freak,' storms Len. 'She's put you up to this.'

'This may astound you, but I am capable of taking some decisions all by myself, without help or influence from anyone else.'

'I knew she spelt trouble as soon as I set eyes on her. Bloody dyke. Did she try and touch you up?'

'If you must know, Dallow is *celibate*.'

'I should think so too, at her age. Geriatric sex is disgusting. She was probably constipated. It happens with old people. No wonder she gobbled all those prunes.'

'She's a mere fifty-two, for heaven's sake. That's only twelve years older than you.'

Juliette slips into the denuded sitting room, her clogs echoing on the bare boards. She intends merely to retrieve her art portfolio and slither away, but her father stops her. Enthroned, sultan-like, on the biggest of the three cushions that now comprise the total seating in the room, he demands, 'You're a bright girl, Juliette. Have you any suggestions as to why your mother has gone right off her head?'

'Take no notice of Leo,' instructs Caroline calmly, rolling up the sleeves of the sweater covering her blue muslin djellabah. 'He is simply approaching the male menopause. It's bound to cause him a great deal of emotional distress.'

'Jesus Christ! What are you – '

'Having a vasectomy is an extremely sensitive decision for a man to make. I appreciate that.'

A vein bulges on Len's forehead. 'I have no *intention* of having a vasectomy.' And, Len signals, you are a right cow to bring this up in front of Juliette.

'Our daughter is quite well aware of what a vasectomy entails,' drawls Caroline. 'She is not at all phased by this discussion.'

This is true. Juliette is far too fascinated to be embarrassed. Boy, how dull life was before Dallow. Shivering, she pokes another log into the black stove.

'We are not having a discussion about vasectomy,' spits Len, 'because there is nothing to discuss. I am not having one. I have never even contemplated having one.'

'Exactly! That's precisely my point. You are quite content for me to go on and on endangering my life by taking the Pill.'

'It's not forever. If I'm alleged to be menopausal at forty, then you haven't got much catching up to do.'

'Women in affluent, middle-class areas like this don't stop menstruating until they are fifty. Statistics and my doctor confirm that fact.'

Len staggers wearily to the drinks cupboard and pours himself a scotch. He must be feeling really downtrodden, Juliette realises. Normally he's a beer man. Scotch is his crisis tipple.

Len examines the half empty bottle. 'Interesting that you didn't heave out the drinks cupboard along with the rest of the furniture.'

'I have given up smoking. It isn't reasonable to expect me to abandon everything at once. In time, I hope to reduce my alcohol intake.'

'You don't want your whisky topped up, then?'

'Don't be petty.' Caroline holds out her tumbler.

Her condescending tone enrages Len. 'Will you wipe that smug sodding expression off your dial and just tell me in plain, simple English what the hell is going on here. What's it all about?'

'There is no need to shout. I keep telling you. I'm hoarse from trying to explain. But you never listen. You just tune in to every other sentence and of course you can't make sense of that so you go around roaring that Caroline has gone potty. Which reminds me. From now on I'd prefer to be known as Cassie.'

'That's short for Cassandra, not Caroline,' Juliette points out.

'I am listening. Explain again.'

Caroline takes a deep breath. 'I simply came to the conclusion – all on my own – that we in this family were suffering from a surfeit of manufactured goods. We were so cluttered with unnecessary junk, we couldn't breathe. The more I thought about it, the more convinced I became that we should get back to basics and return to a simpler way of life.'

'Now hang on. I could understand all that crap if we were living at the level of Annabel and Miles, with swimming pools, yachts and marble baths. But we're just an ordinary family, for Pete's sake.'

'Ordinary! What do you mean, ordinary?' Caroline leaps to her feet. 'Let me tell you. Wendy's husband runs a youth club for underprivileged kids. The boys there kept using the word posh, so Tim asked them what they meant by that. They said that posh was having an inside toilet. In this day and age! Now who are you calling ordinary?'

The long-suffering expression on her father's face makes Juliette laugh. Caroline rounds on her. 'And you're just as bad, young lady. "Oh, we can't possibly watch telly on Gail's portable. It's so boring in black and white!" I think it's about time you got yourself a Saturday job.'

'I don't want to work on Saturdays. It's my lying in and lazing day.'

'You can slope about on Sundays instead.'

'Now what are you on about, Caro? There's no financial necessity for Juliette to have a job.'

'Besides, I'm revising for my exams.'

'You're both missing the point. Apart from giving you a break from academic work, Juliette, a Saturday job will provide you with the satisfaction of earning money of your own. More important, it'll bring you into contact with a different class of people. Your mind could do with some broadening.'

'The kid's still at school, Caro. She needs her rest at the weekend.'

'You never tire of telling us, Leo, about the paper round you did in your salad days. How the canvas bag was so heavy you toppled off your bike into the busy main road. About the day you had a bilious attack and every door on the council estate was painted green or yellow. And how good it all was for your character.'

'We were bloody hard up. I needed the bread. But Juliette's well provided for. She gets a whacking amount of pocket money. And she's a *girl*.'

Caroline stares at him stonily.

Thanks, Dad, thinks Juliette. Now you've really lumbered me. Embracing the inevitable, she enquires

'Where am I to go and work, then?'

'Tim tells me that Fortune Pools employ part-timers.'

'But I don't know anything about swimming pools.'

'Not swimming. Football! It's clerical work, dealing with the coupons. You get six pounds a day. They're always looking for new people.'

'I'm not surprised, at that money,' scoffs Len. 'It'll cost Juliette that much in fares and lunches. Talking of which, I wish to make one thing quite clear. If you prefer to eat rabbit food, that's up to you. But when I come home beat after a hard day's work I want to see a proper dinner waiting for me. Meat, spuds, veg, gravy, pudding. Is that understood?'

Caroline closes her eyes, shutting him out. Juliette resolves to chat up Gail's mother, and have most of her meals round there in future.

Len waves his arms. 'And you will get the furniture and the telly back. I'm not having my house looking like Squatter's Hall.'

'It's not your house. It's mine! When my father gave us the deposit he insisted that the deeds be put in my name. Just as he gave the big Melford house to my mother.'

'We all know why he did that. Because he was a bloody crook and suspected he might come to a sticky end.'

Juliette grabs her portfolio and runs as Caroline's glass smashes against the wall, inches from Len's head.

6

'Lay your drawers on the table, girls!'

Ivy, Juliette has discovered, raises a laugh with this every Saturday at Fortune Pools. Ivy is Juliette's section head. She has cropped, jagged black hair, broad hips and enormous breasts which embarrass her to such an extent that she can't stop drawing attention to them.

'A titter ran round the room!' shrieks Ivy, rolling her eyes and squeezing her nipples beneath the grubby Acrilan jumper.

Juliette and her colleagues obediently slide out the drawers from the long metal tables, to prove to Ivy that they haven't stolen any postal orders. Two hundred females sit twenty to a table in the airless room. Although cigarettes are officially banned, a permanent pall of smoke clings to the grime on the high, closed windows.

'If you're going to be checking the coupons, make sure you turn mine into a winner,' joked Len when he dropped Juliette at the trading estate on her first morning.

But the checking, Juliette discovered, is carried out by an elite band of trusted women on Saturday evenings. All the daytime girls are allowed to do is open envelopes, separate the entry from the postal order, and rubber stamp the coupon with a table number. As a Saturday girl, Juliette has no choice but to accept her role as the most loathed and despised form of life in the entire rickety building.

'It's so unfair,' she complained to Gail. 'Here I am, taking eight O Levels and with my sights set on university. But just because I can't sort and stamp coupons as fast as everyone else, they think I'm thick!'

At first, Juliette's incompetence was deeply resented by Sharon and Shirley, the nineteen-year-old full timers sitting on either side of her. As they snapped elastic bands round their finished bundles and prepared to slither under the table for a quick drag, Ivy would shout:

'Bums in seats, you two, and give the kid a hand.'

'Bleedin' bookworm,' they muttered, mystified by Juliette's intention to stay on at school.

Sharon's dark, finely plucked eyebrows arched in horror at the small print of *Pride and Prejudice* which Juliette had brought in to read with her lunchtime sandwiches. 'A lot of readin', isn't it? No pictures, neither.'

'You should leave as soon as you're sixteen,' Shirley urged, her icing-pink finger nails flashing through the coupons. 'Come and work here. It's good money, with overtime. And you'll soon speed up.'

Juliette, her hands feeling like bunches of bananas, was grateful when the hooter blew for tea break. By her third Saturday, she was beginning to feel less of a sprog. She had learned not to hang back and politely let the others go first. Instead she clattered down the iron fire escape, elbows out, chin forward, a pace behind veterans Sharon and Shirley. In the bustling canteen she was wise enough now not to ask for a saucer with her tea, or wonder aloud why the teaspoons were chained to the chipped trestle tables.

Gradually, Juliette is aware of a change in the full timers' attitude towards her. Sharon and Shirley have become strangely proud of their 'clever clogs' Juliette. They even, with Ivy's permission, volunteer to divide her share of the work between them to give Juliette more time for her revision.

'You get on with your book learning, love, and make something of yourself,' Ivy instructs, kneading Juliette's shoulders with her large, square hands.

The crucial breakthrough comes for Juliette when she is invited to read Shirley's copies of *Tenderness* and *Red Roses* during breaks. Shirley won't allow just anyone to look at her 'books'. Certainly not Jill, the narrow-nosed redhead on the other side of the table. Jill is called a Saturday girl although at twenty-nine she is regarded by all the full timers as over the hill. Sharon once burst her zip laughing when Jill let it slip that she still had it off with her husband.

'I don't know how you can bother with that trash,' sniffs Jill, as Juliette spills sticky bun crumbs over *Tenderness*. 'You with your fancy education and all.'

Juliette tears herself away from the picture heroine with her flowing hair, doe eyes and pouting mouth. 'It's relaxing.'

A mindless job, she has discovered, deadens the brain to such an extent that it will only be assuaged by comics. The monotony of the Fortune routine tires her far more than O Level work. Even a tabloid newspaper is too much of an effort to read on Saturdays.

Fortunately, live entertainment is at hand. More riveting by far than the *Red Roses* romances is the Saturday serial of Shirley's lovelife. A small, curvy girl with dyed, purplish-black hair and, permanently moist mouth, Shirley reminds Juliette of an overripe Victoria plum.

Shirley is engaged to an Irishman, Bren. Every Friday night he beats Shirley up, and at work on Saturdays she unbuttons her blouse and displays her bruises like combat medals. For Juliette, time never drags while Shirley recounts, in her flat, unsurprised voice, how Bren threw the stereo out of the window. Again.

Not even the mighty Bren, however, can provide sufficient excitement for Shirley. On her way to get savaged by Bren on Fridays, she often leaves the train two stops up the line, and walks back along the track to the signal box. The signalman, Juliette gathers, is the strong, silent type. Certainly, Shirley never reports that he has actually said anything. Just that they had it away on the floor, and won't Bren do his nut if he finds out?

Sharon's pert face creases with scepticism. 'It'll be your nut needin' attention, Shirl. Not Bren's.'

'Put that fag out!' yells Ivy. 'And get back to work.'

Shirley scoops up Juliette's pile of coupons and begins stamping, Bren's solitaire twinkling under the harsh fluorescent lights. Juliette tries to concentrate on her novel, but finds that Shirley's dramas hold far more fascination than the tepid adventures of Jane Austen's heroines.

Each of the unmarried Fortune girls lives at home with mum. To Juliette, mum sounds wonderful. Always willing to iron dresses for a special date, help with a perm, come shopping and supply endless plates of sausage and chips. On Thursdays, Shirley takes her mother round the local for a knees up. Sharon swears her mum is her best mate. And a right laugh with it.

'I want you to call me Caroline,' Juliette's mother informed her over breakfast.

'What's wrong?' Len demanded. 'Does the term mother make you feel old all of a sudden?'

'Don't be ridiculous. It's merely that *mother* stereotypes me into a role and denies me free expression as a person.'

Another boo word, thought Juliette, surreptitiously tipping tonight's celery salad into the waste bin.

'After all,' Caroline developed her theme, 'you don't address me as Wife, and I don't call Juliette Daughter.'

The undisputed logic of this rendered Len momentarily speechless. He buttered his toast, then countered, 'Mother and Father are terms of respect. And why isn't there any marmalade?'

'I'm not buying marmalade any more. It's bad for your teeth. Have some cottage cheese. Respect is something we have to earn, Leo. It isn't ours by right.'

'Well as I'm the one earning the crusts round here, I'll thank you to get off your fat arse and provide the food I like.'

'Does your mum go out to work, Julie?' Shirley asks, her rubber stamp poised over a Ladies coupon, garlanded with daisies and horoscopes.

'Course her mum don't work,' Ivy says indignantly as she and the security officer perform a spot check on handbags. 'Neither will Julie when she gets hitched to her rich stockbroker type.'

'What's the point of all this studying, then?' sneezes Jill. She grins as the security man plunges his hand into her bag, which is crammed with nasal sprays and soggy tissues.

Ivy stands arms akimbo. 'So she can talk to all her husband's clever friends. And one thing's for sure. She won't have to clock in at a crummy joint like this to earn pin money, like some I could name.'

Jill bridles. 'I don't need the cash. It's the company I come for.'

One Saturday, Shirley is missing. The following week, Ivy's bosom heaves as she gives them the news. The inevitable has happened: Bren has found out about the signalman.

Ever a man of action, Bren had proceeded to batter Shirley as usual on Friday, marrying her by special licence the next week. Sharon passes round polaroid shots of Shirley at the registry office. She looks less than radiant, with a swollen bruised face and two teeth missing.

'But she is smiling,' Sharon points out. 'So she must be happy, mustn't she?'

Sharon is pathetically limp without Shirley. 'We used to go dancin' at Tiffany's every Wednesday,' she mourns, heaping sugar into the pale grey canteen tea. 'Now I haven't no one to go with.'

Juliette absently snaps a tin teaspoon in half. 'Can I come?'

'You *can't*.' Gail is stretched full length on the goatskin rug in her bedroom. 'Tiffany's has the most awful reputation.'

Juliette finishes copying a sentence from Gail's French translation. 'I thought it would make a change.'

'But what about your revision? And you know the Village Players meet on Wednesdays.' She smiles, fingering her long, tawny hair. 'Edwin says if the committee let him produce *Look Back in Anger*, then I can play Alison. I quite fancy myself in a low cut slip. And if I keep behind the ironing board, no one will notice my thighs.'

'You're welcome. I'm sick of that lot. All those shrieking old prima donnas powdering over their wrinkles, and middle-aged married men trying to get a squeeze at your tits.'

Gail rolls onto her stomach and examines her tapes. 'Kate Bush or E.L.O.?'

'E.L.O.'

'You're only going to Tiffany's to get yourself out of the madhouse. What's the state of play with your ma?'

'Oh, she's quite loony. When I left this morning she was hunched like a witch over a cauldron, brewing up herb soap. And now she's given up smoking she's fanatical, flinging open all the windows and hurling bay leaves onto the fire to cleanse the air. Dad raves and shouts, especially when she dishes up nut cutlets for Sunday lunch. But he knows it won't last. Her fads never do. I just hope she gets over the delirium before Granny comes to stay.'

'My Granny's gaga,' confesses Gail. 'I'm not supposed to tell anyone, but she's in an old people's home. We have to trek over there with bottles of lavender water on the last Sunday of every month. My ma calls it *doing the oldies*. She always comes away in a ratty temper, though, because half the time Gran can't remember who mum is. She drones on about her bunions, and how when she was five she used to watch her mother trimming her corns with a cut throat razor. Oh yawn.'

'It wouldn't be so bad if they rambled on about something interesting. Or decadent. Wouldn't it be marvellous to have a really glamorous grandmother? Someone like Lady Diana Cooper, all feathered and furred, always getting her picture in the gossip columns.'

'I'd choose Augusta's grandmother, from the strip in the *Standard*. She sits in bars, throwing back cocktails, making her lantern-jawed young boyfriend carry her parcels.'

'My Granny swigs Sanatogen and complains because the new curtains are three inches too short. It seems a frightful extravagance to me. I mean, she'll die soon, so what does she need new curtains for? Or new anything?'

Juliette turns up the volume on the E.L.O. tape and rocks on the bed to the rhythm of the music. 'Hey, did you hear what happened when old Frances buried her mother? Her vile son was larking about and toppled into the grave. Frances was *not* amused.'

'That reminds me.' Gail riffles through her loose leaf folder. 'The sixth formers were doing Swinburne today, and Frances read them the most incredible verse. One of the boys copied it out for me. Listen:

> *I will go back to the great sweet mother,*
> *Mother and lover of men, the sea.*
> *I will go down to her, I and no other,*
> *Close with her, kiss her and mix her with me.*

'The entire class was in hysterics. Poor old Frances kept rapping the desk, demanding to know the cause of all the hilarity. She obviously hadn't a clue what it all meant.'

Juliette screams with laughter, though she is not really sure what Gail finds so uproarious about the verse.

'Actually, I'm pro Frances at the moment. She's putting my poem in the school mag.'

'Oh, the one about the lady in the red sequinned dress? Is that how you're togging yourself up for Tiffany's?'

'Don't be daft. Sharon said something about it being a Fifties Rock Nite.'

Gail obligingly swings open her wardrobe doors. 'Let's see what we can dredge up. You'll need something eyecatching. Else you'll be consigned to the wallflower bed.'

Juliette barks, in a Frances voice: 'The diversification of the social plumage of the human female is a contributory factor in the mating ritual. Discuss.'

'You are not going out dressed like that!' bellows Len.

'Don't be so Victorian, Leo. I think she looks charming.'

The Lamberts stare up at Juliette as she pauses uncertainly on the third stair. She is wearing a scarlet felt dirndl skirt and a black sweater with a low, heart-shaped neckline. Her dark hair is pulled into a high pony tail. Poppy red lipstick glows on her mouth, and from her ears dangle long yellow plastic earrings.

'Where's she going, anyway?'

'To a disco in Guildford. And you mustn't cross examine her in such a hectoring fashion. Everyone is entitled to do their own thing in this life.'

'Christ, Caro, she's my *daughter*. I'm *responsible* for her. I *paid* for those tarty clothes she's decked up in.'

'You didn't. I borrowed most of them from Gail.'

'And I used to wear gear like that myself. Besides, I remember your mother showing me pictures of you in Teddy Boy drapes and fearful crepe soled shoes.'

'It was different then. Times have changed. I won't have my daughter looking like a prize slag.'

'Juliette is simply expressing her individuality. If you had to wear a dreary school uniform every day you'd feel like branching out a bit in your spare time, too.'

'I'd have been over the moon if I'd gone to a good school like Juliette's. Wearing that uniform is a privilege. It drives me mad the way she keeps throwing that expensive blazer in a heap on the floor.'

'I shall miss the bus.' Juliette makes a dash for the front door.

'And how are you going to get home? I want you in by ten on the dot.'

'Eleven, Juliette. I've given her money for a taxi.'

'A *taxi*? God, when – '

'We know. When you were her age, you walked everywhere, barefoot. But Juliette is a girl, and if you fancy the idea of her roaming alone across the Hog's Back at midnight, well I don't. I have a stronger sense of responsibility.'

'I didn't say that. All I said was – '

'I mean, stuck out here, it's difficult for Juliette to go anywhere outside Maybrook.'

'Now wait a minute. Maybrook was your idea. It will be wonderful for our child to grow up in the fresh country air, you said. You and your father together – '

'That's right. Drag him into it. Now he's dead and can't answer back, poor sod.'

'You cunning, sly cow!' Lester hurled the diaphragm across the sitting room, impaling it on Rose's darning needle.

Rose laid down the stocking she was mending and murmured dully, 'Now you've punctured it.'

He seized her by the shoulders, shaking her until the hairpins fell from her coiled hair. 'What's the game, then?'

The lie came easily. 'It's just that I was worried about my health if I got in the family way again. The doctor was most concerned about me when I had Caroline. He said any more would be dangerous ... '

'Balls.' Lester flung her back into the chair and lit a cigarette.

Rose shrank back against the cushions. It terrified her the way Lester's moods could switch so suddenly from blistering rage to icy disdain. If he'd shouted and hit her, or smashed the place up, she would have understood. She'd have found it easier, then, to fight back and justify her actions. But this bleak accusing stare defeated her. She felt bereft and helpless in the face of such steely self control.

He didn't even slam the door as he left. She assumed he'd

gone out on a blinder. But what would he do when he came back? Throw her on the floor and rape her?

Frantic, she took Caroline into her bed, and pushed the utility wardrobe against the door. She spent the remainder of the night in a cold sweat, unable to sleep. It was not just Lester she feared, but the threat of fire. If the electrics failed and the house went up, would there be time to move the wardrobe? Would she be burnt alive?

If I am it'll be all his fault, she decided, hugging her one-year-old daughter close. He should never have been nosing about in my underwear drawer. It's just my luck. The one time I forget to put the blessed thing in, he chooses to go rummaging where he shouldn't. Looking for his black socks, indeed. He must think I was born yesterday.

Lester returned at two a.m. 'You needn't bother barricading the door,' he hollered. 'I wouldn't touch you with a barge pole.'

Rose shrank beneath the covers, convinced the neighbours must be listening to every word.

'You needn't fret. I won't put you up the spout again. I wouldn't want anyone as rancid as you to be the mother of my son.'

There followed several weeks of non-verbal combat, while Lester slept in the spare room. Rose felt guilty, as he intended her to, for her betrayal. She lay rigidly awake until the early hours, listening for his key in the lock, petrified that he would demand a divorce. Then she'd really be done for.

But gradually, it dawned on Rose that Lester was not staying out late to seek solace in the arms of another woman. Instead, he was busy making contacts, to help him expand his business. He did not, of course, confide his intentions to Rose. But by steaming open his mail Rose gathered that Lester was about to establish himself as a home planning consultant.

With the war over, Rose's opportunist husband had appreciated that the battle-weary English would now want to concentrate on rebuilding their homes. Lester intended to sell his London shops and set up a comprehensive decorating store in Melford.

This was not all. Lester was also deeply concerned about

the thousands of local residents who had been bombed out. People were desperate for houses. It shocked Rose that homes worth £1000 in 1939 were now selling for four times that price. She was knocked down in the newsagents by customers rushing to buy *Daltons Weekly*. Bulging with property classifieds, the paper was sold out within minutes.

Lester's aim, as Rose interpreted it, was to become the Melford Mr Fixit. If you were searching for a house, then despite the shortage, and the stringent Government controls, Lester would produce it for you. At a price.

The public-spirited Lester would also find you a job. After all, not every homecoming soldier wanted to return to the firm which had employed him before the war. In the intervening six years, men had learned new skills, and forgotten old ones.

It was Lester's intention to liaise, quite unofficially, between Melford companies and unemployed ex-servicemen. From the guarded replies written by company managers, it seemed to Rose that they were in favour of Lester's proposal. They agreed with him that although the Government's own redeployment Scheme was a worthy enterprise, it would be more advantageous for all concerned to have a local man working on the problem.

To assist her digestion of this turn of events, Rose treated herself to a chocolate biscuit with her tea. It occurred to her that if Lester was to establish a respectable, consultant image for himself, then he would have to start socialising with the top men, the professional class in Melford. And he couldn't do that with the scandal of divorce round his neck. Broken marriages were common enough in areas like Eaton Square. But no one who was anyone ever got divorced in suburban Melford.

You need me, Rose informed him silently. Try and ditch me and I'll ruin you. But give me a decent, comfortable life and I'll not let you down.

Over Christmas, Rose sensed that Lester was coming to a decision. They ate their monthly egg ration boiled for Boxing Day tea, and he broke his silence to tell her something of his new business plans.

But it was at the end of the year, when a boatload of

bananas arrived at Avonmouth, that Rose knew she had won. It was the first shipment of bananas to reach Britain for six years and Lester made a special trip down to the dock.

He arrived back in triumph, waving the fruit aloft. 'Would you believe, the Lord Mayor of Bristol was standing on the quay to welcome the bananas.' He grinned. 'Give one to Caroline. She's never seen a banana before. I can't wait to see her try and peel it.'

It was a bizarre way to strike a marital bargain. But by now Rose was a sufficiently experienced campaigner to understand that within a marriage, wars and truces are rarely openly declared.

For ten minutes, she allowed Caroline to run riot with the banana. The child squealed with delight as she tore it open and squeezed the pulp over the floor. Then Rose filled the kettle for some warm water and took her daughter into the kitchen for her bedtime wash.

Fearful that Lester resented Caroline because she wasn't a boy, Rose was careful not to permit her childish antics to get on his nerves. Of course, when they were out in public together, posing as the happy united family, he glowed with pride when everyone petted his pretty daughter. But there were times at home when Rose was sure Caroline's chatter irritated him, and she felt obliged to whisk her into the push-chair for a walk.

Increasingly, then, it bewildered and infuriated Rose that as Caroline grew older, she so patently adored her father. No matter how rarely he was at home, or how abrupt he was with her, it was his smile, his approval for which Caroline strove.

Eighteen months after the end of the war, the housing shortage showed no sign of abating. Prefabs scarred the streets and squatters, as Lester put it, were 'as much a part of our life as spam'. Lester's services were in heavy demand ... not least by one mysteriously persistent househunter with a weakness for what Rose detected as *Moment Suprême*.

Rose could not but admire her taste. Sir Desmond had always presented this perfume to Lady Evelyn on their wedding anniversary.

Rose fell into the habit of going to bed early so she could

feign a doze when Lester came home. Not that he ever tried to bother her any more. It was just that the pretence of sleep made the sexual rift less obvious.

It interested Rose that she had never once looked at another man in that way. She concluded that she was not a very passionate woman. Some people simply had less primitive urges than others. Yet on still, hot summer days she would find her thoughts drawn back to her honeymoon, and the pleasure she and Lester had shared in the long grass at Eastbourne. It was like looking at someone else. Another woman. A person she didn't recognise at all.

She didn't mind Lester having a bit on the side. Just so long as he didn't flaunt it, and embarrass her with their new friends. They were invited, now, to an increasing number of public functions at the Town Hall. For Rose, each social engagement was an ordeal. Especially that winter when the weather men declared it was colder in Britain than in Iceland. In the draughty, unheated hall, the Mayor's wife, shivering valiantly in her rayon evening frock, urged the ladies to get back to haybox cooking during these days of austerity. Rose, her hair crimped into waves with left-over tea, cringed against the wall, sick with apprehension in case the Mayor should single her out for the foxtrot.

'I thought you said everyone would be in 50s gear,' Juliette accuses Sharon. The queue outside Tiffany's is gaudy with girls in shocking pink harem pants, gold lurex cat suits and fake leopard shifts, slit to the thigh. Juliette's skin prickles hotly with embarrassment. She could kill Gail for persuading her to wear the red felt dirndl. All the slick sophisticates sliding into Tiffany's must be sniggering at the sight of her.

Sharon gives a shake to her white circular pleated skirt. 'You look fine, Jule. I think the 50s idea was just an excuse to give the blokes a chance to dress up as Teds. Most of the girls just wear what's fashionable. Anyway, it's a bind tryin' to find out just what they did wear then. Amazin' the number of my aunties who pretend they're too young to remember. Actually, my mum reckons I've got it wrong with this skirt. She says it's pure 60s gear.' She pushed

Juliette towards the chipped, gold-painted doors. 'Shove on. We girls get in cheaper if it's before quarter past eight.'

Sharon hands over her shoulder bag to the burly, black-suited bouncer. 'No bombs in there, mate,' she grins, as frankfurter fingers fumble in her make up case and packet of Craven A.

She rushes Juliette through into the disco, where glass-topped tables are dimly illuminated by amber Tiffany lamps. Disorientated by the gloom and flashing strobe lights, Juliette stumbles, knocking over two red plush chairs.

'We'll bag ourselves a table, then head for the loo and tart ourselves up,' instructs Sharon.

Juliette regards the ton of pancake, courtesy of Max Factor, and wonders what further adornment Sharon can possibly be planning.

With no hesitation, Sharon selects a table half way between the entrance and the bar. 'We'll get a lotta dances that way, because the fellas have to pass us to get a drink. If you sit up the other end, near the Gents, all you get is fast moving traffic whizzing past you to relieve themselves or hurl. And when they come out they're too busy zipping up their flies to notice the likes of you.'

Under soft pink lights in the Ladies, girls are stripping off raincoats to reveal gossamer leotards and tight white satin trousers. Sharon plunges a hand into her mauve sequinned boob tube and hoists up her breasts.

'Wish I had as much on top as you, Jule.'

'Do you think this skirt's all right? I borrowed it from a friend who's acres bigger than me. I've got it hauled in with safety pins all round the waist.'

'Don't worry. It's not your waist the fellas are interested in. They'll all be peering down your front.'

'I've never worn a sweater as low as this before.'

'It looks great. I'm dead jealous, I tell ya. On the other hand, it's you big-chested girls who're more likely to get cancer. Look at Ivy.'

'Don't tell me Ivy's got breast cancer?'

Sharon takes three different sized combs from her bag and teases her curls with each in turn. 'Didn't you know? Well, it was all very sudden. She got a lump, and was whisked in for examination. Then when they told her they'd have to operate she bellowed at the surgeon that he'd better go the whole hog and chop her other breast off as well. Course he refused. Muttered to the nurse that she was hysterical. Then Ivy asked if she could have her old breast to keep in a jar on the table at Fortune Pools ... '

She leads the way back into the disco and fetches two Martinis. A gilt rail encloses the dancing area, which is presided over by a black DJ wearing a white suit and sunglasses. Although the disco is crowded, and the lights flash encouragingly in syncopation to the throbbing music, no one is dancing.

Young men in Teddy Boy drapes lean against the gilt rail, staring myopically at their fingernails. The girls are grouped round the tables, gazing with studied uninterest at the Victoriana. It is as if, realises Juliette, the last thing they anticipate doing is actually getting up and dancing.

The top of the DJ's mirrored control console is lit by fronded lights that resemble silver wigs. To Juliette, these shimmering cascades are the most animated beings in the entire disco. She can imagine them taking wing and whirling luminously onto the deserted dancefloor.

'Seen anything you fancy yet, then?' Sharon lights up a Craven A.

'It's a bit difficult to tell. All I can see of the fellas is their backs.'

Sharon laughs. 'You don't know much, do you. They may look uninterested, but they're sizing us up all the same. You wait and see. You never had a steady, then?'

Juliette shakes her head. 'Just kids from school. Wet kisses in the back of the school bus, that sort of thing. I've never been out with anyone really grown up. But I'm not in a rush.'

'Sensible kid. No point in gettin' a name as the local workhorse.'

Juliette smiles, remembering last night's conversation with her mother.

'I shall quite understand if you want to go on the Pill, Juliette. After all, you are coming up to sixteen. It would be the sensible thing to do.'

'But mum, I don't – '

'There's no point in coming over all coy. If there's one thing I detest it's mothers and daughters who can't discuss sex in a frank, open manner.'

Juliette could imagine Gail's reaction to this remark. 'Demand to know what *her* sex life's like, then. I bet she wouldn't be as free and frank as she wants you to be.'

'Mum, I haven't even got a steady boyfriend. I don't need to go on the Pill. I've never even considered it.'

'I sometimes think you live too much in your head, Juliette. I'm afraid for you. You'll find yourself suddenly headlong in love and you won't know what's hit you. You won't be prepared.'

'Look, it's my life, isn't it? Don't interfere. And stop pressuring me to take the Pill. If at any time in the future I do decide to go on it I'm quite capable of making my own appointment at the family planning clinic.'

God, why can't she be like other mothers and blush and clam up at the very mention of sex. All this unreserved candour is inhibiting me.

'Oh look,' giggles Sharon, 'the Elton John lookalike is giving a demonstration dance.'

The balding, bespectacled young man is jerking rhythmically, half a second behind the beat, alongside a dowdy girl in a crumpled flowered skirt. They are the last couple Juliette expected to be first on the floor.

For the duration of two records, 'Elton John' and his partner dance alone, ignored by the rest of the crowd. But as the DJ mumbles an announcement for the next disc, there is an inexplicable surge towards the floor, led by a striking redhead in thigh-high leather boots and a cossack shirt.

A youth with long winklepicker shoes minces up and mutters to Sharon:

'Dance?'

Sharon jerks her head. 'Can't. I'm with my mate.'

'Oh, it doesn't matter,' Juliette assures her fervently. 'You go ahead.' She nearly adds, 'And enjoy yourself. Don't worry about me. I'll be all right on my own.' Fortunately, the spectre of Granny looms through the Martini haze and stills her tongue.

'OK. Will you look after my bag, then?'

As Sharon is engulfed in the bobbing throng, Juliette sits with a fixed smile on her face, toying with the dregs of her drink. Hell, this is awful. I wish I'd never come. Gail was right. It's a right slime of a joint. No one will ask me to dance. Ever. I shall just sit here for years, all by myself, with everyone staring at me, saying look at that poor little thing in that terrible dirndl skirt, isn't she having a rotten time? Well, what can you expect, she's not really one of us, is she? Pretty soon I shall be the only girl left not dancing. I'll count to ten, then make a dash to the Ladies, and stay there for the rest of the evening.

Sharon returns, mopping her brow. 'I sent 'im off to get us some more drinks. Are you all right?'

'Yes, fine! It's just so absorbing sitting here studying everyone. Really fascinating!' chirps Juliette.

'Goin' to write about us all in one of your school essays, are you?'

'I was wondering, just as a point of academic interest, what would happen if I went and asked a fella to dance.'

'God no, you mustn't do that! He'd think you were right forward. It'd be his cue to take all kinds of liberties.'

Winklepicker returns, accompanied by an acne-scarred youth clad in an acid yellow shirt and shoestring tie. 'Wanna dance then, girls?'

On the dance floor, acne gyrates gravely round Juliette, waving his arms, palp-like, in the manner of a spider signalling to his mate. 'You're a good mover,' he informs her condescendingly.

'You're not so bad yourself,' she murmurs politely. 'Quite the John Travolta.'

He scowls. 'Nah. Don't rate him. He's just a bitta celluloid for the bored middle-aged housewives to wet their knickers over.'

'Really? My mother says he's a pain.'

'Live at home with mum, do you?' he grabs her arm. 'When does she go out, then?'

'Well ... to the shops, you know, or to visit her friends. Any time she likes I suppose.'

'Don't have me on. You get what I mean. When do you have the house to yourself?'

He leers, the fluorescent strobes highlighting the porcelain caps on his two front teeth.

Juliette sighs. What was it her mother said? *You'll fall headlong in love and not know what's hit you.* Chance would be a fine thing.

For the next hour, Juliette is hurled round the floor by a flattering succession of partners. But the conversation, shouted above the deafening beat, is always depressingly the same:

Where do you live? How big's your dad? When do your parents go out?

Sickened by the mediocrity of it all, Juliette abruptly leaves the floor, determined to catch an early taxi home. As she heads for the exit, her arm is caught by a tall, fair-haired Ted.

'Not leaving already?'

'Yes. If you must know, I'm bored out of my skull.'

'Stop and talk to me a minute. There's something I want to ask you.'

'I live at home. My father is a heavyweight boxing champion. And my mother never ever goes out.' She tries to push past the young man, but he whirls her round to face the dancers.

'Look at that girl in the cossack outfit. See the way she's moving? What does it remind you of?'

Juliette stares. The girl is staggering round the floor, arms outstretched, her red curls twitching convulsively in time to the music.

The Ted whispers in Juliette's ear. 'Tell you what I'm put in mind of. Have you ever woken up in a strange house, and leaped out of bed, knowing you were going to be sick but unable for the life of you to remember where the damn bathroom was?'

Juliette laughs. Perhaps the evening isn't going to turn out to be such a disaster after all.

7

The taxi is ordered for 9.30. By five to nine, Rose is waiting by the front door, hat on, coat buttoned up. She is longing for a cup of tea, but there's no milk. She tipped the last of the bottle into her Thermos of coffee. There'll be enough for a cup mid-morning, and another one with her lunchtime sandwiches.

Along with a cheque for her ticket, Caroline included enough for lunch on the train. The idea terrifies Rose. The way those waiters rush up and down sends her all of a flutter. She'll never have the nerve to catch their eye and give her order. And then there's the problem of tipping. It was easy when you had a man with you to take charge of everything. Most enjoyable, then, to have lunch on a train. But when you're on your own, well, it's less bother just to pack yourself up something tasty.

Rose is quite looking forward to her midday meal. She's wrapped up chicken sandwiches (well, you can't go wrong with chicken, can you?) cut nice and thin. There's a packet of Jaffa cakes, and three Mars bars to nibble as a treat after she's downed her pills.

Rose lays her gloves and handbag on the hall table and returns to the kitchen to check once more that everything has been turned off. She cleared out the fridge last night. Been running it down for the past fortnight, of course. Overdid it, really, and left herself only an egg and chocolate mousse for yesterday's dinner.

Everything is in order. All the plugs are pulled out. The cooker switch is up. Doors and windows locked. Mrs Logan next door offered to come in and water the plants, but Rose isn't having any of that. She knows the woman is dying for an opportunity to get inside and have a good poke round.

Rose has met her type before.

'Do call me Morag,' she invited.

'I should get back indoors, Mrs Logan,' Rose said briskly,

'before you catch a chill.' Morag indeed!

She gives the hot tap a quarter turn. Rose is always confused about what to do with the central heating. If you leave it on, you run the danger of flooding the place. On the other hand, if you switch it off and there's a sudden frost, your pipes are liable to burst.

She'll have to consult Leonard. He'll tell her what's best. Though by the time she's able to speak to him, it'll be too late to do anything about it. Should she leave a key with Mrs Logan after all? No she can't. It's Thursday. By now Mr Logan will have taken his wife down to the hospital for her treatment. She had a brain op. last year. Must be terrible to have madness in the family.

Rose feels guilty, making Leonard lose time at work to come and meet her at King's Cross. She should have thought of that when she booked the ticket. But travelling midweek is so much cheaper. She takes Caroline's letter from her handbag and rereads it, to ensure that Leonard really will be looking for her by the barrier. What if the train is late, or there's a crash? What should she do? Will Leonard still wait for her? What will his boss say if Leonard has to spend the entire afternoon ransacking King's Cross for his lost mother-in-law?

Already, the nightmare looms in Rose's mind. Suppose she gets on the wrong train in Edinburgh? Stations are such bewildering places. All that clatter, and whistle-blowing. No one ever seems to have time to help, or point you in the right direction. Lester was marvellous to go travelling with. A born organiser. Porters sprang from nowhere to take the luggage, and he always made sure she had a window seat, facing the engine. And her favourite magazine to browse through.

The magazine! Now what did she do with it? She'd bought *Woman's Own* specially, for the article on that nice Princess Alexandra. Rose rummages feverishly in the plastic shopping bag, squashing the Jaffa cakes in her anxiety. Not there. She darts into the sitting room, remembering that she leaned on the magazine to write the note stopping the milk. Relief. There it is, on top of the television. Is the set disconnected? Rose clearly remembers pulling out the plug after the News last night, but nonetheless she feels compelled to check again.

Rose mops her face. Her felt hat is as hot as a sentry box. She's positive all the perspiration on her forehead is ruining her perm. She should have been firmer with that girl in the hairdresser's. The limp fingered little madam had taken no notice when she said she wanted it curled good and tight. Now it's all dropping out and that's £10 wasted.

The doorbell rings. The taxi. Fearful that the cabbie will leave without her, Rose flings herself into the hall and wrenches open the door.

'Is the traffic bad today, driver? You will get me there by 10.15? I'm going to stay with my daughter, you see, in Surrey, and my son-in-law is meeting me, taking time off work as it is so I don't want to miss the train and put him to a lot of inconvenience.'

'It's only three miles, pet. We've got time for a tour of the city if you feel like it.'

Such impertinence. He'd never have dared speak to Lester like that. She hovers on the front step, clutching her plastic shopper and handbag, convinced she's forgotten something.

Rose closes the door. The driver slams the taxi boot on her case. Rose pales. Her case! What did she do with the keys? Her mind is muggy. She remembers putting them down on the dressing table while she hid her radio under the bed. But after that she'd dusted the bedroom, and she's sure the keys weren't there then. Did she slip them under the bed instead of the radio? Or are they behind the wardrobe with her jewel case? Surely she can't have thrown them out when she emptied the wastepaper basket?

Oh dear, she knew this was going to happen. She just knew it. She's going to be late. The train will have gone. Leonard will be annoyed and Caroline will be *furious*.

'I can't imagine why you're so exhausted, mother. Personally, I find train journeys most relaxing.' Caroline sets down the supper tray on the floorboards, and lights the scented candles.

Len pours three glasses of wine. Poor old Rose. She does

look fagged out, he thinks. Perched like a rubber doll on the floor cushion, with chubby legs stuck straight out in front of her, she views with dismay the bowl of cauliflower cheese Caroline is offering.

Len settles himself on a kitchen stool at the dining table, and tucks in to his steak and chips. When he picked Rose up at King's Cross he tried to warn her about Caroline's new spartan regime. But as soon as she spotted him at the barrier, Rose started gabbling – something about the hairdresser's keys, and Princess Alexandra's central heating – and Len couldn't get a word in all the way home. Supper is an hour late because Rose has been sitting with Caroline in the kitchen spitting blood over some madwoman called Morag Logan.

'Is anything the matter with that cauliflower cheese?' Caroline enquires gently. 'Would you prefer something else?'

'You haven't cooked the cauliflower properly.'

'It's not meant to be all mushy, mother.'

'But when it's hard like this I can't bite into it properly with my dentures.'

'Give her some of my dinner,' suggests Len. 'You'd enjoy a big lump of steak, wouldn't you?'

'What I'd really like, if it's not too much trouble, is some bread and milk.'

'I'll get it.' Caroline eases on her rope sandals.

'With sugar on. And perhaps a sweet biscuit.'

'I'll see what there is. But you do realise we don't eat white bread any more, only granary?'

'Anything will do, dear. I'm not a fussy eater.'

While Caroline is in the kitchen, Len refills Rose's glass. 'I'm glad to see,' she says, eyeing his steak, 'that Caroline isn't feeding you pap. A big man like you needs a proper plateful of dinner.'

Len chokes. A big man! When Caroline had first introduced them, Mrs Scott-Peters called him 'that hulking lout'.

'I shouldn't rest your hand on the floor like that, love. You'll get a splinter. I'm sorry it's not as cosy in here as usual. Though I suppose it doesn't look so bad by this candlelight. But you know what Caroline's like when she gets a bee in her bonnet over something.'

Rose's grey corkscrew curls bob as she sorrowfully shakes her head. 'It's poor little Juliette I feel for. Is she getting proper nourishment?'

'Oh, she spends most of her time round her friend's, scoffing fish fingers. At least,' he looks up as Caroline returns, bearing a steaming dish of soggy, khaki coloured lumps, 'I assume Juliette *is* at Gail's, and not out with this Nick creature?'

'You're being extremely unreasonable about Nick. Just because she met him at a disco.'

'Well would you mind telling me,' Len demands, wincing as Rose slurps down her wine, 'what all this fancy education is for, if she's going to end up with some yobbo?'

'You were a yobbo once,' laughs Caroline, 'and look how well you've done for yourself.'

And you were a randy little bitch with an itchy cunt, Len wants to shout. But he can't because Caroline's mother is waiting for him to top up her glass.

Rose says thickly, through a spoonful of bread and milk, 'I think what Leonard means is that –'

'Mother, I'm very sorry, but I can't hear you if you talk with your mouth full. Anyway, Juliette isn't ending up with Nick. He's merely her first serious boyfriend. In a year's time, he'll be forgotten.'

'But he's seven years older than her!'

'So what? You're five years my senior but for much of the time I feel like your mother.'

'Lester was five years older than me. No, I tell a lie. It was six. Well, five and a half, really, because our birthdays were six months apart. His was in June – '

'That's right, mother. And frankly, Leo, you're only making the situation worse by not allowing her to bring Nick home.'

Aware that he is in the wrong over this, Len changes tack. 'And just how is she going to pass her exams if she's out bopping till all hours?'

'She should get her sleep,' nods Rose. 'You were just as bad, Caroline, staying out late and worrying me half to death. I don't think you ever appreciated how much I fretted over you. It's only when you get to be a Mother yourself you realise how many sacrifices were made.'

'I don't worry about Juliette.'

'Well you should. It's only natural for Mothers to worry.'

'Look, Juliette only sees Nick at weekends, and she's always in on time. We should count ourselves fortunate that she's so mature for her age. And don't forget, Leo, her O Levels start at the beginning of June, so please don't go upsetting her.'

'Me? Why am I always made out to be the bloody villain of the piece?'

'I think I'll go to bed now, dear.'

'But it's only half past eight, mother.'

'Oh, is it? I can't see my watch properly in this gloomy light. Those candles have a funny smell, don't they?'

'They're scented with lemon. I made them myself.'

'Well can I have the electric on while I have my bath?' Rose drains her wineglass. 'I'm not all that steady on my feet, you know. These Nerve pills make me dizzy.'

'Mother, the candles are just to add atmosphere while we dine. Of course the lights are on through the rest of the house. But is it absolutely vital that you have a bath right now? Juliette's left all her tights dripping in there.'

'Yes, I'd rather. I don't want to get in Leonard's way in the morning. I'd feel terrible if I made him late for work after he was good enough to meet me at King's Cross.'

'Tell him to use the downstairs cloakroom', Mrs Scott-Peters had instructed, when Caroline first took him home for Sunday lunch. 'I'm not having him tramping council estate filth into my nice clean bathroom.'

'I'll look you out a towel, then.'

'Don't worry, dear. I packed a hand towel. That'll do me.'

'No, we've got masses of big fluffy bath towels. It's no trouble.'

'And you will turn the light on for me? I don't like candles. They remind me of the power cuts after the war. I remember all that winter you grizzled with the cold, Caroline, it was all I could do to get you dressed in the morning – '

'Talking of the morning, mother, what about food?'

'Oh, I don't eat breakfast, dear. Just half a grapefruit.'

'Good, we've got plenty of those.'

'And some Sugar Puffs first, of course, with milk. Sometimes I add a spoonful of honey as well, for energy. In the winter I make porridge too, just to warm me up.'

'Have you tried muesli, mother? I make my own.'

'I'm not partial to all those foreign foods. Sometimes I fry myself a few streaky bacon rashers. And then I have a slice of toast, with just a scrape of butter.'

'We have polyunsaturated margarine. I'm most concerned about Leo's cholesterol count.'

'And crunchy peanut butter, or chocolate spread.'

'I'm afraid –'

'And two cups of tea. Sometimes three, just to finish the pot. I take milk but not sugar. I brought my saccharine tablets with me. Too much sugar is bad for you, isn't it? I know you believe in keeping fit, Leonard, I do too. I watch my weight all the time.'

'And as you say,' he smiles, 'it's not as if you eat breakfast.'

'No wonder she's so fat,' hisses Caroline later, sliding under the quilt beside her husband.

'Have a heart. She didn't eat much dinner.'

'And do you know why? Because all the way down on the train she was stuffing her face with chocolate bars. I found the wrappers in the waste bin along with the greaseproof from her sandwiches. She's beginning to look like a huge, decorated easter egg.'

Len switches out the light. 'Try and be patient with her, love. It can't be easy for her, not having a man to lean on.'

'I do try. Really I do. I start off brimming with kindly intentions. But she's so selfish, Leo. She's not interested in talking about anything except her own life. You listened to her all the way here in the car, and I spent an hour hearing the saga of poor Mrs Logan. Yet over dinner, because the conversation didn't directly concern her, she turned peevish and said she was off to bed.'

'Mmm, she does like to be the centre of attraction.'

'All I know is that she's turned goading me into a minor

art form. It's a little jab here, another one there. All tiny pinpricks, but enough to perforate my great bubble of goodwill and send me screaming to the scotch.'

For the first time in months, Len feels his wife's hand running up his thigh. He takes her in his arms. Her nipples are hard to his touch.

'Thought you couldn't do it with your ma in the next room?' he whispers, burying his face in her long dark hair.

'Sod her. This is my house. If she doesn't like it she can poke a Mars bar down each ear.'

'She seems to be behaving herself pretty well,' comments Len.

Despite the rain, he feels buoyant this morning. It's Saturday. He and Caroline have had a few good fucks this week. Quite like old times. And against the odds, for the past nine days his mother-in-law has not proved to be the trial he'd anticipated.

Caroline stretches, and plumps up her pillow. 'Don't be deceived. She's just been playing herself in. Anyway, it's been all right for you, taking yourself off to work, and darts matches, and your allotment. It's been hell for me dreaming up things for her to do every day.'

'Didn't she enjoy the trip to Salisbury?'

'No. I had an awful job just persuading her to get out of the car and have a look round. She shows no interest in anything. I've taken her to Guildford and Arundel and Winchester. We have lunch. I coax her up the high street. Look, I say. There's the river, the castle, the cathedral. She complains there are too many tourists. We have tea. "Is it time to go home yet?" she whimpers. I feel like a tyrannical seaside landlady evicting all the guests between nine and five. Basically, all mother wants to do is loll in bed like a great big slug, gobbling chocolates when she thinks I'm not looking.'

'What about Juliette? Has she been giving you a hand?'

'She very sweetly spent hours arranging a beautiful display of American currant and daffodils for mother's room. I put it on the pine chest and it looked quite lovely. Mother barged in, took one look at the flowers and turfed the whole lot out. Flowers in bedrooms are unhealthy, she said.'

Len pulls on his scarlet track suit. 'What are you doing with her today, then? I thought one of your libber friends had invited you round for tea.'

'Mmm, Wendy. But her baby's due any time, so I don't want to impose. I must phone later and see if there's any news. God, you're not going out for a run in this weather?'

'Course. Coming?'

Caroline tugs the quilt up over her head and groans. Len slips a hand underneath and pinches her bottom. She laughs. He loves to see his wife like this, her body pliant and her eyes still luminous from the going over he gave her this morning.

He takes the stairs three at a time. Outside the rain has stopped, the sky is clearing, and the road ahead is beginning to steam gently in the April sunshine.

Len's route takes him past an apple orchard, round the lush pastures of a stud farm, through the wood and down sleepy lanes canopied by spreading oaks. On working days he is out running by six-thirty, intoxicated by the luscious, fruity scent rising from the dew-frosted orchard. But most of all, Len savours the sounds of the early morning countryside. The song of the birds, wind gusting through creaking pines, horses whinnying a welcome in the fields, the gentle drip of moisture splashing down through the trees, and the rushing of clear water in the roadside streams.

Today being Saturday, he has allowed himself an extra couple of hours in bed. Instead of quiet, deserted streets, Len suffers the squeal of Volvo tyres as silk headscarved ladies rush to their early appointments at Mane Line. Already, a long queue is snaking round the corner from the butcher's, where rabbits frieze the window, their heads encased in green plastic bags.

The paper boys, their rounds completed, lounge against the sports pavilion on the village green. They strew sweet papers in Len's path and shriek their usual taunts about training for the Olympics.

'Anyone care for a race?' Len challenges.

'Wouldn't be fair, mate. Have to give a geriatric like you a head start.'

The little graveyard round the church is ablaze with daffodils. Len waves as the vicar careers past in his Landrover. In so doing, he almost collides with the local middle-aged tart, pedalling her rusty bicycle. 'Not in your shorts today, then?' she flutters coyly, treating Len to a glimpse of stringy thigh.

A worse menace than randy ladies are the dogs. Hungry-eyed dalmatians, bounding labradors, sprinting alsations and yappy spaniels.

'Here's sport!' they cry, as the sucker in the red track suit enters the woods. 'After him, chaps!'

Teeth bared, they pound exuberantly after their quarry, whilst a hundred yards behind their brogue-shod owners neigh ineffectually, 'Tarquin! Caspar! Heel this instant, I say!'

Every Saturday Len mourns the passing of the lovable, friendly Lassies and Rovers of this world. One morning, an Irish wolfhound shot out of the bracken and pinned Len to a birch tree. Her camel-coated owner galloped up, glaring accusingly at Len.

'What are you doing with Sheba? I thought I'd lorst her.'

'The police,' Len informed her cuttingly, brushing muddy paw marks from his shoulders, 'run first class dog-training classes. Shall I put your name forward?'

The woman smiled indulgently, as Sheba shat on the path. 'She's awfully naughty. Can't do a thing with her. Trouble is, she's not very partial to men.'

Today, however, Len is well ahead of the pack. He leaps easily over the wide stream, leaving the beasts to skid to a halt on the opposite bank. They quickly lose interest in him, and race off in pursuit of a squirrel.

With the danger past, Len heads down a peaceful, winding lane which in a few weeks will be heady with the scent of May blossom. For Len, the lane is full of pleasurable reminders. Already the hedgerows are freckled with green, prompting him that once the hawthorn comes into leaf, it is time to start sowing his allotment. As he regards the cobwebs, strung like fishermen's nets across the roadside gorse, Len realises that he must start thinking about holidays. Yugoslavia again this year, or should they try somewhere different? Trouble is, Caroline always seems so set on the Dalmatian coast. Says the food agrees with her there.

Len quickens his pace towards one of his favourite houses: a whitewashed thatched cottage, set in a wild garden of long grass, with chickens running free under the pear trees. A doll's pram and toy train lie overturned near the wooden gate. What an idyllic place to bring up kids, dreams Len.

This morning, a gleaming new Volkswagen is parked beside a hedge which in June will be ablaze with deep pink roses. A woman with silver meringued hair is mincing up the path. The peeling yellow door is flung open, revealing a distraught long-haired girl holding a child in each arm.

'Mother! What are you doing here? Is anything wrong?'

The woman clutches the lapels of her navy blue costume. 'I'm running in my new car. I thought I'd drop in and lunch with you.'

'Lunch! We haven't had breakfast yet. Samantha's teething, and Benjy has measles. Honestly, I do wish you'd show a bit of consideration and ring before you come.'

Len grins. Another happy family Saturday has begun. As he rounds the corner into the village he puts on a spurt. The paper boys give him a sarcastic cheer.

Len pokes his head round the kitchen door of Lavender Cottage. 'Is Juliette ready?' On Saturdays, he gives his daughter a lift to Fortune Pools.

Caroline looks up from her mixing bowl. 'She's already left. Nick said he'd drive her.'

'That dance hall lout? Christ, I – '

'Where are those peanuts I just chopped up? They were in a little blue dish.'

Rose, squirting washing up liquid into the blue dish, says blandly, 'They're gone now, dear. I mixed them in with the peanut butter for my toast. You've only got the smooth sort and I don't like that.'

'But you saw I was making a nut cake for Juliette's birthday. They were the only nuts I had in the house.'

'I'll buy you some more from the village store,' soothes Rose. 'And I'll get myself some crunchy peanut butter and sugar puffs while I'm at it.'

Caroline throws down her spoon. 'Now there's no need for you to go spending your own money on household things while you're here.'

'I like to pay my way, dear. What with poor little Juliette being sent out to work, I thought you might be feeling the pinch.'

'Mother, please put your purse away. You're our guest. And of course we're not hard up. Juliette's Saturday job is just to help broaden her horizons.'

'Well let me fetch you some nuts. I'd like a little walk.'

'The village shop only sells salted peanuts. I prefer the natural ones from the health store in town.'

'Mmm, I thought they tasted a bit funny.'

'Mother, I haven't finished with that spoon. Why don't you leave the washing up till I've done the cake?'

'I was only trying to help. Anyway, I thought you said you couldn't finish the cake till you'd got some nuts?'

Len ducks out, dashing upstairs to take his shower. The peanut dispute has reminded him that his daughter will be sixteen next week. Sixteen! Whilst he is forty. And dance hall Nick is a mere twenty-three.

Len peels off his tracksuit, flings himself onto the carpet and grunts his way through twenty-three press ups. In the shower, he soaps himself down, then turns the dial to cold.

Rose takes herself off for a little walk round the village green. Best to get out of Caroline's way when she's in one of her paddies. Odd, really, the way she's turned out. As a girl, she had such a cheerful nature. Everyone said so.

'I can't tell you how uplifting it is to have such a happy mother and daughter for my neighbours,' trilled Mrs Sprett-Davies when they moved into the big house in Laurence Drive. Caroline must have been about ten, then. Such a neat little thing in her pigtails.

That was the year they promoted themselves to Scott-Peters.

'If we're going to be rubbing shoulders with the Sprett-Davieses of Melford, then we'll do it on equal terms,' Lester announced. He had a cousin Scott in Australia, so they could legitimately claim it as a family name.

103

Lester's business was booming. He could now afford to buy properties himself, do them up and let or resell them at a vast profit. Rose never bothered to ask him about his work. Well, she had enough to do running the new house. It featured everything Rose had ever dreamed of. Central heating. Tudor beams (mock, but you really couldn't tell them from the real thing) and little latticed windows. They took all day to clean, but Rose didn't mind.

'Get the best,' Lester instructed, when she asked about furnishings. 'Chuck out all the utility, and we'll start investing in antiques.'

Rose's face fell. Who wanted all that old stuff? The Mayor's wife was going in for the new modern look. Rose yearned to have her sitting room decorated with two different wallpapers, and curtained in a bright, contemporary print. She'd got her eye on some fabric in an abstract red and blue pattern, though here and there you could pick out a vintage car. A mosaic-tiled occasional table would be nice, too, and instead of those bloated armchairs, a lightweight suite with screw-on legs you could sweep under properly.

'Use your head,' said Lester. 'Would Lady Evelyn choose to have ballerinas twirling round her hall wallpaper? Of course she wouldn't. Quality, Rose. That's our image.'

The mention of Lady Evelyn had, naturally, swung it for Rose. While Lester attended furniture auctions, Rose bought best quality chintzes and velvets. She had them made up by an upholsterer on whom she could rely to gossip freely round the neighbourhood.

After a year in Laurence Drive, Rose felt she was becoming a woman of substance. She had an imposing house, and a husband in property. Her charming daughter Caroline had just passed her Common Entrance and would soon be walking down the road in a blazer adorned with the County School crest.

When Mrs Sprett-Davies invited her to a coffee morning, Rose knew she had arrived. After all, Mr Sprett-Davies wasn't in trade, like the mayor. He was a stockbroker, whilst his wife was related to an Honourable. That made her only a step or two down from Lady Evelyn herself.

Caroline was so sweet during her first year at the Grammar. They were let out at three thirty, so she'd be home by four, throwing her big leather satchel on the kitchen floor and announcing that she was *ravenous*.

They'd have tea together. Something tasty on toast, and Caroline's favourite orange fairy cakes. Caroline would chatter on about having to eat frog spawn for lunch, and Bella being told off for passing notes, and the games mistress showing all her knickers when she demonstrated the western roll.

After tea, Caroline spread her books on the kitchen table, flicked back her plaits and got on with her homework. Rose always read it through when she'd finished. Not to make any corrections. She wouldn't have dreamed of interfering. But just because she was interested, and liked to keep tabs on what was being put into her daughter's head.

There wasn't anything about Caroline she didn't know. Rose was aware of what she liked to eat, and wear, who her friends were and what they said to one another. She could monitor Caroline's progress through every minute of the day. Rose knew what Caroline was learning at school, and precisely how much of that information was understood.

Their easy, companionable relationship was made all the more special because Lester was out so much. And when he was home he and Rose didn't have a great deal to say to one another.

'You and Caroline are really like sisters,' Mrs Sprett-Davies carolled, watching Rose and her daughter laughing over a gaffe Gilbert Harding had made on *What's My Line*.

At first, Rose was unconcerned when Caroline came home later and later from school. When they got to about fourteen, their classes went on longer, and Caroline was an active member of the debating society and drama group. Rose was glad her daughter was so popular.

Although Rose missed their cosy teatime chats, she understood when Caroline shut herself in her bedroom, saying she must have peace and quiet to do her homework. Not that Rose could comprehend much of the syllabus any more. All that algebra, French and physics was beyond her.

It seemed daft, really, filling girls' heads with complicated stuff like that. What was the point when they'd all be married with babies by the time they were twenty? Rose thought they should concentrate on domestic science and needlework. But Caroline made a face and muttered that you only did Homecraft if you were thick.

Whatever Rose said, it seemed, was wrong. When she asked Caroline if it was really a good idea to play Everley Brothers records while she wrote her essays, the girl flung down her pen and worked herself up into a right temper. 'You're just like Bella's mother! Nag, nag, nag. I'm not a child! Why can't you leave me alone?'

Her monthlies had started around that time, but Caroline hadn't confided in her mother, the way a normal girl should. Rose only found out when she discovered the half burnt sanitary towels in the boiler. By then Caroline was in such a moody state that Rose was afraid to broach the subject. Rose justified her abdication of responsibility by telling herself that Caroline was bound to have been given all the facts either in her biology lessons, or by that Bella.

Sly, almond-eyed little madam. She was the one who'd enticed Caroline away from her. Without Bella goading her on, Caroline would never have had the nerve to cut off her plaits and bleach her fringe.

Bella was the one who got expelled from school for taking off her blouse and bra during prayers. 'But how did they know what I'd done when we're all supposed to have our eyes shut?' Bella protested. 'The headmistress should have been setting a pious example, not standing there like a great bat, spying on me.'

Rose fretted constantly about what the pair of them got up to, closeted together upstairs for hours.

'Bella and I are going to play records in my room, so *don't come in.*'

Of course Rose had gone in. It was a Mother's duty to supervise her daughter. But after all that fuss, the girls were merely sitting on Caroline's bed, laughing as they flicked through magazines. It was the laughter which pained Rose most. Lester was so engrossed in his business affairs he rarely had time to share a joke with her. And now Caroline, too, was shutting her out.

The smiles vanished as soon as Rose entered the room, to

106

be replaced by expressions of sullen wariness. Rose hovered for a few minutes, drawing the curtains, throwing some crumpled paper into the wastebin. The girls lolled against the pillows, peeling long strips of red varnish from their nails as they waited for her to go away. At last, defeated by their silence, Rose retreated, snapping at them to get off the bed as they were dirtying the counterpane.

As she closed the door she heard them giggling again.

'Oh, there you are, mother. Did you have a nice walk? Look, Leo's just driving me to the shops. Would you like to come? Or will the Saturday crowds be too much for you?'

'I'll be all right here, dear. You two go off and enjoy yourselves.'

'Mother, we're only going shopping. Not out on the razzle. You're very welcome to come.'

Rose mutters darkly, 'I know where you're going. Don't think I don't. I shall only be in the way.'

Len is suddenly touched by the sight of her too-short green trousers, and the hankie tucked like a little girl's into the sleeve of her beige cardigan. Impulsively, he slips an arm round her sagging shoulders.

'Come on, love. Hop in the car. We'll whizz you round town and pick up some fish and chips for lunch on the way back. How does that suit you?'

'I never eat fish and chips, dear. The batter sticks to my teeth. But get some for you and Caroline by all means. I'll be quite content with a Ryvita. I never have much for lunch.'

Exasperated, Caroline slides into the Jaguar and slams the door.

Len says helplessly, 'Will you be all right? Treat the place as your own, won't you? Make yourself some tea ... '

'Don't you worry about me,' sighs Rose. 'I'm used to being by myself.'

As they drive away Caroline lights a cigarette and exhales noisily.

'I thought you'd given it up.'

Caroline laughs. 'I'm in a state of shock, seeing you of all people putting a comforting arm round my mother. How did it feel?'

'Like embracing a tree.'

8

'Christ, Caro, every bog in this house has got a body in it.'

'I'm sorry. Juliette's shampooing her hair in the bathroom, and mother's using the downstairs cloakroom to wash her clothes.'

'But she's going home tomorrow.'

'What if there's a train crash, she argues, and her case bursts open, revealing a heap of soiled knickers?'

'Wouldn't it be more convenient for her to fling everything in the washing machine, instead of scrubbing away in a handbasin?'

'Of course it would be easier. But now she's had her holiday, mother isn't playing Happy Families any more. She alleges she won't use the machine because she doesn't want to get in my way. She scores more points by commandeering the cloakroom for an hour so no one else can use it. Then she'll trail through the kitchen with armfuls of wet vests which will drip all over the floor while she fiddles ineffectually with the tumble dryer. She won't ask me how to work it because she doesn't want to be a nuisance.'

'Can't you ask her to hurry up? I must go before I set out for work.'

'I'm not giving her the satisfaction of admitting she's causing us aggro. And you mustn't hustle Juliette. She's washing her hair specially for our birthday dinner tonight. You'll have to go in the garden.'

'In this rain?'

'Don't be so soft. But keep away from the roses. Go up the end. Urine is very beneficial for compost heaps.'

Len pauses at the kitchen door. 'Who the hell told you that?'

'Oh ... just the husband of one of the women in my group.'

*

'Are these pearls all right, dear? I wasn't sure what to wear.'

Intent on basting the duck, tasting orange sauce and salting broccoli, Caroline says absently, 'You look fine, mother.'

Len sneaks a walnut from the top of the trifle. 'Belle of the ball, love. But it's only going to be a small family birthday party, you know. Nothing special.' He notices that his wife looks different. 'Hey, you've had your hair done. It's great piled up like that.'

She smiles. 'Thanks. It went all curly in the rain so I thought I'd make the most of it.'

'My hair looks horrible, doesn't it? I had it permed just before I came but the girl didn't do it tight enough. The curls dropped out the next day. That was ten pounds wasted.'

'A tenner? Can't you get it permed cheaper if you show your pensioner's card?'

'I've never accepted charity, Caroline. Your father would turn in his grave – '

'Don't be silly, mother. It isn't charity, it's your right.'

'Talking of the underprivileged,' grins Len. 'I met Miles on the train. He's just bought a Piper Aztec.'

'I know,' laughs Caroline. 'When Annabel told me, I said my God, you must really be one of the jet set now. She replied gravely that possessing a private plane was nothing. To be considered filthy rich you need to have your own airport.'

'Ooooh! Oh dear!' Rose doubles up.

'What's wrong, mother?'

'Nothing ... just a little pain I get sometimes under my heart.'

'Wind. I'll mix you up some Milk of Magnesia.'

Len guides her to a stool. Gratefully, she clutches his arm. 'It doesn't seem so bad, now I'm here with you. When you have your own people around you, the pain isn't so frightening. It's when you're by yourself you start imagining things.'

Caroline hands her a glass of cloudy liquid and says mildly: 'Mother, nobody forced you to go and live all that distance away in Edinburgh. If you feel nervous, you could always buy yourself a nice little cottage near us.'

Rose's voice trembles. 'Oh no. Leonard wouldn't want his mother-in-law living on the doorstep.'

Len clears his throat, prior to a diplomatic protest.

'Happy birthday to me!' Juliette sings from the doorway.

Len experiences a rush of pride as he looks at her. His daughter. Sixteen! He can't believe it. And what a little smasher she's turned out to be. The grubby jeans and clogs have been discarded in favour of a delicate Indian print dress, and pretty, high heeled sandals. Shiny black hair tumbles to her shoulders. With her blue eyes alight with excitement, Juliette seems to Len so poignantly poised on the threshold of her life. God, how he envies her.

'You mustn't mind me, dear. Granny's not very well.'

'I'm sorry, Gran. Won't you be having dinner with us?'

'If you're not up to it, mother, I'll willingly bring you something up on a tray.'

Len watches Rose hesitate as he pours the wine. 'Oh, I wouldn't want to spoil the party. It cheers me up to be with you all. I'll just nibble at a little duck breast, Caroline. And perhaps a small glass of wine would settle my stomach.'

As they draw up the garden chairs to the dining table, Rose confides to Juliette, 'I wasn't sure what to wear. I thought you might be allowed to invite some of your friends round, and I didn't want to let you down.'

'I'm sharing a party with Gail on Saturday. Her birthday is the day after mine, so she's having a bash at her house.'

Len has overheard the two girls moaning because Gail's parents refuse to do what the girls regard as the decent thing and go out for the evening.

'And as today is a schoolday, mum said we should just have a family celebration here, with me choosing the food. And where we eat it.' She glares at the abandoned floor cushions.

'What are you going to spend your birthday money on?' asks Len.

Juliette swirls the skirt of her dress. 'I've already blued it on this.'

'That reminds me, Caroline. Don't let me go off and leave

my things in the airing cupboard. I'd better take them out tonight and put them straight in my case, just to be on the safe side.'

'Whatever suits you best, mother.'

Len spears a potato. 'Seems incredible to think you're an old lady of sixteen, Juliette. Your mother was only two years older than you when I first met her.'

Caroline flashes him a *watch it* look. They have always taken pains to ensure that Juliette is unaware of her mother's wedding day pregnancy.

'Let's just hope Juliette doesn't turn out the same way,' mumbles Rose.

Caroline bangs down her glass. 'Just what is *that* supposed to mean?'

Rose tilts her head to one side and says sweetly, 'Merely that Juliette seems to be the studious type. I hope she keeps her eyes on her books instead of boys. I really do. You think you're very modern in your ideas, Caroline, but believe me you'd be just as shocked as I was if your daughter came home and said she was in the family way.'

Len is gripped by an infuriating impotence which normally only occurs during a row with his wife. It is as if his anger boils up into a thick strong glue, which seeps into his brain, clogging his furious eloquence into an incoherent stutter. Christ, what a bunch of savages they are. How could the old cow let the cat out of the bag like this? And on Juliette's birthday as well.

'Mother, this is unforgivable of you,' whispers Caroline, her face as white as the cloth. 'Juliette, I – '

'It's all right. I've known for ages,' says Juliette, gnawing at a bone. 'I sort of guessed from the way you were so vague about when you first started dating daddy. It really doesn't matter. I mean, we've just been learning in Social Studies that even at the time Granny got married, just before the war, nearly one third of all first-born children were conceived out of wedlock.'

Rose's teeth clack indignantly. 'I hope you're not suggesting, young lady – '

'Of course it doesn't matter, Juliette. It's very mature of you to take that attitude. But I'm sure you understand that it was impossible for us to tell you before you were adult enough to appreciate what was involved?'

'Oh sure. Actually Gail was positive you'd fill me in with the news soon after I was sixteen. Is there any more orange sauce?'

Len, almost bursting with rage, admires his wife's control as she enquires, with cool restraint, 'You've already discussed all this with Gail?'

'Of course. We tell each other everything. We've got something in common in a funny kind of way. Her mum was forty-one, you see, when she had Gail, so she was an afterthought.'

'You used to have a friend you told secrets to, Caroline. Bella, her name was. I wonder what happened to her? I always thought she'd come to a sticky end.'

'We lost touch for a while. But now she flies around over Guildford with her wealthy second husband.'

'Is that Auntie Annabel? I didn't know you were at school together.'

'That's because Annabel likes to make out she's years younger than me. And you know she winces when you call her Auntie.'

Observing his wife and daughter laughing together, Len realises that no further effort will be required from him this evening. His role now is of admiring spectator. The women are running the show. With malevolent Mother upstaged, Caroline and Juliette are now closing ranks to portray a harmonious family unit that no wicked witch has the power to destroy.

'Gail was running for a train at Waterloo last week and saw Annabel in a passionate embrace with *a man who was not her husband.*'

Juliette, Len muses, is getting drunk on the wine of her mother's encouragement. Normally she would never dare speak so freely in front of him.

Caroline, however, welcomes the opportunity to demonstrate mother-daughter rapport. Blue eyes meet blue conspiratorially across the table.

'Frankly, I suspect that Annabel has a positive squadron of lovers.'

'She's not the only one,' mutters Rose.

'Leo, don't give mother any more wine. It doesn't seem to agree with her.'

'I feel perfectly well, thank you. You're frightened in case I say too much, aren't you?'

'You're babbling. I'm sure none of us have the faintest idea what you're on about.'

'Leonard certainly hasn't. I can vouch for that. What would he think, I'd like to know, if he knew what you were up to with the husband of one of your girlfriends?' She drains her glass. 'I've got eyes in my head. I've noticed you always wait till Leonard's not here before you phone your gentleman friend and I heard you inviting him round to dinner on the night your husband will be out.'

'For heaven's sake! I was ringing Tim for a report on his *wife* who is in hospital having a *baby*. With all the rushing about he's been doing, I thought he'd be glad of a hot *meal*. He's coming on *Thursday* because that's the only evening in the week we're both *free*!'

Rose purses her lips, triumphantly unconvinced.

Len retreats to the bog. He could have sworn that when Rose hurled the gentleman friend accusation, Caroline looked guilty, and wouldn't meet his eye. Her too-indignant denials held to Len an undertone of relief. Naturally, there couldn't be any question of her having it off with Tim. Nice bloke and all that. But too wet to satisfy Caroline.

But what about the husbands of the other women in her group? Frances is hitched to an egghead lecturer called Elliot. Has Caroline been seduced by his intellectual waffle? She's always nagging Len to read something more demanding than page three of the *Sun*. Then there's Babs, the pretty one. Though if you express such a compliment she's apt to spit at you. Babs isn't married . . . but doesn't she live with some art student layabout? God, surely Caroline hasn't started cradle snatching?

Hang about. What was that odd remark she made this morning about peeing on compost? Now which of those jerks could have told her that? Len resolves to keep a closer eye on Caroline. If his wife is putting it about, he wants to know who with. Anyway, he thinks grimly, returning to the fray, two can play at that game.

*

'*Just to let you know I got back safely. Thank you for driving me to King's Cross. I know how nervous London traffic makes you but I still don't think you should have shouted at that Bus Driver the way you did, I hope Leonard wasn't too angry about the dent in the door. As it turned out it was lucky I asked you to pull up and get me that loaf because I had to wait half an hour for a taxi and all the shops were closed and I had no food in the house. Fortunately the milk had come so I had bread and milk for my supper –*'

'There's an Indian takeaway just down the road,' says Len. 'Why didn't she pick herself up a curry?'

Caroline turns over the page. 'You know she's suspicious of *them darkies* . . .

'*. . . for my supper while I watched TV. Not that I felt the lack of it at all while I stayed with you, I don't believe in sitting glued to the set all the time but after being with my Family I missed the sound of voices.*

'*Do wish Juliette every Success with her exams. She's growing prettier every day isn't she. You must feel the passing of the years, Caroline when you look at her I know I do. But that is just one of the burdens we Mothers have to bear. The Old must always give way to the Young it is one of the great Lessons of Life that Mothers must learn to accept with Grace.*

'*Well I will sign off now and post this on the way down to collect my prescription, I am as ever, Your Loving Mother.*

'*PS. Enclosed is £2 to cover what you spent on petrol.*'

Len decides on a neutral comment. 'She got back OK then.'

'However much I fight against it, I can't help feeling guilty about mother,' sighs Caroline, braiding her hair. 'She looked so pathetic at King's Cross with a sliced loaf under her arm and her ticket clamped between her teeth in case she lost it.' She glances across to the wardrobe. 'Oh Len, you can't wear a suit to this do tonight. You just can't. You'll show me up.'

Len is tempted to tell her to stuff the sodding party. But instead he hangs up the suit, and selects some casual gear. No point in provoking a row before they get there. They are bound to have their usual bust up in the car coming home.

Dallow has rung to say she is back in London. All the

women's group, plus partners, are invited for a get-together. It is the men Len intends to have a good butcher's at. Caroline, he notices, is togging herself up in a new dress. For whose benefit?

Len is not too happy about Juliette tagging along. A weirdo like Dallow is not, he feels, the best influence on a naive girl of sixteen. On the other hand, Juliette is deserting hooligan Nick tonight, which is a step in the right direction.

'Won't your boyfriend miss you this evening?' he asks as Juliette, in her new Indian print, scrambles onto the back seat of the car.

'Nick's working up north for a few days.'

Working at what, ponders Len. He wishes he hadn't shown so much initial hostility towards the lad, for Juliette now stubbornly refuses to give her parents any worthwhile information about him. She meets him at a secret rendezvous, returning at ten-thirty alone. It riles Len that he hasn't the foggiest where Nick lives, what he looks like or how he earns his living.

'Don't forget we agreed to pick up Babs and her man,' Caroline reminds him.

But Barbara is standing by herself outside her flat. She is wearing a red crushed velvet skirt and top. Her pert face radiates a bruised, though purposeful energy. Caroline winds down the window and converses with her in whispers.

'Drive on, Leo. Babs can't come. She's had a tear up with lover boy and is heading round the pub for a showdown with him.'

Len listens intently to the note of Caroline's laugh. But it reveals not a twinge of disappointment that the young art student is otherwise engaged tonight. That leaves Frances's know-all husband. Len accelerates towards the motorway, reflecting that after a few stiff scotches he'll be just in the mood for a very interesting dialogue with Elliot.

'What do you mean, there's no booze?'

'Leo, you know perfectly well that Dallow is teetotal. Of course she wouldn't offer alcohol at her party. I'm surprised you didn't think of that before you came.'

It is clear from Caroline's stridently self-righteous tone

that she herself has not previously given the matter a thought and is wondering desperately how she is going to get through the evening without a drink. Had it been anyone else but Dallow, then he and Caroline could have slipped round to the off licence and smuggled in a couple of bottles. But tonight such an act would smack of unsisterly betrayal.

The women's group are the first to arrive at the crumbling terraced house in Bayswater. But the hostess is making no attempt to welcome her guests, or even help them to a mugful of fresh orange juice. Dallow is sitting cross-legged by the French window, lost in a smiling, vapid daze. It comes as no surprise to Len that the room is devoid of furniture or decoration, apart from long wooden benches erected on the rush matting. The skull-crushing music, Juliette informs him, is Bob Marley and the Wailers.

'Very middle of the road,' sniffs Juliette. 'I'd expected something more way out from Dallow.'

Her own tape recording of a Bantu war chant, perhaps? Len is beginning to wonder just what he's doing at this arid gathering. It's not even as if there'll be any talent to chat up. They'll all be raving women's libbers making him feel a heel for having been born male.

Frances strides across the room, followed by a balding man in a cream linen suit. Ah, the mighty Elliot. Len brightens at the prospect of a verbal skirmish.

'Evening, Frances. I didn't know you were bringing your father with you?'

Frances's retort is muffled by Juliette's giggle. Coolly, the deputy headmistress turns to Caroline. 'Isn't it good news about Wendy's baby? What are they going to call him?'

'Originally, Wendy couldn't decide between Barnabus and Piers. Then she read the *Telegraph* birth announcements and realised that all the trendy Hampstead offspring are Piers this year, so she's doing a turnabout and calling him Arthur.' Caroline shakes a cigarette from the packet. Elliot glides forward, flicking his lighter.

Neither Caroline nor Frances makes any attempt to introduce Len to Elliot. Frances takes her husband's arm. 'Come and meet Dallow.'

'I hope Elliot's semaphore is up to scratch,' observes Len.

'Dallow hasn't said a word to anyone yet.'

'She's stoned,' volunteers Juliette.

'How do *you* know?' Len demands. God, that Nick has a lot to answer for.

Juliette shrugs and wanders off to sample the nuttolene salad. Len edges past Dallow and steps out into a long, narrow garden. His objective is to find a back entrance leading to the salvation of the nearest pub.

'If you're looking for a back gate, you're doomed to disappointment.'

The girl is sprawled on top of a red brick wall, framed by sprays of overhanging lilac from the neighbouring garden. Len approves the shoulder length blonde hair, and long slim legs. But at this moment, by far her most beguiling feature is the bottle of scotch gripped in her red-nailed hands.

'Like some?'

He jumps up beside her. 'Len Lambert.'

'Fay Lawson.'

With the formalities out of the way, he feels free to swig at her scotch. What a stunning bird. He notices her nipples are hard beneath the thin white dress. She can't be wearing a bra, the bitch.

'Fay's a pretty name. It suits you.'

She smiles at him as she curves her lips round the bottle. Len stares, fascinated. It's rare to meet a woman who throws back neat scotch. Even Caroline usually takes a splash of water with it.

'What are you doing here?' he asks.

'I came with a friend of a friend.'

'You're not one of the bra burning brigade, then?'

'Certainly not. I give you fair warning, I don't want to be equal with men. I want to exploit them.'

You can manipulate me any time you like, darling. 'I think that's a very intelligent approach.'

She wriggles on the wall. Len catches a glimpse of snowy lace panties as she shifts her legs.

'Not very comfortable is it?' he says. 'Tell you what, why don't I find us some cushions and a rug? Might as well make ourselves at home while they're all in there having a dull time.'

'Don't be long, then.'

Feeling considerably uplifted, Len weaves through Dallow and the courtiers sitting heaped at her feet. On the other side of the room, Caroline is dancing cheek to cheek with Elliot.

He taps Elliot on his cream linen shoulder. 'Hi. I'm Caroline's husband. You may have heard of me.'

'Of course. Glad to meet you.'

'Leo, have you been drinking?' Caroline sniffs his breath accusingly.

'Chance would be a fine thing,' he grins, backing away. He knows he's winning. Outside, under the lilacs, there's a willing young blonde and a bottle of scotch waiting for him. Whilst all Caroline's got is Elliot, with his sweaty top lip.

He takes a blanket and pillows from one of the beds and throws them down into the garden. Emerging from the French windows, he finds that Fay has settled herself under the blanket at the far end of the clover-covered lawn.

She laughs as he slides in beside her. 'Dallow and Co will think its some mystical astral vision – pillows and a rug raining down from heaven.'

She passes him the scotch, but he only permits himself a sip. Foolish to spoil his chances by getting pissed. He is beginning to warm towards Dallow. Never, at any party in Surrey, has he found himself lying on the lawn with a delicious blonde. Oh, a lot of the bored middle aged wives often fancied a grope in the shrubbery, of course. A last frenzied fling before the deadly strike of the first hot flush. But Fay is young (in her mid-twenties he guesses) and her left hand is ringless to his touch. She edges closer. Encouraged, he kisses her.

'Do you live on your own, beautiful?'

'Mmm. In West London. Just a small place, you know.'

'I work quite near there,' he lies.

'Then you must come up sometime – see me.' Len remembers there has been a recent revival of Mae West films.

He finds it hard to believe all this is really happening to him. Knowing his luck, in a moment the rug will be

wrenched aside and a snarling skyscraper will pick him up
and hurl him head first at the wall.

His hand caresses her breast. She eases down his zipper.
His cock feels ready to explode.

'Does anyone know where Dallow keeps the lavatory
paper?' Caroline's voice lasers through the scented night air.
'My daughter has diarrhoea and she's getting pretty frantic.'

'Mother, you don't have to *tell* everyone.' Juliette sounds
near to tears. Reluctantly, Len sits up.

'There is nothing to be ashamed of in your bodily
functions, Juliette. I'm sure Dallow would agree, if only she
could see or hear us.'

'Have you had a good look in the bathroom, Juliette?'
Crisp, no-nonsense Frances: *have you really lost your gym
shoes?*

'Of course she has. All the poor child could find to wipe
herself with was an empty crisps packet.'

'Mother! I'm all right now. I just want to go home.'

'Unfortunately, your father appears to have made off into
the night with the car keys.'

'I'll drive you, Caroline.' Elliot.

'I'll have to go.' Len stands up, hoping his cock will have
shrunk to normal size by the time he reaches the house.
'How about your phone number, Fay? Perhaps we could
have a drink, or a meal, sometime?'

She takes a pencil from her bag and writes her number on
the torn off scotch label.

'Thanks for the drink. I'll ... call you then.'

'You do that.'

She smiles. She knows he won't phone. He knows he
won't. How can he? He's a married man. He's expected
home in the evening for meals. His wife has a strong sense of
smell and can detect deceit five miles away under water. He
has never been unfaithful to Caroline. The ripped scotch
label is burning a hole in his trouser pocket.

The following day, Caroline pauses in sorting out the
washing and says, 'I'm thinking of taking mother on a little
holiday.'

'What's brought this idea on?'

'Oh, I feel so rotten thinking of her stuck up there all on

119

her own, slurping down bread and milk. Elliot was telling me about a really cheap little taverna he can get us into in Corfu. It will do mother good to go abroad.'

Fay. A romantic meal. Wine. Candlelight. Back to her place. Perhaps he can persuade her to tog up in black stockings and suspenders. She's a game bird. She'll play along. 'Do you really think you'll be able to stand your mother for an entire fortnight?'

'It'll be different in a holiday atmosphere. I'm sure we won't row as much. After all, I used to go away with her when I was a kid, and she could be quite good fun when she put her mind to it.'

Even now, Len can taste Fay's ripe young tits. 'When are you thinking of going?'

'Early June. I'll make sure the freezer's stocked up. You'll be able to manage without me for two weeks, won't you?'

'I suppose so.' Dear God, what the hell did he do with Fay's phone number?

Every year Rose took Caroline away for three weeks, to a cottage on the south coast. Lester always promised to come down and join them, but he could usually only manage a couple of weekends away from his work.

Not, of course, that running a cottage was much fun for Rose. She would have preferred a nice hotel. But the cottage was available through a client of Lester's, and anyway, he loathed English hotel food. If there was one thing Lester did love Rose for, it was her cooking.

Away from Melford, and the influence of that pert Bella, Rose found Caroline an agreeable companion. Inevitably, she acted sulky about having to do her share of the housework, but once they got down to the beach and settled on their patch, Caroline was Rose's own sunny little girl again.

If only the evenings hadn't proved so tricky. Caroline was so infuriatingly restless. No, she didn't care to sit and read, or listen to Ruby Murray on the wireless. She was fed up with playing whist. She pined for the telly and that infernal record player. Above all, Caroline itched to go dancing, and that Rose would not allow.

The year she was fifteen, the little minx slipped out. Rose

thought Caroline had gone to bed early, and only realised the truth when she heard a car draw up outside. At first she believed Lester had arrived, and flew to the larder to rustle him up a meal. Yet there was her daughter, brazenly, getting out of the car and kissing a man goodnight. Nasty, greasy specimen he was, too.

Rose was so enraged she grabbed Caroline as she came in, and lashed at her with a hairbrush. Hit her hard on the backs of her stockinged legs all the way up the stairs.

'You wait till I tell my father,' Caroline screamed. 'You just wait!'

'What are you going to tell him? That you've deceived your own mother? That you've given yourself to men?'

'I was out having some harmless fun. Daddy will understand that. When he takes me out we have a good time together. You're just jealous because he never wants to take you anywhere.'

Caroline adored her father. Well, no wonder, when she only saw one side of him. What young girl wouldn't be dazzled by a father who swooped in and declared, 'Pack your bags, girl. We're flying off to Amsterdam. I've got business to do there. I'll give you some cash, and you can wander round the shops. Then in the evening, your Daddy'll show you the sights.'

He never encouraged Rose to accompany him. She pretended she didn't want to go anyway. She assumed he only asked Caroline because one of his lady friends had let him down.

It worried Rose that he and Caroline were so physical with one another. Forever tickling, teasing, touching. 'You ought not to let her sit on your lap like that,' she warned him. 'Caroline's not a child any more. She'll be sixteen next year. You should encourage her to be more ladylike.'

But Caroline never did tell her father that Rose had hit her. They were forced to return home early that summer, because Lester was rushed to hospital with pneumonia. For the next two years, Caroline spent her vacations in Spain with Bella and her parents. Then when she was eighteen, Caroline met Leonard, and Rose realised sadly that the nearest she'd get now to a proper family holiday would be through the pages of her old photograph albums.

9

'It seems a bit rough and ready. Not at all what I expected.'
Rose stares with distaste at the fading Marlboro posters
stuck to the peeling green distemper.

'We're in a taverna, mother. Not the Grand Hotel at
Eastbourne. You have to make allowances. And tomorrow
we'll be able to eat our breakfast sitting outside under the
vines. Won't that be lovely? Look, there's a little garden out
there. Aren't the geraniums gorgeous?'

'Funny kind of garden, with geraniums blooming side by
side with dahlias in June. Doesn't seem natural, somehow.'

Caroline kicks off her sandals, and cools her feet on the
smooth, tiled floor. 'Everything's bound to seem strange at
first. You'll feel more in the swing of things when you've
had a drink. Would you like to try the retsina?'

'I'm dying for a nice cup of tea.'

'Oh mother, you can't. Andreas has offered us the first
drink on the house. He'll feel insulted if you ask for tea.'

Andreas, the walnut-faced owner of the taverna, presides
behind a large, well ordered desk in the corner. While his
mouth beams the traditional welcoming smile of the island
host, his eyes are flickering in ruthless assessment of how
many drachmas he's likely to squeeze out of the new English
arrivals.

'I'll have a small port and lemon, then.'

'The Greeks don't drink things like that. Try an ouzo
and lemonade.'

When the waiter has taken their order, Rose comments
loudly, 'They must be terribly poor here. The shirt that
boy's wearing is at least two sizes too small. You can see all
his chest straining through.'

'I think that's the idea,' murmurs Caroline, observing the
admiring eyes of a group of pale East London girls as Spiros
poses near their table. 'And mother, please try and keep

your voice down. The waiters speak very good English and can understand every word you say.'

'That wasn't what your father used to tell me,' pouts Rose. 'When he took you off on all those foreign trips he said it was because your French and German was useful for dealing with stupid waiters who couldn't understand English, however loud he spoke.'

Caroline is determined not to be drawn into an argument about her father and those contentious weekends abroad when Rose was left to sulk at home. She says cheerfully, 'We're lucky to have such a pleasant room, aren't we? With a balcony overlooking the sea, too. And those pine slatted beds look really comfortable.'

Rose snaps at the elastic gripped round the plastic tablecloth. 'I shan't be able to sleep a wink. I never do in strange places.'

Don't I know it, muses Caroline, sipping her chilled retsina and thinking back to those teenage holidays in Bridley Bay. God, how I longed for you to take an afternoon nap, or nod off after tea, so I could skip out on my own for a few hours. It was so frustrating, cooped up in that cluttered cottage, seduced by the music drifting out from the dance halls, and not being able to join in. You insisted on treating me like a child all the time, when I was longing to be grown up. You didn't realise I was past the stage of buckets and spades. I wanted to make love, not sandcastles.

Admittedly, when I did break out that night, the great adventure turned sour. I sat in a coffee bar, drinking espresso with filthy grey scum on top until I felt sick. And all the boys in their sharp Italian suits were more interested in admiring their new scooters than picking me up.

It was even worse in the ballroom. Standing there in my dress with the bow at the back, rooted with all the other wilting wallflowers round the fountain. Smiling vivaciously at the floor, trying to look really fascinated by the pattern on the carpet, as if the last thing in the world one had come for was to dance.

Inevitably, I ended up with an oily shorty with garlicky breath. He pushed me round the floor as if he were working a water pump. And when the band played the last dance,

Always, he pulled me close and stuck his tongue in my mouth.

Still, it was something to boast about to Bella. I never let on how I loathed that smelly kiss, or how mother went at me with the hair brush when I got home.

'I don't know how you can drink that stuff,' Rose grimaces as she sets down Caroline's tumbler of retsina. 'It tastes just like Izal.'

'Mother, just sit calmly and the wasps won't bother you. Eat your egg.'

Rose's plump arms flail like windmills as the wasps hover over her breakfast jam. 'It's all hardboiled and horrible. I wish I'd thought to pack my Sugar Puffs.' She shoots to her feet as a wasp crash lands on her hand. 'We must buy an insect repellent. I can't stand much more of this. I was bitten all over by mosquitoes last night.'

Caroline slices her hardboiled egg into a roll. 'That was your own fault. I did warn you not to leave the bedroom light on and the door open when you went to peg out your undies on the balcony. I can't imagine why you had to start washing the minute you got here.'

Rose retreats into the taverna, and shouts from the door, 'I don't like to see it piling up. What will the maid think?'

'She'll do the laundry for you for a few drachs.'

'You know I don't understand this foreign money. In any case, I'd never let a darkie touch my underwear.'

'Greeks are not darkies!' hisses Caroline, aware of Andreas broodily adding two percent to their bill for every insult hurled by the elderly English lady. 'And even if they were it doesn't mean they ... oh, come on, let's go and explore the village.'

The single long winding street of Siditses, shadowed by olive and mimosa trees, is jammed with a strange assortment of transport. Men on rusty bicycles, old ladies leading hay-laden donkeys, tourists crammed into tiny Fiats and local girls riding demure side-saddle pillion on their brother's motorbikes. Outside the shuttered houses, women in black hang out their newly washed sheets, blindingly white against a madonna blue sky. Chickens run free, scratching at the dry earth between the courgettes and potatoes, while a goat with devil-eyes cuts loose from his rope and wreaks havoc munching the lilies by the East London girls' villa.

Rose peers past the water cart, through the open door of one of the whitewashed houses. 'How can they live like that, Caroline? I've not seen such slums since those days after the war. They've hardly any furniture!'

'They all own a bed, a chair, a table, and something to cook on. What more do you need?'

Much, much more. Rose cannot envisage an existence without her carpets, curtains, television and glass fronted cabinets. She is about to voice her protest, when just in time she remembers that Caroline has just flung out most of the furniture from Lavender Cottage.

Best not to make an issue of it then, Rose decides. If Caroline turns huffy she won't come with me to buy the insect repellent, and I couldn't face going into that Greek shop all on my own.

Gazing with appalled fascination at an old woman tilling the stony ground with a piece of bent iron, Rose reflects bitterly that even Flo had a better life than this, in that terraced Fulham hovel.

Ironical to think I spent all those years fighting my way out of poverty, struggling to better myself and make something of my life. And now my own daughter has laid out all this money flying me to Corfu, where I'm supposed to stand and marvel at the primitive simplicity of it all. There was nothing charmingly rustic about Artillery Road, I can tell you.

'At least,' she admits grudgingly, 'their washing looks nice and clean. Which is more than can be said for the beach. All this seaweed, and thistles! You'd think the local council would clear it up.'

'But that's what's so special about the place, mother. If you have an army of people deodorising the beach you're just inviting the rot to set in through souvenir stalls and kiss-me-quick hats.'

Caroline slips off her sundress and flops down on the warm sand. Her bikini strap digs into her back. She closes her eyes, resolving hazily to swim every day and lose some weight.

And I must try to be more patient with mother. After all,

she's done remarkably well so far. No fuss over her first air trip apart from the hassle over how the plane loo flushed. (The stewardess was most understanding). And now here she is, installed in a foreign country, with her first Greek meal inside her. Well, some of it. Admittedly, the souvlaki at dinner last night wasn't a raging success. But it wasn't mother's fault that she grew impatient trying to ease the meat off the wooden skewer and it shot all over the floor.

There's no point in my getting irritated because she refuses to acknowledge the existence of drachmai, and responds with a frosty stare when any of the locals greet her in Greek. She'll adapt in time. Everything is bound to seem alien to her at first. But I invited her, so it's up to me to ensure that she enjoys herself.

She glances at her mother, sitting stiff legged in her striped Marks and Spencer frock. 'You'd be far more comfortable in a swimsuit. I saw some really pretty ones in the village store.'

'Oh no. I'm too old for that lark.'

'Nonsense. Look at Beth over there, fooling around in those flippers. She's magnificent in that black costume.'

Although Beth and Joshua are nearing their seventies, they are the most active of the guests at the taverna. Wiry Joshua, whose flowing white beard lends him the startling appearance of a prophet, told Caroline that he and his wife have already walked most of the northern paths on the island.

Beth, Caroline decides, is the type of woman who looks her best undressed. Meet her in the street and one regards a dumpy woman of faded beauty. Yet the black swimsuit reveals a splendidly sturdy body, still well muscled, with firm, lightly bronzed skin.

Rose purses her lips as the flippered Beth, laughing maniacally, flaps into the sea. 'Embarrassing, a woman of her age, cavorting about like that. She should cover herself up. Personally, I wouldn't dream of going out without my corsets.'

Sticky in the midday heat, Caroline walks slowly into the sea, enjoying the torture of the cold water shocking its way up her thighs. She waves at the East London girls on their orange pedallo, and settles into what Leo would mockingly describe as Caroline's ladylike breaststroke.

If he were here now, he'd be diving down under me, pulling off my bikini pants under the waves ...

No, it's years since he's played a trick like that. Caroline rolls onto her back and floats, her salty face turned up to the sun.

That first summer, when we met, he took me down to Brighton for the day on the back of his new motorbike. I wore a blue Orlon jumper and a cream pleated skirt that flirted up round my stocking tops. We limped across the pebbles, and I deliberately gave him a flash of my tits when I changed into that one-piece with the ruched top. He threw me in the sea. God it was freezing. But I was so hot for Leo I'm surprised the water didn't sizzle.

I was different then. Sharper. More forward, my mother would say. Going around with Bella helped. After I told her about that dance at Bridley Bay, we went every week to the Palais. Rows of us, standing four deep under the pink lights in the powder room, intently lacquering our backcombed hair.

Staggering to think that when I met Leo I was still a virgin. Just. But I'd been fingerfucked so often, I was raging for the real thing. Dying for it. Poor Leo couldn't understand why I wouldn't let him do it in his old van. He assumed I found that moonlit riverbank more alluring. But I had to choose a spot where it wouldn't show if there wasn't any blood.

Leo was always the romantic one, not me. It took him ages to recover from the shock of me shoving my hand into his overalls just an hour after I first set eyes on him. But I only did it to impress Bella.

We made a good pair, she and I. Her father in electronics, mine in property, and on the local council. Our families mattered in Melford. We knew it, and played up to it. I loved queening it over Leo's Rocker mates. Persuading Dad to let me take the Daimler to drive the gang down to the coast for a confrontation with the Mods ... being the only girl in the bowling alley wearing a real fur jacket and genuine suede skirt ... pretending I didn't know they were all fascinated by my accent ...

Caroline stands up and splashes through the shallows.

Hell, what a pain you were in those days. Wallowing in the reflected glory of being big-shot Lester Scott-Peter's daughter.

When her father was arrested, and news of the embezzlement was splashed across the papers, Caroline was shocked at the extent to which his public disgrace affected her. She had been married for fourteen years. She was no longer even living in Melford. Yet she felt as if not only her prop had gone, but all the masks, glamour and glitter, too.

It stunned her to realise that for all her married life she had never for a moment regarded herself as Mrs Leonard Lambert. Always, she had faced the world with supreme confidence, as Lester Scott-Peters's daughter. But with his conviction and imprisonment, she lost the identity which had bolstered her for so long. Even her sex drive diminished. All that's left, she muses, is a person known as plain Caroline Lambert. But who on earth is she?

'That's a sensible bikini you've got on,' remarks Rose, averting her face from the spray as Caroline wrings out her hair. 'Much more suitable than the postage stamp that red haired madam is wearing.'

Caroline instantly resolves never to wear this particular bikini again. The red haired girl has a fantastic body, she admits, towelling hard at her spare tyre and wishing she'd swum more energetically. The guy with her is easy on the eye, too.

Young, fair, well muscled, his hand rests lightly on the curve of the girl's behind. No litter of plastic beachbags, sand encrusted goggles, lemonade bottles and soggy paperbacks surrounds them. Instead they lie on pristine Yves Saint Laurent monogrammed towels, raising an occasional languid arm to anoint smooth limbs with expensive continental sun oil.

The Beautiful People. Caroline squirts Boot's sun screen over her burning cheeks, reassuring herself that presumably they must lead perfectly ordinary lives just like everyone else. He's probably a used car salesman and she's a secretary in a bank. Yet somehow it seems impossible to imagine this gilded pair ensconced in a semi, engaged in a routinely mundane clash about who blocked up the drains.

Rose rams on her cotton sunhat. She wonders how she is going to tolerate two weeks of sitting on a scalding beach with nothing to look at but disgusting mounds of naked flesh. Her corsets are killing her.

I was slim like you, once, she silently informs the prone redhead. But I lost my figure when I had Caroline. One of the many sacrifices a Mother makes. You'll find out. When it's too late.

She looks down at her daughter, noticing with grim satisfaction that the tops of Caroline's legs are mottled with thread veins.

The East London girls have recklessly ignored warnings not to drink the local water. Over breakfast each day, they shrilly compare the state of their bowels.

'Brenda's a bit loose this morning, but not half as bad as I was yesterday. Honestly, it was coming out both ends at once. That cement stuff works a treat, though. Really clogs you up. Poor Ellie, now, she's quite the other way. How many days has it been now, Ell? I shouldn't worry. There's a girl in my typing pool only goes once a fortnight and her breath don't smell. Oh, here's Bren, several tons lighter by the look of her. What's that, love? Well I told you not to use the taverna loo, Bren. It's always bunged up. Have a couple of hardboiled eggs. 'Ere, Mrs Scott-whatsit, if you're not eating your egg can our Bren have it?'

Rose pounds across the vine-shaded terrace, armed with an aerosol, waging war on the wasps. While Caroline shops in the village store for their lunch of rolls, cold meats, olives and fruit, Rose busies herself tidying up the bedroom so the maid won't have to bother.

Mornings are devoted to lying on the beach, on the opposite side of the sand dune to the Beautiful Couple. Joshua has discovered that the young man is a pop star. His Scandinavian girlfriend, Elsa, solemnly explained that they chose remote Siditses to avoid being hounded by the world's Press. The pop star is allergic to the glare of publicity. It is crucial that he should rest, and assuage his grief over the death of his drummer from an overdose of drugs. He can bring himself to talk to no one.

The pop star is so overwrought that even the click of the East London girls' Instamatics is enough to send him scuttling back to the taverna, with his monogrammed towel shielding his famous face. Rose is quick to note, however, that, not all the pop star's senses are numbed with despair. After a hearty lunch washed down by three bottles of beer, he and the redhead retire to their room each afternoon and are not seen again until dinner.

Caroline enjoys a siesta after lunch, falling immediately into a delicious, drugged sleep. Rose, unable to rid herself of the notion that it is sinful to close her eyes during daylight hours, sits out on the balcony, nibbling at the Battenburg cake she brought with her from Edinburgh.

Around five, they take a stroll through the olive grove, with Caroline suppressing her mounting irritation at her mother's refusal to pick her feet up. It's all that slopping around she does in slippers at home, Caroline realises. Thank you, mother. Now my memories of this walk won't be of silvered, age-old trees filled with the sound of birdsong. Instead all I'll recall will be *shuffle*, bloody *shuffle*.

'Weird trees, aren't they, these olives,' says Rose. 'They look as if they've got varicose veins.'

They saunter back to the taverna, and sit with cool drinks, Caroline idly, Rose critically, watching the world go by. Schoolgirls in blue cotton dresses barter urchin shells for sweets. Andreas cruises past in his large red Fiat, blaring his horn at the bronzed holidaymakers careering down the street on dilapidated scooters. The stocky owner of the village store stands in the middle of the road, waving his arms in vehement argument with a fisherman. Just when it seems they will come to blows, the men laugh, smack one another on the shoulder, and go their separate ways. Spiros, haggard after long nights and afternoons spent servicing the villa girls, wobbles back by bike to lay up the taverna tables for dinner.

Caroline sips her cold retsina and thinks back to all the other pavement cafes where she's sat, with a drink and a cigarette, revelling in the last golden hours of the day. Paris, on honeymoon with Leo. And before that, Rome, Amsterdam and Copenhagen with her father. If his business

130

affairs had been successful he would be in an expansive mood, entertaining her with scandalous stories about his colleagues, choking over his cigar as he bellowed with laughter. How sophisticated he made her feel.

The trips with Lester were always fun. A blessed far cry from those childish holidays with mother at Bridley Bay. Even so, Caroline was ever acutely aware of her father's disappointment that she was not a boy. Instinctively, Caroline tried to make it up to him by looking pretty and always having something pert and amusing to say. His approval meant everything to her, and even his wrath was welcomed as an alternative to being ignored. The more outrageous her behaviour, the more he noticed, and, yes, admired her. But in turn, the more father and daughter's eyes met in shared laughter, the more jealous mother became.

'Caroline, don't fuss round your father like that. Can't you see he's trying to finish his tea? ... Lester, should you really allow Caroline to drive the Daimler? It's so big for her to handle. If she had an accident I'd never forgive myself...'

Yet despite the rapport with her father, Caroline could never suppress the irrational fear that she had let him down by not presenting him with a grandson.

'I was hoping you'd call him after me,' her father admitted. 'But there's no female equivalent of Lester, is there?'

Caroline drains her glass and scribbles postcards to Leo and Juliette. How she envies those of her correspondents who are capable of summing up the holiday scene in witty one-liners. With her creativity dulled by too much sun and resinated wine, Caroline finds herself once more reduced to platitudes about the flight, the bougainvillea, the eccentric Greek plumbing.

The only way Caroline can coax even a trickle of tepid water from the shower is by detaching it from the hook and lying down on the bathroom floor. The culprit, she discovers, is the girl in the room next door. Sandra is in the habit of dashing back from the beach at four o'clock and using the taverna's entire water supply to wash her long blonde hair.

Rose is prepared to be magnanimous about the water situation. She takes her shower in the mornings. And she approves of Sandra and husband Brian.

Brian is a tall, darkly intense accountant who Caroline suspects was force fed on the *Boys' Wonderland of Knowledge*. Already the taverna guests have learned never to express in Brian's hearing even the vaguest interest in subjects ranging from the midnight sea temperature, the mating habits of the crab or Albania's chief agricultural crop. (Potatoes.)

'He's so polite and well informed,' whispers Rose as they make their way down to dinner. 'He sat with me for an hour this afternoon explaining why it's so unusual to get wasps here at this time of year. And he even knew how Battenburg cake got its name.'

The wait for Spiros to stagger round with the lemon soup would be tedious without the suspense of wondering which dress Sandra will be modelling tonight. Will it be the dramatic red flounced skirt, the off the shoulder number . . . or the starkly sophisticated black and white shift?

The East London girls, in T-shirts and shorts, lounge against the soft drinks crates. Bra-less Elsa idly disentangles a fly enmeshed in the string vest she's sporting over skin-tight black satin pants. Caroline feels pleasantly peasantlike in her cool cheesecloth. All eyes swivel expectantly towards the door as Sandra steps over the mangy taverna cat and makes her entrance.

The creation tonight is full length smocked pink gingham. She carries a matching, lace edged shawl, and from her wrist swings a dainty chrocheted evening bag. The high heeled silver sandals ti-tup down the dusty tiled floor in counterpoint to the soft squish of Brian's solid leather sandals. With a flourish, he pulls up the sleeves of his white shirt and eases out the rickety chair. Smiling graciously at the assembly, Sandra takes her place, resting her immaculate bag on the plastic table cloth.

Behind her on the flaking wall is a lurid print depicting four Italain girls on a bridge. Their carmined lips smile enticingly at the men in the gondola below, though the proportion is so awry that the gondola would get stuck if it tried to glide under the arch. The frame is fashioned from shells, some of which have come unglued, and the entire masterpiece is wrapped in cellophane to ward off the flies.

'Doesn't Sandra look lovely again tonight?' sighs Rose, slurping her soup in a manner which sets Caroline's teeth on edge. 'She has such exquisite dress sense. And he treats her like a princess.'

Caroline wishes Juliette were here, to act as accomplice in an enjoyable bitch about HRH. Clearly, when Brian's wife is not busy arranging candlelit dinner parties with an artistic rose centrepiece, she props up her little manicured feet on a fringed footstool and studies the fashion magazines for advice on Your Holiday Wardrobe.

Pretty, practical pink gingham! Perfect for those sultry Greek nights spent dining under the stars. Yet with our generously cut matching shawl it will see you through a chilly English evening, too. And here's an added bonus! From just the one pattern you can make yourself the négligé you've always dreamed of (at a price HE can afford!) ...

The pop star, draped in a hand-tucked lawn shirt, sits with his broad back to the rest of the room. Elsa, looking beautifully bored, bends the tin spoons into mini Loch Ness monsters. They are receiving, in full measure, all the peaceful anonymity Elsa declared they crave for. Displaying a triumphant mixture of British reserve and sheer bloody mindedness, the other guests have spoken not a single unnecessary word to the glitterati. By unspoken mutual consent, they have refused to probe for details of the pop star's group, records or films. Even his name remains a mystery no one is anxious to solve.

On the first dull day, Caroline and her mother take the local bus into Corfu town. The ride is enchanting, through green hills splashed with yellow broom, scented with oregano and wild thyme. Despite the cloud, the light is bright enough to make Caroline's eyes water.

I shouldn't have gorged on that moussaka last night, she realises. The cheese topping is going to bring on a migraine later.

Like a distant drum in the far recesses of her head, Caroline feels the first warning tremor of pain, which if left unchecked will soon be beating mercilessly against her skull. Through blurry eyes she studies her Greek phrase book, memorising the word for aspirin. Rose has borrowed her sunglasses, as she was bitten on the eyebrow by a mosquito last night.

At Corfu town bus station Caroline fights her way through a crowd of noisy Corfiots in order to buy tickets for their return journey. When she reaches the desk she is laconically informed that she is in the wrong queue. Rose emerges tight-lipped from the public lavatory, her handbag firmly clasped in both hands.

'It's disgusting, Caroline. Just a hole in the floor, and that's all blocked up with bits of smeared cardboard. And the smell! I had to take a deep breath before I went in and hold it all the time I was doing my business. What do we have to wait here for? But why can't we buy our tickets *on* the bus like in England? They have a funny way of carrying on here, I must say.'

Caroline dearly longs to wander alone through the colourful winding lanes and markets of the old town. Through the gaps between the Venetian houses she catches tantalising glimpses of cool, wisteria shaded squares, where dreaming churches whisper a promise of peace to the hot, tired explorer.

But Rose will not leave Caroline's side even to glance in a shop on the opposite pavement. Dog-like, she follows two paces behind her daughter as they drag from street to street, stopping where Caroline stops, gazing with glazed suspicion at the filigree silver, handpainted pottery, woollen shawls and leatherwork.

Pressured by the weight of her mother's increasing boredom, Caroline pays more than she intended for Juliette's leather sandals and Leo's superb Aran-type sweater. For herself she chooses a single personal memento: a tile in glowing blue, green and white to remind her on drizzly English winter days of the sundrenched brilliance of the sea, hills and whitewashed houses of Corfu.

Rose complains that her poor feet have swollen up like

boiled puddings after all that walking. Caroline should have warned her to wear more comfortable shoes. She flops down with a sigh of relief at the only vacant table outside a restaurant overlooking the tranquil cobalt water of the harbour.

The sun breaks through the clouds, beating down on Caroline's bare, throbbing head. She swallows the aspirins. 'I imagined you'd enjoy a change of scene today, mother. But it's all been a complete waste of time. You haven't bothered to buy a thing. I should have thought you'd like a little vase as a souvenir of your holiday. Or a new pair of slippers. You know how fond you are of slippers.' Shuffle, shuffle, shuffle. All morning long.

'I don't need another vase. It's only something extra to dust. And I've got enough pairs of slippers to see me out. Besides, those Greek shopowners put me off, prancing round all the time, trying to make you feel guilty if you don't buy their tatty pottery. At least in Princes Street they give you time to browse.'

When the mullet is ordered, Caroline fetches an ashtray from a nearby table.

'You should wear a petticoat under that thin cheesecloth, Caroline. With the sun shining through all the men can see your pants.'

Caroline exhales. 'If they don't like it, they needn't look.'

The cigarette is certain to aggravate her headache, but she is past caring. With detached interest, she appraises the battle raging behind her brow. Exacerbated by the cigarette, the bright light, the smell of cooking food and a morning of Rose's unceasing chatter, the band of pain is attempting to tighten its grip round her head. But the strong Greek aspirins have set up a smoke screen, in the form of a soothing, cotton-wool type mist which absorbs and anaesthetises the worst of the ache. It eases the migraine, but has the counter effect of dulling all Caroline's other senses, also.

When the meal arrives, she is unsurprised at her lack of appetite, and pushes the plate aside. If I can just keep my head in the shade, and sit here quietly and calmly, I shall be all right.

Rose, horrified at the waste, devours both portions of mullet and chips.

'Very bony fish, this,' she mutters. 'I must say, *clack*, I like a nice bit of cod myself but it's getting *click* so dear. A couple of weeks ago it was such a ridiculous price *tick-tack*. I said to myself *clack* well I'm not paying that, I'll have coley instead *click*. It's not the same of course, has a greyer look to it than *tick-tack* cod but if you do it with a lemon sauce and parsley it's quite tasty *click clack* – '

'Mother, please *please* will you let me buy you some new false teeth?' Caroline is on the edge of her chair, her nails rending the paper tablecloth.

Rose calmly dabs her mouth with a paper napkin. 'Why? I'm used to these ones. And you know I'm frightened of dentists. Mind you, I'm very careful with my dentures. Mrs Logan next door threw up and lost her set down the toilet.' She lays down her knife and fork. 'I enjoyed that. It's the first hot lunch I've had since I've been here.'

'But I thought you enjoyed our picnic lunches on the beach?'

'I did at first. But you always bring the same food every day. Rolls, cold meat, fruit. It gets boring. You never thought to ask me if I'd like a change now and then.'

'Well really! Every damn morning I'm the mug who stands in a long queue, Greek phrase book in hand, to buy all the food. I'm the one who fills the rolls, washes the fruit, packs it up and carries it all the way down to the beach. I also lumber myself with your beach umbrella, your towel and your infernal Battenburg cake. All you have to do is sit back and lap up the sun. And now you're bitching!' Caroline bites her lip, instantly regretting the outburst. Her head is starting to throb again.

Rose's chin tilts aggressively, 'Well why shouldn't you do these little things for your Mother? I waited on you hand and foot when we used to go to Bridley Bay.'

The words tumble out before Caroline can stop them. 'Are you joking?' She laughs mirthlessly. 'God, I remember those so-called holidays. Every morning I wanted to rush down to the beach and get a tan. But no. We had to make the beds. Wash up. Dust. Hoover. Walk a mile to do the shopping. Trail back. Peel the vegetables for supper. Rinse out the drying up cloths. Debate whether we'd got enough bread. By the time we did get down to the sands the best spots were taken and the sun had gone in. Then you'd drag me off the beach at four to go back to the cottage for a sit down tea. I'd have been happy to munch a bought meat pie by the sea, but you'd insist that we lay the table and nibble garden party sandwiches, neatly cut into triangles with the crusts sliced off.'

'What's wrong with eating decently cut sandwiches? All my life I've slaved to try and show you the right and proper way to do things. Now I find all my sacrifices thrown back in my face. I don't mind telling you, on my last visit to Lavender Cottage I felt right ashamed to see my own daughter living in such squalor. There's practically no furniture and I found cockroaches under the sink.'

'That's your own fault for poking around under there.'

'You've no standards. I watched you wield a *fish slice* to serve up the apple pie. And that lovely Victorian soup tureen Lady Evelyn gave you is being used as a chamber pot.'

'That was Leo's idea. Quite right too. We both thought it was hideous.'

'And don't think I didn't notice what you've done with that heated hostess tray I gave you for your tenth wedding anniversary. I saw it lying in the mud when Leonard drained the fish pond.'

'I've never been the After Eight type, mother.' Perhaps Sandra would like the heated tray. No, Sandra will already have at least three. Indispensable for keeping the petit pois warm while Brian bores the boss's wife with the saga of this unspoilt little fishing village they've discovered in Corfu.

'It's not just meant for entertaining. If Leonard is late home – '

'If Leo can't be bothered to ring and say he's delayed, then he gets a burnt dinner and that's that.'

'You'll lose him if you're not careful. You haven't got the first idea how to treat a man. I see a lot more than I let on, I can tell you.' The narrow-eyed, knowing look is wasted behind the sunglasses Rose has borrowed from Caroline.

'That's rich, coming from you. Your marriage was hardly idyllic.'

137

Rose blows her nose. 'My marriage was the most wonderful – '

'Stop burbling like a *Womans Weekly* heroine, mother. Be realistic. I got on famously with my father, but I'd be the first to admit that he could be difficult to live with. He was moody, unpredictable and spent most of his time out of the house, so he was hardly a companion for you. In many respects your life is easier now, without him. You can please yourself much more.'

Rose's voice trembles. 'I'm afraid I don't have a selfish nature like you. I'm not afraid of wanting to feel needed. You don't know what it's like being totally adrift in the world, with no family or friends.'

'But no one forced you to uproot and run away to Edinburgh.'

'I felt harassed by all those newspaper reporters when your father's trial was on. They even sneaked into the house, you know, and stole my framed snapshots from the top of the china cabinet. And I do have strong ties with Scotland. My mother was Scottish – '

'But she died when you were tiny. It's not as if she ever took you there – '

'And Lady Evelyn always favoured Edinburgh for a holiday. I don't dislike the place itself. It's just that I get so lonely.'

'Well would you rather come and live with us?'

'You wouldn't want me anyway.'

Caroline ignores the undisputed truth of this. 'Leo has frequently said that you'd be more than welcome.'

Rose scrabbles in her bag for her pills. 'He made me feel definitely surplus to requirements when I took care of you all after Juliette was born. I remember I starched and ironed every one of his shirts, and put them in his drawer all neatly folded. Two minutes later I caught him shaking them all out and slipping them on hangers. After all my hard work.'

'Mother, you can't still be harbouring a grudge for a trivial incident that happened seventeen years ago!'

'It doesn't seem that long. As you get older, time appears to telescope. I can recall every detail of my wedding day as if

138

it were yesterday. Course, I wasn't to know then that I'd end up all on my own.'

'I thought you prided yourself on your independence.'

'Oh I do! I never want to be a burden on anyone. Even when I get really old and crippled I'll just put myself away in a home somewhere. You won't have to worry about me.'

Caroline pleads, 'Why not try and make some friends, mother? Mrs Logan next door seems very pleasant.'

'I want no truck with her. She's the sort who hangs her washing out on a Sunday.'

Confused, Caroline murmurs, 'Oh ... I had no idea you have religious convictions, mother.'

'I don't. But why can't she do her washing on Mondays like the rest of the world? It irritates me beyond words, Caroline, looking out of the window on a Sunday and seeing her smalls flapping in the breeze, spoiling my view. It isn't decent.'

'Yes ... well, to get back to your social life. There must be loads of pensioners' associations and clubs in a place as big as Edinburgh. You'd go on outings and trips to the coast. They'd come and pick you up – '

'I don't want a herd of strangers galloping into my house and poking about. I like to keep myself to myself.'

'Don't whine at me that you're lonely, then.'

'Sorry I spoke, I'm sure.' Rose glances round the crowded restaurant. 'Keep your voice down, Caroline. Everyone's staring.'

'I think we'd better make our way to the bus station.' The entire left side of Caroline's face feels veined with pain. 'If we miss the damn thing I think I'll just go away quietly and smash my head against the nearest wall.'

'It's the weight of all that hair giving you migraines. Seems ridiculous to me, a woman of your age, and a Mother, trailing around with shoulder length tresses. You should have it razor cut. It would take the pressure off your head.'

Caroline spends the journey back with her eyes closed, planning, with feverish, illicit pleasure, every detail of her mother's funeral ...

10

The morning brings a blessedly clear head, and the sound of her mother singing in the shower. She's always at her most cheerful after a row, Caroline realises. Everyone else feels wrung out like wet rags, whilst mother, who has usually provoked the upset in the first place, is smiling, happy and infuriatingly purged.

But Caroline is glad to accept the truce, and allow the soothing Corfu air to envelop her in lethargy once more. To Caroline's relief, her mother is befriended by Joshua and Beth, who take her off for peaceful walks through the olive groves.

Treasuring her solitude, Caroline lolls contentedly on the beach, so relaxed that even turning the pages of her paperback seems too much like hard work. When her mother mentions Maybrook, a sleepy, sun-drugged Caroline has a struggle to remember that this is the village she calls home. She smiles in sympathy at the memory of that other, English Caroline. The efficient wife and mother, with her mind cluttered with junk.

Pay milkman Saturday, collect bread Monday and Friday, take Leo's suit to cleaners, Juliette's dental check due end June, dustman Wednesdays, remember to stay in Thursday for electricity man, defrost fridge, phone insurance people about dent in car, arrange washing machine service, plant out geraniums, repair Leo's work apron, have chimney swept, remind Juliette to sort through her jumpers for Tennis Club jumble sale, write shopping list, buy christening present for Wendy's baby, check garden hose for leaks, try and snatch an hour on Sunday afternoon for quiet nervous breakdown ...

Yet out here, away from the treadmill, nothing seems to matter. When we missed the boat for the round-the-island trip because the courier was slow changing our travellers' cheques, we just shrugged and said never mind, we'll go

140

another day, another year. In England I'd have thrown a fit and gone screaming for my migraine tablets.

Their inertia is indulged until the last night, when Andreas storms at his listless guests, 'The trouble with you English is that you have no idea how to enjoy yourselves. This evening, we will have a party. I shall push all the tables together and my mother will prepare special traditional food. Spiros will teach you to do our Greek dancing. You will take home the happy memory of a warmhearted Corfiot evening.'

The taverna has a festive air, with candles set in wine bottles on gay red cloths, and insistent bouzouki music blaring from the loudspeakers. But the British guests are sullen and unresponsive, resentful at being bludgeoned into a turmoil of typically Greek fun.

Joshua and Beth have been drinking on their balcony since four. Joshua protests his eyelids feel as heavy as up and over garage doors. Elsa is angry because Spiros has spilt coarse red wine on her white dress. No chain store mode this, but a stunning creation fashioned from a single length of silk jersey.

'She told me the name of the designer, but it's slipped my memory now,' Beth confides in a slurred whisper to Caroline. 'It sounded like someone being sick.'

Yuki, thinks Caroline jealously, feeling frumpish in the neat little flowered print she is wearing to appease her mother over the see-through cheesecloth incident. Her temper is not improved when Rose nods approvingly and remarks that Caroline looks 'much tidier' tonight.

HRH, exotic in South Sea Island cotton, complete with coral necklace and white flowers twined in her hair, is in the middle of a domestic dispute with Brian.

Caroline gathers that the royal bowels have at last succumbed to what Leo would term the Aztec two-step. But Brian has refused his wife permission to borrow the East London girls' medicine.

'Scientific tests have proved conclusively that the stuff merely paralyses your insides, Sandra. You're over the worst now. But if you do feel an attack coming on, there's a Ladies just at the end of the room.'

'But it echoes in there,' HRH protests tearfully. 'Everyone will hear.'

'I think that's most unlikely. I estimate that the accumulative decibels of sound issuing from those loud-speakers, and Andreas's mother shouting in the kitchen, is in the region of – '

Sandra turns her back on him and applauds Spiros wildly when he takes the floor and demonstrates a dance which involves him leaping backwards over two chairs. Encouraged, Spiros pounces on HRH, lifts her onto a table and gyrates round her in an elaborate Greek courtship ritual.

Joshua wakes up and claps enthusiastically. 'Show a leg there, Sandra! Let's see the South Sea siren do her stuff!'

Wooden with embarrassment, Sandra stands stiff as a bobbin doll, tossing her blonde hair in a token expression of seduction. The other women cringe low in their chairs, praying it won't be their turn next. When the record ends, a perspiring HRH bolts for the Ladies, with Caroline hot on her silver-sandalled heels.

'Those Greeks have no respect for a lady,' mutters Sandra. 'I'm surprised at Brian, allowing that waiter to become so familiar.'

'Bit more boisterous than the Young Conservative wine and cheese parties, isn't it?' murmurs Caroline, watching the trembling Sandra fluff powder over her shiny nose.

Is your puff as spotlessly clean as your face? Remember, your powder puff can speak volumes about you!

By the time HRH has snapped shut her engraved gold compact, she has regained sufficient poise to bestow a condescending smile on Spiros as he embarks on his *tour de force*. This is a frenzied dance which will climax in him balancing a glass of water on his head, whilst picking up a table with his teeth. Bereft of a dramatic roll of drums, Andreas is reduced to turning up the stereo and shrieking triumphantly the Greek translation for allez-oop!

HRH slides into her chair and begins to clap, smiling vivaciously to demonstrate her kindly patronage of native art. The set of her shoulders indicates that she is quite prepared to lend her support, just so long as the filthy wogs keep their distance.

No one else is paying any attention to Spiros's heroics. Joshua is regaling the pop star with an account of a recent fracas on a Manchester bus. The pop star, crushed between Beth and Brian, sits in a state of stunned incredulity at this his first close encounter for years with ordinary, real people. Head down, Brian is scribbling figures on a paper napkin, costing out how Andreas manages to make enough profit to run that large red Fiat. Beth, taking advantage of Andreas's attempts to hype up Spiros, is feeding the skeletal taverna cat with Elsa's untouched meatballs.

On the other side of the table, Rose and the East London girls are swapping mosquito bite horror stories. 'Oh, I've got millions on my eyelids. Wait till you get them right in the crack of your you-know what like Bren. Show her, Bren ...'

Spiros lurches gamely round the room, eyes bulging, the table clamped triumphantly between his white teeth. The applause is muted enough for Elsa's Swedish monotone to be heard distinctly, 'He was cheating. One of the table legs was resting against his groin.'

Frowning, Andreas signals the sweating Spiros to round up all the girls for a hectic communal dance. But before he can change the tape, Joshua has leaped to his feet, roaring,

'Enough of this foreign exhibitionism! Come on, Brits, let's show these Greeks. We'll do the hokey-cokey!'

It is as if he has lit a fuse under the British guests. Cheering, they stampede into a circle, leaving just two of the women sitting at the long table. Swedish Elsa has never heard of the hokey-cokey, while Sandra mutters that she won't be seen dead doing it.

As the pop star drags Elsa onto the floor, Caroline prods Sandra encouragingly on her bare back. To her disgust, it feels spongy.

After muddling through the hokey-cokey, Joshua organises the Gay Gordons and a riotous Dashing White Sergeant. No one knows the steps, and no one cares. Rebelliously united against a glowering Andreas, the laughing guests head out towards the moonlit sands for a drunken midnight swim. Back at the taverna, Spiros sinks gratefully into bed, for his first and only early night of the holiday season.

143

Their euphoria carries them through until Monday afternoon, when they reach Corfu airport.

'The place is like the Black Hole of Calcutta. What's gone wrong?'

'There's a strike. All the planes are delayed at least five hours,' says Joshua. 'In my view we can count on kipping down here for the night.'

At last, the pop star speaks: 'But I'm due at the studio early tomorrow morning.'

'And *I* have a crucial board meeting at ten,' snaps Brian, wheeling smartly towards the Information Desk.

HRH smiles serenely. 'Don't worry, everyone. If anyone can sort this mess out it's Brian.'

Brian returns to announce that he has spoken to the Duty Officer *personally*. He has been assured that their aircraft will be taking off at 9 p.m.

'I want to sit down,' quavers Rose.

Every seat has been commandeered by other waiting passengers, their faces drawn and pinched under their tans. Brian removes a lilo from his holdall, and blows it up with huge manly breaths.

'When you travel as much as I do you learn to be prepared for this kind of emergency,' he informs the circle of envious eyes as Sandra sinks with regal grace onto the puffed up air bed. 'This time next week I shall be in Venice.'

Joshua shrugs. 'You're welcome. Venice reminded me of Sheffield under water.'

'And then I shall be flying onto Shanghai.'

The pop star rushes to save the day. 'I been there. Didn't rate it. If you're really desperate to hob nob with all those chinks you might as well save yourself the fare and go to Slough instead.'

At a quarter to nine Brian marches across to enquire of the Duty Officer why their flight has not yet been called. He storms back with the information that the Greeks are inefficient, lazy idiots. He has made a mental note never, under any circumstances, to employ them. They are muddle-headed, prevaricating –

'Perhaps,' suggests Elsa, 'it would be a kindness if you volunteered to run the airline for them?'

Resigned, the party settles down to a cramped night on the floor. The departure lounge is now pervaded by the warm mutton smell that emanates from too many people crammed into too small a space.

Until the small hours, the pop star busies himself making long distance telephone calls. Elsa adopts the lotus position and goes into a trance. Joshua and Beth doze with their arms wrapped round one another, oblivious to the East London girls' giggles as they drink themselves into an ouzo stupor.

Caroline persuades a sympathetic Ladies Room attendant to find a canvas chair for Rose. Her mother flops into it and snores loudly, causing Caroline to wake up with a start, dreaming she is under rifle fire. Brian does not close his eyes at all, but spends the night patrolling the airport, fearing that if the plane is ready for sudden take off, the inept Greeks will forget to wake the passengers.

The flight is finally called at eleven the following morning. Immediately, the grumbling stops, and the party is engulfed in a wave of sentiment. Addresses are scribbled on the backs of Greek phrase books. Everyone promises faithfully to write, to send on snaps, to keep in touch.

How we've changed, smiles Caroline. A fortnight ago in the Gatwick departure lounge we were pale, wary strangers, sizing one another up and thinking dismally, 'God, she looks a pain. Hope she's not staying at my taverna ... '

Yet here's suntanned Beth, clinging tearfully to my arm, telling me to look her up any time I'm in Manchester. And in five years' time when she rifles through the photo album, she'll peer at the dark-haired woman squinting into the sun and ask Joshua, 'Who the hell was that?'

The air hostesses, looking consumptive beside their bronzed passengers, purr in unison through the oxygen drill.

Rose chatters, 'So well turned out, those girls. Isn't it nice to be flying British Airways? So reassuring. Just like being back on home soil, somehow. I wonder if they'll give us lunch? We had chocolate mousse on the flight over, didn't we? I did enjoy that. It'll be good to have some plain English food again after all that foreign muck. I'm glad I bought that copper frying pan for my pancakes. Not that I eat pancakes of course. Well, not very often. Shrove Tuesday I make them, and sometimes of an evening – '

'Mother, shall I recline your seat for you, so you can have a little nap? Frankly, I'm absolutely bushed.'

'Yes, well I'm sure we're *all* tired. I know I didn't close my eyes for a single moment last night. You'd have thought that Sandra would have offered me her air bed.'

HRH has effected a quick change in the Ladies. Garbed in an embroidered kaftan and mu-muus, she looks poised enough to entertain an exotic eastern potentate.

At Gatwick, Caroline's case is the last to topple up onto the caravel. There are no porters, and Brian has snapped up the last trolley. Caroline prays he and Sandra will be stopped going through Customs. But it is a furious Elsa who is required to tip out the contents of her Gucci luggage.

It takes Caroline half an hour to heave the two cases to the car park. Rose wanders on ahead, clutching her handbag and complaining that Caroline keeps grazing the back of her heels with the luggage.

A further twenty minutes is devoted to coaxing the car to start.

'Are you sure you've got enough petrol?'

'Mother, you were in the car with me when I had it filled up in Reigate.'

'I knew we should have taken the train. Cars are always letting you down.'

'There *is* no direct rail link between Maybrook and Gatwick.'

'Would it help if I got out? Perhaps we should lessen the weight on the engine?'

'It's all right. Stay where you are.'

'Don't you think you should have a look under the bonnet?'

'No.'

'You could phone Leonard and ask him what to do.'

'No!'

'How has he managed without a car while you've been away?'

'He enjoys the opportunity to ride his old motorbike. He says it makes him feel twenty-one again. There!' The car splutters reluctantly into life.

'It doesn't sound very healthy. I just hope we're not going to break down on the way home. You read such awful things in the newspapers about poor defenceless women being raped and murdered on lonely roadsides. Oh, why look who it isn't!' Rose knocks Caroline's shoulder as she turns to wave at the pop star and Elsa gliding past in a silver Rolls Royce. 'What a lovely car. Chauffeur driven, too. Funny how life turns out. I remember your father insisting on naming you Caroline because he hoped you'd marry into the aristocracy. Lady Caroline, he said – '

'Mother, please could you help me navigate? The light's so dim after the brilliance of Corfu, the road signs look all blurred. Does that one ahead say Reigate?'

'I don't think so, dear. It just shows two little children hand in hand. Lester always wanted you to have a brother, you know, but – '

'The green sign, mother! What does it say? Oh hell, now I've missed the turning.'

'You should have told me you meant the green sign. I think it did say Reigate. But I can't see properly without my reading glasses.'

'Could you put them on, then?'

'No, dear, I'd rather not. They make me feel all dizzy if I wear them in the car. I suppose now we're going miles out of our way. Not that I can see much. The inside of the window is all fogged up.'

'I know. The demister isn't working, and if I open a window you'll complain of the draught. There's a cloth in the glove compartment if you'd like to clean the window for me.'

'It would be better if you did it. I'm frightened of jigging about in moving cars.'

'You might make an effort to be a bit more helpful. You've just spent two weeks sitting on your backside being waited on hand and foot. Now you can't even rouse yourself to clean a sodding window.'

'There's no cause to use bad language, Caroline. I realise how much it goes against the grain for you to look after your

Mother like a daughter should. Ever since you made such a song and dance about a simple matter of fetching the rolls for our lunch, I knew how much you resented having me along on this so-called holiday.'

'Are you trying to tell me you haven't had a good time?'

'How could I enjoy myself when you made it obvious that I was just a burden to you? Don't think I don't know how relieved you were to shove me off with Joshua and that Beth woman.'

Keep a grip, Caroline. She's just trying to wind you up.

'I thought you'd like being with people of your own age for a bit. And you had some lovely walks with them.'

'A gooseberry, wasn't I?'

God, if she goes on like this much longer, I swear I'll drive the car straight into a tree. Let's try a lighthearted remark . . .

'After forty years of marriage you can hardly call them spooning honeymooners! I'm sure they were very glad of your company.'

'Which my own daughter, my own flesh and blood, most obviously wasn't.'

'That's not true. What did you expect, that we'd troll around the entire time like Tweedledum and Tweedledee? Why can't you look at life more positively? Most people regard their first trip abroad as a thrilling experience. You've had marvellous weather, a lovely rest and seen some of the most beautiful scenery in the world. But all you do is moan.'

'I don't see what's so incredible about going to a slummy village like Siditses. I was appalled by the way those people live. And there was no night life at all. Just a scabby taverna down the road with washing strung in one corner and chickens running across the floor. You must be mad if you think there's anything picturesque about that.'

Caroline slams on the brakes at Reigate traffic lights. 'I'm sorry, mother. I had no idea you were expecting a Palm Court orchestra, and Pearl Carr and Teddy Johnson doing the cabaret. I just thought you might like an all expenses paid fortnight away from it all, in the sun. Obviously I was wrong. I shan't make the same mistake again . . . *Now* what are you doing?'

Rose has stumbled from the car, and is dragging her suitcase from the boot.

'Thank you for paying for my ticket and everything, Caroline. I want you to know I'm very grateful. There's a station over there. I'm going back to Edinburgh.'

'Don't be absurd ... '

Other drivers are hooting impatiently. Suddenly overcome with fatigue and frustration, Caroline has not the strength to argue any more. She winds down the window and calls helplessly at her mother's receding back:

'Have you got enough money for your fare?'

'Don't worry about me. I shall manage perfectly well on my own.'

Wearily, Caroline slips the gear lever into first, and heads for home. Extraordinary the way rows with mother reveal so many hidden resentments, which have built up over the years like layers of old polish. Caroline reflects back over the holiday, and traces the pattern of this latest dispute.

It had begun over lunch that day in Corfu town, when mother said she was sick of their beach picnics. This led to an argument over teenage holidays in Bridley Bay ... Caroline's failure as a Wife and Mother ... Rose's idyllic marriage and current loneliness ... and Leo's ingratitude over the way she'd ironed his shirts, seventeen years ago.

It can't be true, Caroline thinks, bemused. All this couldn't have started just because of some wretched bread rolls for lunch?

But it had.

Juliette is frying a chicken leg. 'You look fagged out. Where's Granny?'

'Sulking on her way back to Edinburgh.'

'I get it. You're very brown, anyway. Thanks for the card.'

Caroline catches the sarcastic note. 'Oh, I'm sorry. I did send you both one, but the post takes years from Corfu. God, I need a scotch.'

'Before you go into the sitting room I should warn you that the telly is back, as is the rest of our furniture. Dad and I rebelled.'

'A *large* scotch.'

'And while we're on the subject, I want you to know that I'm not eating that vegetarian crap any more.'

'Don't fret. I jacked all that in on holiday. It was unbearable watching mother chomp her way through succulent kebabs while I toyed with a stuffed tomato.'

Sipping her whisky, Caroline battles against the familiar backwash of guilt over her mother. *I shouldn't have snapped at her. I should have been kinder, more understanding. I ought not to have let her go off on the train on her own.*

She watches Juliette sullenly arranging the chicken with onions and carrots in a casserole dish. 'Eating alone?'

'Well I thought you'd just want a salad. And Dad's been working late most nights while you've been away.'

Oh really? Peering out of the bathroom window at Dallow's London party, Caroline had spotted her husband with a leggy blonde. She knew that variety. They always planted themselves in a stiff breeze so their bra-less nipples went hard with the chill. And Leo had fallen for it. Trust him to go for the obvious type.

Caroline has often pondered on how she would cope if she returned home and found Leo in bed with a blonde.

Would she remain cool, amused, composed? 'I've just mixed a jug of dry martini. Help yourselves when you're ready.'

Or how about a topspin backhander: 'Don't let me disturb you. I only popped in to pick up my diaphragm.'

In fact, she'd probably let rip, creating the most spectacular scene, hurling *her* clothes out into the road and *her* out naked after them.

But it's all academic because Leo patently isn't going to let me catch him at it. What now? Months of injured silence and furtive raids through his jacket pockets? Or shall I confront him? And if so, how?

Perhaps a sudden, knock-out blow, out of the blue while he's absorbed in something mundane like cleaning his shoes: 'I suppose *she* sucks you off?'

Or subtle barbs: 'Barbara's lover has gone off with a bottle blonde. Poor Babs, one daren't advise her, but really it's just his age. All men go through a stage of lusting after the brassy types. But when they get older they learn to value

150

experience and sophistication in a partner. Of course, some unfortunate men never achieve the maturity to attract real, grown up ladies, so they're stuck with the peroxide tart all their lives . . . '

Alternatively, a floating scarer might be amusing. 'Did you hear the big joke about Dallow's party? Apparently there was some blonde tart in the garden and the blokes were taking it in turns to go out and lay her. Even by the time we arrived she'd entertained five of them . . . '

'I *said*,' Juliette bangs the oven door shut, 'that it's all gone quite well, *thank you*.'

'Sorry, I was miles away. What's gone well?'

'My O Levels. While you were loafing in sunny Corfu, I've been incarcerated in a stuffy examination room.'

Christ. 'Juliette, of course I hadn't forgotten. I simply didn't want you to feel pressured by me keeping on about it, that's all.' Oh Caroline! 'How did the French oral go? You were most worried about that one, weren't you?'

'I haven't done it yet. French is the last one, tomorrow.'

'Oh. Well I'll tell you what. Next Saturday, we'll celebrate. We'll have a fantastic party. You've worked so hard, you deserve a treat.'

'Will you and Dad go out?'

'Definitely not.'

'Don't you trust me, then?'

'It's not that. But if we're going to all the expense of a bash, we may as well ask our friends too.'

'The two age groups won't mix.'

'Well your lot can have a disco in the meadow at the end of the garden. And we old fogies can foxtrot across the patio.'

'Can I bring Nick?'

'Of course.' That will be one in the eye for Leo. I wonder if he'll have the nerve to invite his blonde?

11

'It's your age,' declares Leo, ransacking the chest for a clean pair of pyjamas. 'All women get depressed when they're heading up to forty. You should take more exercise. Get your circulation moving. Why don't you go for a run round the block tomorrow? Oh, what shall I do with this sweater? There's a hole in the elbow.'

'You've had a difficult year, coping with your mother,' sympathises a hollow-eyed Wendy, shovelling soiled nappies into the washing machine. 'God, I'm whacked. My health visitor assures me that babies who are active after dark are usually the most intelligent. My own view is that a really bright child would surely have the consideration *not* to brawl all night.'

Her tone is indulgent. Caroline realises that Wendy revels in feeling needed at three in the morning.

'But what do you do when you feel low?'

'I talk to Tim about it, of course.'

'Follow my example. Get yourself a lover,' Barbara advises. 'It would give you no end of a boost.'

Caroline perches on an upturned paint tin, sipping home-made rhubarb wine. She feels staid and middle-aged compared with the radiant young girl stretched out on the tiny, cluttered balcony.

'And where am I to find this dose of male Sanatogen? We're not all in a position to engage in an affair with the new driver of the travelling library.'

'Surely you must know just one fanciable man?'

Caroline remembers Adrian. God, I can't go through all that again.

'Anyway, I'm sure someone will turn up. They always do. Just send out a few sexy vibes. Or wear some musk. It never

152

fails.' Lazily, Barbara turns up her face to the sun, and moans languorously, 'Oh, doesn't this heat make you feel randy!'

Caroline beats a retreat, seeking the shady side of the street for her walk home. Barbara's scorching, youthful optimism makes her feel like cutting a vein.

'It's been a trying time for you, nursing Juliette through her O Levels,' murmurs Frances in a voice as French polished as the cabinet which conceals her television. 'Have you ever thought of taking a job?'

'But what can I do, Frances? Before I married Leo I had a year fooling about at art school. You can hardly call that a qualification. Then when Juliette was young I had my hands full with her, and two miscarriages.'

'I'm sorry. I had no idea you wanted more children.'

Caroline shrugs. 'Too late now. The ironical thing is that Juliette's got a great nostalgic fascination for the sixties. She's burning to know if I was into flower power, and drugs, and did I wet myself screaming at a Beatles concert. I feel such a fuddy duddy admitting that the only swinging I did in the sixties was over the pan, flushing away the mess that might have been Juliette's brother.'

'Yes. Quite. Now what about Leo? Has he never encouraged you to work?'

'He says he hates coming home to an empty house.' An empty dinner plate, more like.

Frances smiles over her steepled fingers. 'But what would *you* like to do? We all have some kind of secret, unfulfilled ambition. What's yours?'

'I don't know. That's what's so worrying. I have no raging desire to write the definitive English novel, or paint a great masterpiece. I just seem to drift along, feeling guilty at having no goals. Then I get depressed, and lethargic, and I despise myself even more.'

'Why not try and accept yourself for what you are,' counsels Frances. 'We can't all be achievers in life.'

'But every magazine I pick up, every programme I watch is urging me to get out and do something. I feel such a parasite. But what can I do? What am I good at? All

I've done in the last seventeen years is be a mother. I've no experience at anything else.'

Frances's eyes stray over Caroline's head to the hands of the grandfather clock. 'Why don't I put you in touch with one of our careers guidance people? I'm afraid they're up to their ears in school leavers at present. But if I put in a word, they'll probably have time to fit you in later in the year.'

'Unemployment is running into millions,' announces Juliette, slashing at the sleeves of the summer dress she's renovating. 'Nick says it's wicked the way all these bored housewives are taking the bread from school leavers' mouths.'

'Then what do you suggest I do with myself?'

'Get your hair done. Buy some new clothes. Sign up at an evening class. It puts years on you, dragging around like this. I do hope you're not going to turn into the kind of mother who keeps the Valium parked next to the Bisto in the larder.'

'I'm always depressed,' intones Annabel, intent on tweezing out the hairs straggling from her bikini. 'I just seem to lurch from one emotional crisis to the next.'

Caroline climbs out of Annabel's sea green pool. 'Don't you have any remedies?'

'My dear, I've tried them all. Lovers, pills, alcohol, pot, fat farms, meditation, yoga, new clothes, new furniture, new babies, exotic holidays, ski-ing lessons, cordon bleu courses, moving home, voluntary work, primal scream therapy – the lot.' Deftly, she wraps a silk chiffon scarf round her face to shield it from the sun, and settles back on the flowered hammock. 'Nothing works for long.'

'Thanks. I knew you'd be a tower of strength.' Caroline splashes iced dry Martini into a glass.

Lazily, Annabel stretches out a manicured foot and presses the knob which turns off the underwater music in the pool. 'I do get a temporary lift each day when I read the newspapers. All those starving millions, and murders, and bombings and those poor battered women in Chiswick. I feel so damned glad it isn't me. It quite bucks me up.'

154

'So your get up and go got up and went, eh? Well why don't you treat yourself to a little holiday, Mrs Lambert? A break from routine would do you a power of good.'

'Doctor, I've just come back from Corfu!'

He smiles nostalgically. 'Ah, Greece! No wonder you feel so unsettled. Hellenic air is potent stuff. Bound to be a struggle for you, slipping back into domestic harness. But physically you're as sound as a bell. Come back and see me in a month if you're still not feeling your old self.'

'Throwing a party?' grunts the delivery boy, heaving the last case of wine through the kitchen door.

'I can't think why,' mutters Caroline, removing sixty roasted chicken drumsticks from the oven.

'What I always say,' he informs her cheerfully, 'is that if you're feeling low, you can count on a party to make you feel worse.'

Glowing tubs of geraniums, lobelia and fuchsias garland the patio. Caroline sits on the low patio wall, savouring these last few peaceful minutes before her guests invade the waiting house. Everything is ready. Through the French windows, she watches Leo finishing his conversion of the sideboard into a bar. Down in the meadow, Juliette shouts contradictory orders to the boys she has pressganged into setting up her disco.

Caroline holds her gin and tonic up to the light, admiring the sunburst of lemon sparkling with bubbles as it floats above the ice. Too warm tonight for scotch. Drugged with the scent of cut grass, honeysuckle and roses, Caroline realises with relief that the black fog of depression has finally fled. Instead of lethargic despair, she is engulfed by ... what? Melancholy? No, that's too autumnal. Too heavy an emotion for a fragrant summer evening filled with the melody of birdsong. What I feel is more of an elusive, gossamer sensation. Sad, yes, but sweetly so. It's more in the nature of a yearning. But for what? She closes her eyes and absently crushes a geranium leaf between her fingers as she tries to pin down that for which she seeks.

> *'The woods are green with branches*
> *And sweet with nightingales*
> *With gold and blue and scarlet*
> *All flowered are the dales.'*

The speaker is a tall, fair young man in his early twenties. He leans with coltish grace against the clematis, and continues,

> *'And yet when all men's spirits*
> *Are dreaming on delight,*
> *My heart is heavy in me,*
> *And troubled at her sight.*
> *If she for whom I travail*
> *Should still be cold to me,*
> *The birds sing unavailing,*
> *'Tis winter still for me.'*

Caroline smiles, feeling deeply content. The young man must be Babs's new librarian lover. She should rise gracefully, introduce herself, fix him a drink and sparkle with sociable, bookish chat until Babs finishes spraying herself with musk.

But unwilling to break the spell he has cast, she says lazily, 'Wouldn't it be delightful if no one else turned up at this party? We could take a bottle of wine, sit under the apple tree, watch the sun go down, and see what develops.'

He moves towards her. As he sits down on the wall, his thighs strain against the white drill of his trousers.

Oh Babs, you lucky bitch! With an effort of will, Caroline tears her eyes away from his crotch. So much for poetical romance. She bangs down her glass. Go easy on that gin.

'I'm Caroline Lambert,' she says briskly. 'I don't believe we've met?'

His blue eyes meet hers. 'I'm really glad to know you, Mrs Lambert. I'm a friend of your daughter's. Nick Walsh.'

Caroline's voice is strangled. 'Oh ... I ... I thought you'd be different ... I mean, Juliette told me she'd met you at Tiffany's.'

He nods, the fair hair falling over his brow. Caroline resists an urge to smooth it back again. 'That's right. I'm a journalist, you see. I was doing a piece on the disco scene. I can tell you, I was having a lousy time until I met Juliette.'

Caroline feels murder in her heart towards her daughter. The little rat. All along she has pretended that Nick is some common Tiffany lout. At least, she didn't contradict her father when he raged on about her yobbo boyfriend. And all the time, he was a blueprint of the young man any parent would approve of. Personable, intelligent, good looking, broad chested, wide sensitive mouth ... oh God.

Still groping for words, Caroline senses she has lost Nick's attention. He is gazing down the garden, past the apple tree, to the meadow gate which Juliette is closing behind her.

Caroline's stomach lurches as she regards her daughter. The freshly washed hair ... the slim yet womanly figure ... the breeze catching the skirt of her lavender blue dress. It's me. Oh hell, it's me, nineteen years ago, looking newly minted and beautiful, stepping lightly through a summer scented garden to greet my handsome young man.

No, it isn't me. It's as I wish I'd been. When I was sixteen I was a posturing pseudo sophisticate. My hair was streaked orangey-blonde. My skin was hidden under an inch of pancake make up. I wore grippingly tight skirts over stockings with daggers up the ankle. And all my boyfriends were roughneck Teds, not clean-cut charmers like Nick.

She lights a cigarette and watches through a haze of smoke as Nick and Juliette move towards one another. Really, this is all too much. The good looking couple. The lovely English garden. The setting sun. It's like a slow motion Diamonds are Forever ad.

Juliette reaches up and kisses him lightly, confidently on the lips. Caroline hopes Leo hasn't witnessed this.

'Didn't mother get you a drink?'

'We were too busy talking.'

'Oh. Well never mind, we've got masses of wine down in the meadow. Sharon's just arrived with an Elvis Presley lookalike, and Gail's halter neck keeps snapping ... '

The invasion has begun. Guests are spilling out of the sitting room on to the patio, flicking cigarette ash over the petunias and dibbing the lavender border with their stilettos. Caroline collects another gin and tonic from the bar. In the kitchen, she finds Miles and Elliot wedged up against the cooker, devouring devilled chicken legs and prawn bouchées.

'Smashing nosh, darling,' Miles raises a gnawed chicken bone in salute. 'Does one gather that the back to basics bit has been abandoned? I lived in dread, you know, of accepting a Lambert dinner invite and being dished up with potato peeling pie.'

Nettled, Caroline tries to summon the energy to argue, explain, justify. But forceful defence is impossible in her current bruised, vulnerable state. She has a sudden longing to confess: 'Can't you see, I've just discovered I'm jealous of my teenage daughter. I despise myself. I hate her. I want to be admired, soothed, petted, flirted with.'

Elliot runs a finger along the thin black strap of her silk jersey dress. He whispers, 'Any chance of you raiding the pantry for some yellow pickle, love? Cold chicken never tastes quite the same without a good dollop of Piccalilli.'

In the sitting room, Wendy is stuck with Annabel. Draped in a large flowered print that makes her look like a jumble sale cushion cover, Wendy is blinking hard and talking very slowly – a sure sign that she feels intimidated. They are discussing babies. It is fashionable this year to refute the existence of instinctive maternal love. There is fierce competition amongst the new mothers of the neighbourhood over how soon they each began to loathe their offspring.

Gallantly, Wendy does her best. 'It makes me laugh now, Annabel, to think of all the romantic notions I entertained about breastfeeding. The bonding between mother and child. The life juices passed from one generation to another. The truth is, of course, it's just like having your nipples rubbed down with sandpaper.'

Wendy's nose is beginning to run. But she daren't reach into her bag for a tissue in case Annabel notices the treasonable Polaroid shots of Wendy soppily cooing over Arthur's crib.

'I wouldn't know about breastfeeding,' drawls Annabel,

sleek in chocolate brown raw silk. 'My two survived courtesy of Cow and Gate. Mind you, I always think I would have loved my babies more if only they'd been born furry.'

Caroline drifts by, making no hostessy intervention to rescue poor, open-mouthed Wendy. She reasons that Annabel will soon tire of this nursery conversation, and abandon Wendy for the nearest available man.

Caroline takes her drink into the garden. She intended merely to enjoy a breath of fresh air, but finds herself drawn towards the music in the meadow.

'Don't come interfering,' Juliette instructed that afternoon. 'We don't want all you wrinklies spying on us.'

It's lucky Leo didn't hear her say that, Caroline reflects. Fortunately, he's happy dishing out the booze up at the house. Barricaded behind the bar, he has the perfect excuse for refusing to dance with all the predatory middle-aged ladies wanting a grope. No doubt he's saving himself for the blonde popsie he didn't have the guts to invite.

The meadow looks enchanting, illuminated by lights strung in the silver birch trees. The girls are achingly pretty, with enviably unlined faces framed by clouds of curly hair. To Caroline, there don't seem to be any plain girls left in the world any more.

Nick is up at the barbecue, cooking the steaks. In the firelight, Caroline can see the fine fair hairs downing his arms. Nick glances up, an expression of laughter and tenderness in his blue eyes. Instinctively, Caroline arches her back, pushing forward her bosom. But that intimate look is directed at Juliette, the daughter, lying sprawled in the grass. Caroline, the mother, he has not noticed at all.

Caroline's glass is empty. She stands by the gate, eyeing the full bottles of wine and cider littering the meadow. Her hesitation infuriates her. Damnit, it's my wine. I paid for it. It's ridiculous to feel intimidated about venturing into that bloody field.

Nick and Juliette are dancing. Her hands are linked behind his neck. Her young, firm breasts brush against his chest.

Caroline turns away towards the house, wondering who it

was who said that parenthood is feeding the hand that bites you.

'Leo, I want a gin and tonic. Not a tonic with the gin waved in front of it.'

'All right. But I warn you, you're looking distinctly glassy eyed.'

Caroline seizes the bottle of Gordon's. 'And who was it at Frances's party who blundered into her son's bedroom and threw up all over his toy typewriter?'

'It was simply that in the dark, and an unfamiliar house, I mistook the hard edge of the typewriter for a handbasin. Listen, I think I'd better go down and keep an eye on things in the meadow.'

'They're OK. I checked. Oh, and I met the mysterious Nick. He's not a lout at all. He's a journalist, and really very presentable.' His thighs are lovely. Have some more gin.

Leo waves at some new arrivals. 'I forgot to tell you. I bumped into your friend Sue, and invited her and her old man along.'

Adrian and Bianca. The stillborn lunch at the Green Man. There he is, compost heap Adrian, smoothing the fold of his checked cravat. Thank God Leo comes out in a rash at the sight of any man wearing a blazer and cravat. If he hears Adrian call me Bianca, he'll just look scornful, thinking it's a middle-class stab at a humorous remark.

Adrian's wife, fraught and fragile in puffed sleeve cotton, breathes her first apology. 'I'm awfully sorry we're late, Caroline. Adrian was showing some Arabs round a property.'

'It's nice to see you, Sue. How are you?'

'Oh, Adrian's doing fearfully well, you know. He's just opened a new country house office in Chertsey. And Luke's starting play school in September.'

'Good. And how are *you*?'

'Well I feel so guilty about not coming to the women's group any more. But little Luke gets so upset if his mummy isn't there in the evenings. If he peers downstairs and sees so much as my gloves on the hall table he screams the house down. Luckily, he's staying with his grannie this weekend,

160

otherwise I'd never have made this party at all.'

Caroline smiles. 'Sounds as if he's growing up to be just like his dad.'

Sue beams. 'That's right! It's sweet, really. Adrian often says that if I'm not there, then our house is not a home.'

Caroline stretches out an arm and lassoos Frances's husband. 'Sue, have you met Elliot? He's a marriage guidance counsellor. Elliot, Sue here is a mousewife. Her problem is that she has a husband who doesn't know what he wants to be when he grows up.'

Frances is in a skittish mood. She is tickling Leo in an attempt to budge him from the bar and dance with her. Caroline is amazed to see that the lacing on her blouse is undone, revealing a flattish, freckled chest. Leo seems amused by the spectacle. Caroline suspects he's spiked Frances's drink, relishing the prospect of diverting his darts team with the story of how the local deputy headmistress tried to seduce him.

Caroline rests her ice-filled glass against Frances's bony back. 'Frances, have you seen Barbara and her new man? I saw them arrive, but now they've disappeared.'

The deputy headmistress giggles. 'They're probably having it away astride your chimney pot, my dear.'

'Would you like to dance, *Bianca*?'

Caroline stares blearily up at Adrian. Perhaps all that gin wasn't such a good idea after all. The room is beginning to spin, and Adrian's black and white checked cravat is dancing before her eyes in the most alarming fashion. She feels as if she's approaching the finishing line at Le Mans. But somewhere round the track, she seems to have mislaid the brake.

Caroline summons a weak smile. 'What can I say?'

Adrian sips his dry Martini. 'Why say anything? I was most entertained. The odd thing is that I'd heard so much from Susie about this girl Caroline who ran a local ladies' group. But when I met you at the Green Man and you introduced yourself as Bianca, I just didn't connect you with this person Susie had talked about.'

What has that little rat Sue been saying? 'Apart from the

161

name, in what way were we different?'

'Oh, Susie always referred to this Caroline bird as some quite fearsome, self assured, organising sort. But the Bianca I met was vulnerable, soft, very unsure of herself.'

Vulnerable? *Unsure?* What do you mean? I was cool, sophisticated and sexy, damnit. I'd have carried it all off with élan if the sun hadn't been shining. And it was you who looked deep into my eyes and murmured tenderly about peeing on compost heaps.

Adrian nods towards the settee. 'I say. Who's that gorgeous woman?'

'It's Annabel. We were at school together.'

He raises a sandy eyebrow. 'Really? She seems to be giving the young man with her some advanced tuition.'

Annabel is twined round Wendy's husband. Her mouth is clamped to his, and the desperate expression in Tim's eyes reveals a fear that Annabel's saliva is formulated like a powerful fixative, bonding their lips together for eternity.

Caroline realises that Annabel is retaliating, because Miles's eyes are roving like cockroaches over a stunning tawny haired woman by the French windows. Woman? Girl. *Gail* ... Juliette's schoolfriend, with rosy nipples just visible below the curve of the peach-coloured halter neck dress.

'Hello, dear,' croons Caroline. 'I hope Miles isn't boring you?'

'Oh not at all, Mrs Lambert,' breathes Gail. 'Miles was just helping me with my biology.'

'Her O Level paper,' explains Miles hastily. 'Gail didn't feel she'd done too well. But it seems to me that these examiners expect the kids to cram their pretty heads with an impossibly wide range of facts. On Gail's biology paper, for example, four consecutive questions ranged from dry rot, to birth control, to sheep's kidneys to food energy intake in the 1930s.'

'Miles, I'm sure the last thing Gail wants to talk about is O Levels. She'd much rather be rocking away to Elvis, down in the meadow with her young friends.'

Miles lights two cigarettes, and passes one to Gail. 'Interesting you should mention Elvis, Caroline. I was just remarking to Gail on the interesting social significance of the fact that she belongs to the first generation who actually approve of the music enjoyed by her parents in their youth.'

'Isn't that fascinating, Mrs Lambert? I mean, would you say that this rock revival is to our credit, or do you believe that it shows a certain lack of initiative in the youth of today?' Gail glances at Miles, the eyelashes sweeping fit to clean a window.

'I shouldn't worry, Gail,' murmurs Caroline. 'I think the only thing you lack is a degree in inexperience.'

Wendy marches across the room, elbows the hovering Adrian out of the way, and plants herself firmly on the sofa between Annabel and Tim.

'Hi!' she says, in a bright, high voice, her eyes showering steel splinters at her husband. 'You look as if you're having a good time.'

Tim croaks, 'Ah. Annabel was just telling me an awfully amusing story about her flying lessons.'

'Really? Well we ought to be jetting home, Tim. The babysitter charges extra after midnight, remember. And I think we ought to put a poultice on the boil on your poor neck.'

Out underneath the apple tree, Miles is kissing Gail. Caroline tops up her glass, and lies on the long patio wall. In the distance, the lights glimmer in the silver birch trees. Somewhere beyond, in the long grass of the meadow, her daughter is lying in the arms of a strong young man with sunbleached hair.

It isn't fair.

Miles walks back to the house, alone. He looks pleased with himself. Well, why shouldn't he have his fun? Annabel does all right for herself. All the women I know have something good going for them. Annabel has her money. Wendy her baby. Frances her career. Babs her lovers. Juliette has her youth, and Nick and every damn wonderful thing ahead of her.

So what about me? What will I be like in five years' time? Maudlin, middle-aged, migrained, menopausal and mediocre. Novels are teeming with forty year old Caroline

Lamberts, tippling sherry for elevenses and harbouring a suppressed, self pitying resentment at their futile existence.

In the living room, Frank Sinatra is informing the departing guests that he'd done it his way.

Why does no one write witty lyrics about women in my situation, mourns Caroline. When Sinatra sings, the tone is one of noble, bittersweet nostalgia. A woman warbling similar lines would merely sound pathetic.

It's just the same with getting drunk. If I were a man, people would be looking at me now with indulgent affection. 'Good old Charlie. Stewed again and about to roll off the wall into the lavender border. Such a character, our Charlie. Invite him to dinner and you can always rely on him to have one too many and pass out under the table.'

But I am Caroline Lambert. My guests – my friends – are pretending I do not exist. They are scuttling out through the front door and as they click on their safety belts they'll murmur, 'Poor old Caroline. Did you see her, pie-eyed on the patio? Something rather disgusting about the sight of a drunken woman, isn't there? You'd think at her age she'd have learnt when to put the cork in.'

'Caroline! Who the hell's been sleeping in my bed?'

The patio is deserted, and dark. Leo is shouting from the bedroom window.

Caroline giggles. 'Hi, there, Daddy Bear! I think the culprits must have been Babs and her new man. I thought it strange that I hadn't seen them all evening.'

'Well they've left the most diabolical mess on the sheets. Trust your women's lib friends to behave like bloody animals.'

Caroline laughs. She is still smiling as Leo wrenches the stained sheets off the bed and hurls them out of the window on top of her.

'What was that Leonard doing in your room?'

'Nothing. We were looking at photographs.'

'Don't lie to me my girl. You were up to no good with him, under my roof, while I was out.'

'Don't be daft.'

'Do you have the nerve to deny it, you filthy little slut?'

'Don't you call me names! I told you, we weren't doing anything.'

'Then why were your sheets still warm?'

'How dare you go in my room and spy round my bed?'

'This is my house. I'm your Mother. It's my duty to know what you've been up to. I'm accustomed to you treating the place as if it's a hotel, but I'm not having you using it as a brothel as well.'

'Don't be so melodramatic, mother. Honestly, it's impossible to have a civilised conversation with someone as illogical as you.'

'That's precisely my point. You don't talk to me. You spend most of your time in sullen silence, and when you do speak you tell me lies. Little wonder, then, that I have to employ my own methods to find out what you've been doing.'

'Bloody gestapo.'

'Where are you going?'

'Out.'

'I'm warning you, Caroline. You're turning into a right trollop. If you land yourself in the family way, you needn't bother coming back here!'

Of course, when she got herself into trouble, it was her father she went to. Lester never could resist that 'Daddy, I've been a silly little girl' routine.

Lester told Rose, 'It'll do Caroline good to be married. Settle her down a bit. Frankly, she's been getting out of hand. You haven't been able to control her, and I'm not here enough to wield a father's proper authority. Len's a big strapping bloke. He'll keep her in line.'

'But I hoped for something better for Caroline. He's nothing but a common manual worker.'

'There's good money in printing. I'll give them the deposit for a house, and in a few years' time they'll be well enough set up. And having a baby on her hands will stymie all Caroline's gallivanting ways.'

'She gets all her wildness from you,' Rose blurted. 'None of my family have that wayward streak.'

He grinned. 'Aye, she's my girl all right. We'll give her the biggest wedding this neighbourhood has ever seen.

Caroline's got the guts to brazen it out.'

With the situation forced upon her, Rose had done her best to be gracious to Leonard. She introduced him to the other families in Laurence Drive, and even invited his parents up to the house for tea. She thought tea would be a less intimidating occasion for them than lunch or dinner, coming from a council estate as they did.

They turned out to be remarkably nice people. Mr Lambert wore a shiny blue suit and perched on the edge of his chair, as if frightened that if he sat back it would swallow him up. His wife chattered nervously, and dropped an egg mayonnaise sandwich on the carpet. Rose kindly pretended not to notice. Tragic, really, to think that almost five years to the day since they sat taking tea with her, the Lamberts died in a coach trip to the Lakes.

They caused no trouble over the wedding, and agreed to leave all the arrangements to Rose. She had feared they might insist on inviting the entire estate either to the church or to a knees up afterwards. But in fact the Lamberts proved sensibly amenable when Rose pointed out that Caroline was such a popular girl ... and they were all so well known in the neighbourhood ... and they could not disappoint all Lester's influential clients who would wish to see dear Caroline wed ... so there would not really be enough room in the church for a large Lambert contingent.

Leonard, regrettably, was harder to handle. He was stubbornly adamant that all his loud mouthed drinking cronies should attend. The worst of them, a scar-faced Ted whose front teeth had been knocked out in a fight, Leonard chose as his best man.

'Leave him alone, mum,' Caroline instructed. 'Let him invite who he likes. It's his wedding too, remember. I think he's being very good about it all, considering neither of us wanted a poxy white wedding in the first place.'

Rose insisted on accompanying Caroline up to London to choose the wedding dress.

'You'd better have something loose. And a lot of interest in the veil to take the eye away from your front. Tiers of veiling would be nice ... '

But perversely, Caroline had chosen an Empire line

166

gown, with the glistening white satin stretched taut across her stomach. 'I shall only be three months gone on the day. And I don't think I'm the type to show all that much,' Caroline declared, in a voice the blushing Rose was convinced half of Regent Street could hear.

At least she managed to sway Caroline away from the style which was fastened with press studs across the shoulders. 'Lady Evelyn's daughter got married in a dress like that. When she was coming back up the aisle, the organist played rather fast, and everyone started to gallop a bit. The result was that the best man trod on her train, the press studs gave under the strain and the dress was ripped half off her back.'

Caroline thought this was hilarious. In fact, Rose recalled that Lady Evelyn had seemed grateful for the diversion. While the bridegroom struggled out of his jacket to cover the half-naked bride, Lady Evelyn took advantage of the confusion and helped herself to a strengthening swig from the gin flask in her crocodile handbag.

While Caroline and Leonard were away in Paris, on the honeymoon paid for by Lester, Rose enjoyed herself sticking photographs into her Our Daughter's Wedding album. The only one she tore up was the shot of the bride lolling back in the white Rolls Royce, lighting up a fag.

It was lonely in the big house without Caroline. Rose felt oddly bereft, not hearing the constant blare of the Beatles records, not having the trail of teenage clothes to pick up, wash, iron and put away. Lester had never been the stay-at-home type, but since his appointment as Treasurer to the local council Rose saw less of him than ever.

Being a council official's wife was very gratifying, of course. Tradesmen were so much more respectful. Not that Rose would every buy anything on credit.

'Out of debt, out of danger,' she told Lester, when he laughed at her for sneering at people who furnished their houses on the HP.

That year, Treasurer Scott-Peters's wife was asked to present the prizes at the primary school Christmas concert. Imagining that they might expect her to make a speech, Rose was too frightened to accept. But it was flattering to be asked.

She did consent to join Maud Sprett-Davies's Famine Relief Committee. But then she discovered that the new Spanish rug Maud was always going on about only served to hide a frayed edge of the carpet. And once Rose heard Maud shouting at her husband for not paying the phone bill.

'Really, Ronald. I do my best to try and cultivate all the right people in Laurence Drive, and then you allow those men to march in here and have us cut off. What will everyone think?'

Rose thought she'd been taken for a sucker. It was best, after all, to keep yourself to yourself. Especially if you were a person of influence in the neighbourhood. Otherwise people only took advantage.

'I don't know why you find it impossible to get on with people,' Lester sighed. 'There must be someone in this town you could be friends with.'

But Rose had never made a friend in her life. She had not the first idea how to set about finding such a thing, let alone keeping it.

'I don't have time for all that socialising,' she said. 'After all, when the baby arrives, I shall have my hands full. You don't imagine Caroline will have the faintest clue how to look after it?'

Juliette. Six pounds four ounces, and crying all through the night just as Caroline had done. Caroline, ill and exhausted after the birth. Leonard worried stiff. Everyone so very grateful when Rose moved into Lavender Cottage to take care of Mother and Baby.

12

Dear Caroline,
I had thought to hear from you by now to find out if I got home safely. Well I did, but no thanks to you. I caught a chill on the train and the Doctor said I didn't look as if I'd had a holiday at all. I told him that was the last holiday I shall ever have anyway as you won't want to take me away any more. It's at times like this I wish I had been able to bear more children but it was Not to Be. Mrs Logan next door died last week. I closed my curtains as a sign of Respect. She has a Son and two Daughters who will be a great comfort to her poor husband. No one knows better than I the misery of being on your own after a lifetime seeing to the needs of others and putting them First.

It is bitterly cold up here for July. Soon it will be Autumn and the clocks will go back and we shall be thinking of Christmas and that will be another year over and done with. Mrs Logan was cremated. I don't fancy the idea of being burned though they do say it's more hygienic. I pass the cemetery every week when I collect my pension and I don't mind telling you there are times when I look forward with longing to lying in peace and at rest in there. My Funeral should not cost you a penny as I have an insurance policy to cover it and one for you too when you die. You needn't worry that I shall leave you any debts as all my life I have paid my way I even insist of paying for my Daily Express every day instead on running up a bill. The lady in the newsagent's says she wishes there were more people as considerate as me and I told her make the best of it, my dear, because I won't be around for much longer not with my Nerves as bad as they are.

Well now my hand aches with all this writing and I still have my ironing to do so I will sign off as always
Your Loving Mother.

'I don't know why you let her get to you so much,' comments Juliette, as her mother uncorks the sherry. 'You can't go hitting the bottle every time she sends one of her whining letters.'

'Hitting the bottle! You sound just like your father at times.'

'You must admit, ten o'clock in the morning is rather early to be knocking it back.'

'It's just that she makes me feel so damned guilty all the time.'

'You should be grateful she lives four hundred miles away. At least we don't have to endure any more of those grisly Sunday afternoon teas at her place.'

Caroline waves the sheets of blue Basildon Bond. 'But even at that distance she's still adroit at hurling giant spanners into the machinery of our family life.'

Juliette shrugs. 'Look on the bright side. At least Granny is reasonably fit. Remember poor old Frances when her mother came to live with her. If she was two minutes late home from a staff meeting the old biddy invariably had one of her turns.'

'Frances used to say her mother had more turns than a spinning top.'

'Gail is convinced Frances did the old cow in, you know. I'm surprised you haven't considered it yourself. Just a pillow over the head, or a few yew berries concealed in the fruit salad ...'

'You worry me sometimes, Juliette. Is that what I've got to look forward to, then?'

'It depends how you turn out. But I warn you, I've no intention of putting myself on the rack agonising over your emotional blackmail. If you get crabby and querulous I shall either emigrate somewhere a long way away and ignore all your bleating letters. Or I shall do you in. Oh, can I borrow your hair dryer? Mine's on the blink.'

'Yes dear. I'll throw it into the bath with you. Where are you off to, then?'

'Nick's taking me on a picnic.'

Nick and I are going to spend the entire afternoon lying in the sun, making love.

Juliette cherishes the days when she has hours to devote to getting ready for Nick. On weekdays it's a question of rushing in from school, throwing on some clean jeans and tearing out again to meet him. But today is Saturday. Time to linger in the bath and revel in the promise of all the sensations her body will have experienced by the time she comes home.

Enveloped in a thick, fluffy towel, Juliette watches her mother bicycling down the path. She is frowning, still clearly preoccupied with Gran's stupid letter. How awful to be at her stage of life. Not to know any more all the delicious anticipation of preparing to greet your lover ... that tingling, soaring excitement, so intense it makes you want to turn cartwheels all the way down the street to meet him.

How lucky I am. Poor mum. She must feel dead inside.

Juliette had expected her mother to be furious when she told her she was giving up working at Fortune Pools. 'Saturday is Nick's only day off from the magazine, you see. And it seems pointless to waste the summer stuck in that stuffy big room at Fortune.'

Caroline merely nodded, and said that Juliette was old enough to take charge of her own life. Encouraged, Juliette admitted that of course she would miss the money she earned at Fortune. Caroline sat down with her, then, and devised an allowance system. In future, she would give Juliette an adequate amount each month to cover everything except her school uniform and lunches, which would remain Caroline's responsibility.

'But don't tell your father about this allowance. You know he likes to imagine you perpetually in white organdie with red ribbons in your hair – and him doling out cash on a grace and favour basis, according to the sweetness of your smiles.'

'Mum's been in a really weird mood recently,' she tells Gail the following evening, as they lie across Juliette's bed. 'All pleasant and chummy one minute, then totally bitchy the next. Yesterday I felt incredibly close to her when she was being so understanding about giving me an allowance. Then two minutes before Nick was due, she started on about him being too old for me.'

'I expect it's the menopause,' asserted Gail, lighting a cigarette.

'Don't be disgusting. Anyway, she's only thirty-five.

Women round here don't get into the hot flush scene until they're at least fifty.'

'I shall have committed suicide by then. I expect to reach my peak at thirty. By that age I shall be fully experienced and mature, but still devastatingly beautiful. I shall entertain my lovers in a converted windmill, and tie tufts of their pubic hair to the sails, as trophies.'

Juliette stares at her. Gail embraces a pillow and continues, contemplatively, 'I suppose being forty would be just about the top limit. I mean, people like Jane Fonda seem to carry it off quite well. But let's face it, when you hit fifty, what have you got to look forward to? Being sixty.'

'It's different if you're a man, of course,' says Juliette, sipping her Coke. 'Age is quite immaterial once you're beyond your teens.'

Gail flicks her cigarette ash into a geranium pot.

'I could never date anyone of my own age. I'd hate some callow, fumbling youth practising on my body.'

'Impossible. Nick says he finds it hard to believe that I'm seven years younger than him. I suppose I've matured a lot since I've known him. All the other girls in our class, except you of course, seem incredibly childish now.'

'Mmm. Is Nick getting on any better with your father?'

'A bit. They seem to stick to certain safe areas of common ground, like cars and real ale. But dad's been in a strange mood recently, too. Usually he and mum tend to bicker a lot. It doesn't mean they're on the verge of divorce or anything. It's just their way of communicating. But since mum came back from Corfu they've been insufferably polite to one another. He didn't even kick up his routine ruck about going over to spend the whole day with Annabel and Miles.'

'So that's where they've gone,' smiles Gail.

'You're having an affair with Miles, aren't you?'

'How the hell did you find out? I haven't told a soul!'

'I'm not as daft as I look, you know. You told me yourself when you mentioned the converted windmill. Miles has lived in a converted oast house, a renovated coach house, and everyone knows he's lusting after a windmill. But Annabel has put her foot down. She says the sails will make her feel seasick.'

'I take it you don't approve?' enquires Gail archly.

'Hardly! Miles is nearly as old as my father.'

'Oh, don't sound so suburban. It's not as if I have any intention of making him divorce Annabel and break up the happy home.'

'That's just as well. I should think you'd find Annabel more than a match for you.'

'Crap. She's getting past it. Miles says she's talking of flying to some secret Yugoslavian clinic to have her face, tits and bum lifted. Poor old boiler. It's not her Miles cares about, but the *children*. We've had long talks about it all and he's impressed with my mature understanding of the situation. Annabel suspects he's involved with another woman, of course, but she doesn't know who. I expect she's confiding her fears in your mother at this very moment!'

Juliette gets up and closes the window against the rain. 'Sounds like a heavy scene to me. You'll be starting your A Level course in September. How are you going to cope with all that work, while you're dodging around having a clandestine affair with a married man?'

'I'm not doing A Levels. I've decided to leave school and go into modelling.'

'But you're too fat! When we were sunbathing the other day you were moaning that your thighs looked like sausages. You said you didn't need any Ambre Solaire, you'd just stick a fork into your legs and let the oil ooze out.'

Gail sits up, and tugs down her skirt. 'OK, so I am a bit overweight for photographic work. You have to be really skinny for that. But Miles says he has lots of contacts in the promotions field. You work at exhibitions, conferences, motor shows. The money's good, and I'll be able to travel.'

Juliette struggles with feelings of dismay, envy and loss. 'It'll be awful at school without you, Gail.' Outside, the village is deserted and silent, save for the rain dripping from the trees. 'God, I hate wet Sunday evenings. At about eight o'clock there's always the leaden realisation that it's school tomorrow, and I haven't finished that geography essay.'

'Never mind. End of term soon, and then I shall throw my velour hat on the bonfire.' Gail stands up. 'I must be off. I don't fancy bumping into your ma after her heart to heart with Annabel. Aren't you seeing Nick tonight?'

'He's working. He's very ambitious, you know. There's a job he's applied for on the *Birmingham Post*. Nick thinks it'll be a good jumping off point for Fleet Street.'

'Birmingham! What a dump.'

'It's a big conference centre now, I believe. I expect your modelling assignments will take you there quite a bit.'

'Oh ... yes ... well I hope Nick gets the job, then. It'll be nice to see a familiar face up there.'

The Head Girl is making a last ditch effort to perfect the opening bars of Schumann's piano concerto in A for the end of term concert this afternoon.

'De dum! De dum de dum ... de dum dum *dum*!' sings Gail in the adjoining Fifth formroom, wrinkling her nose as she hauls a sweat-stained T-shirt from the back of her desk. 'Phew, what a pong! Valiant of you not to complain, Juliette, when you partnered me at gym.'

'No, no, Penelope!' wails the music mistress. 'That first downward rush must be crisp and authoritative. Try again.'

De *dum*! The T-shirt is consigned to the wastepaper basket, along with an exercise book gummed with boiled sweets, a picture of Rod Stewart and a pencil case lined with chemical formulae, which Gail used as a crib in her chemistry exam.

Juliette is neatly parcelling up the pile of books which form her holiday reading project. She places it alongside her tennis racquet, gym shoes and a bulky folder of A Level art work. 'There'll never be room on the bus for all this junk.'

'You should have got Nick to pick you up.' Two apple cores and a mouldy orange are hurled into the wastebin.

'I hate him to see me in my school uniform. How can anyone look sexy in green gingham? I feel as alluring as Wendy's kitchen curtains.'

'Penelope! This will be the last piece you will ever play at this school. Everyone in the hall this afternoon will remember you for this alone. You must give it more *attack*!'

Gail bangs down her desk lid and holds up a lemonade bottle. 'Fancy a tot of vodka? I raided my pa's drinks' cabinet this morning.'

'Better not. I've got my end of term interview with Frances.'

Juliette hurries past the music room, where the harassed Senior Prefect slumps with her head on the keys. At the end of the corridor, she taps on a panelled door. Frances is seated at her desk, studying an enormous timetable, drawn in multi-coloured inks.

'Ah, come in, Juliette, and sit down. I imagine you must be feeling extremely elated, knowing that when you return next term you will have earned your place in the Sixth form. I shall not, I regret to say, be guiding you personally through your A Level courses, as in my new post as Headmistress I shall be more concerned with the wider running of the school.'

'Congratulations, Mrs Standish.' Champagne all round at the women's group tonight, then. Must remember to look in before Nick picks me up.

'I hope you enjoy the holiday reading I've set you, Juliette. No point in allowing one's brain to ossify during the summer break, is there? Are you going away with your parents this year?'

'I expect they'll take off for Yugoslavia as usual, Mrs Standish. But I'll be staying at home, with Gail.' Nick and I will have the run of Lavender Cottage. We'll make love everywhere. On the floor, on the stairs, on the dining table and oh, the bliss of doing it in bed after all that manoeuvring in his car! The joy of being able to spend a whole night together. Waking up in his arms . . .

' . . . pleased to tell you that we will be making you a prefect next year. Naturally, this will give you certain important privileges. You will have access to the orchard during lunch breaks. The prefects' room will, of course, be available to you, with the comforts of easy chairs and the tea making machine.'

'Thank you, Mrs Standish.' I'll bring him tea in the mornings, and we'll cook huge breakfasts together. Sausage, egg and fried bread. We'll eat it out on the patio, naked in the morning sun . . .

' . . . attendant responsibilities. Discipline in the dining room, for instance, has been extremely lax of late. It is up to the prefects to set an example . . . '

175

Juliette returns to the formroom to find Gail method-ically snipping her blazer to bits. She has reached the breast pocket. Juliette winces as she slices through the school crest. She remembers her first day at the school, walking down the drive in a blazer two sizes too big, which her mother insisted she would grow into. It seemed impossible then that she would ever reach the giddy heights of the fifth year, and wear deodorant, and possess womanly curves. That her creakingly new leather bag would one day be scratched and worn, with the handle broken from the weight of textbooks.

Now it's all behind me ... all those years of freezing on the hockey field ... cringing at the back of the physics lab hoping I wouldn't be called to the front to demonstrate, ... listening to the third year's cheer when I served to win the tennis tournament.

Next year I shall be in the sixth. A prefect. Another girl will sit at this desk, and break her nails on the rough wood at the side, and warm her hands on the radiator, and watch the cherry tree by the school gates coming into blossom.

'Don't you feel in the least bit sad or nostalgic that this is your last day?' she asks Gail.

'No. Why should I?'

'I don't know. I feel all mixed up and melancholy. It's almost as if it's me who's leaving, not you.'

'De *dum*! De dum de dum ... de dum *dum* DUM!'

'Better, Penelope. Much, much better!'

'Caroline, can't you turn that radio down? You'll wake Juliette, and it's taken me ages to get her settled.'

'Stop fussing, mother. The child must accustom herself to the normal sounds of the house. She can't go through life having radios tuned to a whisper just for her benefit.'

Fussing. The word was constantly on Caroline's lips. Never a hint of thanks, or gratitude, thought Rose, for the way I kept her household running smoothly while she lay around reading magazines. All this talk of exhaustion and the blues after having a baby! In my day, with the bombs falling around our ears, there wasn't time to feel depressed. We were all too busy pitching in and making the best of it.

176

You'd have thought she'd be pleased having her Mother there to help with the baby and show her the right way to handle things. But no, everything I did or suggested was wrong.

'I feed her when she's hungry, mother. All this rigmarole of set times is old hat.'

'Mother, please don't keep popping that disgusting dummy in Juliette's mouth. It's so unhygienic.'

'I know there's a cold wind, mother, but I must take Juliette out for half an hour. Fresh air won't harm her. She's warm and snug in her pram.'

Rose tried to do her duty as a Mother should, but goodness knew, it was hard going when all your efforts were totally unappreciated. Caroline never seemed to notice that the house was spotlessly clean, with the ironing kept bang up to date and all Leonard's socks neatly mended.

Not that you'd be favoured with so much as a grunt of thanks from him. Every day Rose made sure there was a hot meal waiting on the table when he returned from work. If Caroline was busy putting the baby down, Rose did her utmost to entertain him with little stories about the events of the day – how she'd had to chase down the road after the milkman because he only left two pints instead of three, and Mrs T in the bakers said little Juliette was the spitting image of Caroline, and how the wind got up and blew a tile off the roof, such a fright we got, it only just missed Juliette's pram but she just lay there and laughed, such a good natured sweetheart she is. But Rose might just as well have been talking to a brick wall. Unnatural, she called it, the way he wasn't interested in his own daughter.

And then there was that business of not having Juliette christened.

'It's shameful and heathen of you, Caroline. After all, you were married in church, before God.'

'Only because dad wanted to sock the neighbours in the eye. Anyway, you know Leo and I aren't believers. We don't even attend at Christmas.'

'I always go to the carol service. Even if there's a snow storm, I still battle my way through to the church. They dress the little choir girls up as angels, with golden halos and wings. They look so pretty it never fails to bring tears to my eyes.'

'If Juliette wants to be a choirgirl when she's old enough, and be christened, and go through all the rest of the mumbo jumbo, that's up to her. But I'm not making the choice for her.'

'It's lucky for you your father's away on a business trip. I dread to think what he'd have to say on the subject.'

'He'd thank me for saving him a tedious Sunday afternoon being polite to the vicar.'

Lester arrived home from Europe and spent two hours parading Juliette round the village green, telling everyone he met that she had her grand-daddy's blue eyes. Then he wheeled the pram back to Lavender Cottage and ordered Rose to pack her bags.

'But Caroline will never cope on her own,' Rose protested as the Daimler swept her away. 'She can't manage the house and a baby. Why, only this morning I found she'd forgotten to wind the child after her feed. You mark my words – '

'You're to stop interfering,' said Lester firmly. 'In my business, I show someone how to do a job, and then I leave them alone to get on with it. If you keep poking your nose in, they only resent it, and get slack.'

Rose did not dare point out that Caroline was not a junior clerk learning how to sort mail. She was a Mother. She had responsibility for a New Young Life.

But they'd find out. Within a week Caroline was bound to be on the phone pleading for her to come back and help out. Well I might, and then again I might not, thought Rose. If I did agree to sort out the mess, there would have to be changes. I couldn't stand things the way they were. It was affecting my nerves. Caroline so hostile all the time, and that husband of hers treating me like a servant. Worse, really. Sir Desmond would never have been so cold and ungrateful. It was quite touching the way he always had a smile and a kind word for me. But then he was a born gentleman. Not an upstart from a council estate, like Leonard.

After a month spent sitting by the silent phone, Rose formed the habit of taking the bus over to Maybrook once a

178

week or so. 'Just popping in to keep an eye on things', was how she put it to herself, convinced that stubborn pride (inherited from her father, of course) was preventing Caroline from admitting defeat.

Yet against all the odds, Caroline developed into a remarkably competent mother. As the healthy baby grew into a sturdy, cheerful toddler, Rose sensed that Caroline was deliberately putting distance between herself and her mother.

'She told me today to stop giving Juliette so many sweets,' Rose complained to Lester. 'I don't see that just one or two will make her teeth fall out. I never had sweets at all when I was a girl, yet all my teeth went before I was thirty.'

Lester merely repeated that she shouldn't meddle, and left for the council offices.

Rose washed up the dinner dishes, rinsed out the tea towels, and settled herself in front of the televison for the evening. She had an unfinished box of soft centres, and a new Barbara Cartland to read while the documentary was on.

She found as she grew older that she didn't mind Lester being out in the evenings. It was peaceful having the house all to herself. When Lester was home he was always so restless. He'd switch over to BBC just as Rose was engrossed in the ITV programme, spill cigarette ash on his chair arm, demand endless cups of tea and bang about if there was none of his favourite cake left in the tin.

But at least now they had Juliette to talk about. He was always interested in her progress, and every other Sunday they had a family get together, which was nice. Rose always gave them tinned salmon, fruit salad and chocolate cake for their tea. They never failed to say how much they enjoyed it.

Sitting by herself every evening, Rose had time to plan every detail of those Sunday visits. Which table cloth she would use. Which recipe for the cake. What she would wear. When she'd polish the sideboard. How much extra bread and milk would need to be ordered.

With all the arrangements straight in her mind, Rose would turn off the television and take her cocoa and biscuits up to bed. Lester usually came in shortly after midnight.

Rose was never asleep, though she pretended to be. She'd lie there in a light doze, listening to the clunk of his watch and cuff links on the bedside table, bracing herself against the draught of cold air as he flung back the covers.

She waited while he shifted position three times beside her, and began to snore. Then she was able to drift into sleep.

13

Fay flings open the bedsit door. She is wearing a see-through lace blouse and a tight satin skirt slit up the sides to reveal black stockings gripped round her thighs with purple garters.

Dismayed, Len dutifully thrusts his hand up her skirt and squeezes his eyes into a passable imitation of a sexy leer. Christ, doesn't she ever leave off? It never seems to occur to her that he might have had a heavy day and not feel up to a marathon of sexual athletics.

While Fay teeters back into the kitchen and stirs chestnut purée over a dish of unidentifiable grey meat, Len splashes a good measure of scotch into a glass. He places an extra patchwork cushion on the cane chair before he sits down.

At first, he'd been fascinated by Fay's little bedsitter. Charmed by the immaculate dolls' house kitchen, with all the bottles and jars neatly labelled in her italic handwriting. Intrigued by the long frilled curtain that concealed her clothes and the row of shoes all neatly stuffed with plastic trees. Yet the bed, by contrast, was covered in red satin sheets and a fake leopardskin rug. Overhead, a pink warmlite bulb glowed in a black fringed lampshade.

In the beginning, gratefully wrestling with his blonde mistress amidst a sea of scarlet satin, he had congratulated himself on landing such an exotic little piece. He couldn't wait to tell his mates at work about her.

But now the whole set up is beginning to look plain pathetic. Fay, poor kid, can't seem to make up her mind which role to play. Is she the budding *femme fatale*, drenched in Chanel No. 5, aiming to spend her spare time swinging from a chandelier? Or is she a girl just two years out of gymslips, keeping her home nice and clean and tidy just like her mummy does in Tring?

He pats Fay's plump backside as she darts in and out of

the room, lighting jasmine scented candles. It wouldn't be so bad if she'd only learn to steer a middle course. Stuff all this tarty, split skirt gear for a start. Or at least not tog up like that every time he comes round. It gets monotonous.

He's tried to tell her, too, that there's really no need to go to a lot of trouble cooking him gourmet meals. He's perfectly well fed at home. Frankly, he'd be just as happy to take her down the pub and get a fish and chip takeaway. But she looked so hurt, and went on in a small, disappointed voice about cooking with love for him, that he dropped the idea.

It makes him feel a heel, though, the way she spends so much on food, and booze, and sweet peas daintily arranged in little pottery jugs brought back from Lloret. Fay is only a receptionist. She can't earn much. On the other hand, there's no sense in making a rod for his own back by getting into the habit of taking her out for expensive meals. Caroline is no fool. She'll soon suss him out if he has less bread to throw around than usual. Or worse, if she finds a restaurant bill in his suit pocket.

Len had often wondered what Fay herself was getting out of their affair – apart from a hefty weekly ration of cock. What did she want from him?

The answer came when he was idly looking through one of Caroline's magazines one evening. Utter drivel most of these women's rags, but some of the photographs were surprisingly fruity. Then he came across a picture of Fay. Not her really, of course, just a busty blonde, garnished with a few bits of flimsy lace. She was decorating an article on *How to Win as a Mistress*.

If you are having an affair with a married man, Len learned, you must never, ever, attempt outright emotional blackmail on him. There must be no tearful scenes. No distraught calls to his office or home. And no bitchy remarks about his wife. It is essential to remain sexy, available, undemanding, and above all, cheerful.

Len threw down the magazine, feeling as if he'd just stumbled across his own death warrant. The article described Fay to a T. Especially all that guff about not shitting on the wife. And being an attentive listener.

Fay's jug-eared all right, Len realised. She clings to my every remark, sucking in the words, embracing them, analysing them, working out how to turn them to her own advantage. Yet when I mention Caroline, Fay listens in a different way. Then her silence is landmined with unasked questions, barbed with suppressed jealousy and spite.

As Fay bears in her steaming cordon bleu creation, Len opens the bottle of Beaujolais he's brought.

'It's Venison Ardennaise,' Fay explains anxiously. 'Only I made it with pork. I do hope you like it.'

'It smells out of this world,' grins Len, balancing the Royal Doulton plate on his knees. The meat tastes like stewed vinyl.

Fay's filled the plate too full. If she doesn't stop sticking her foot in his groin he's bound to tip the scalding gravy down his trousers. Doesn't she realise the sight of purple crotchless panties is offputting when you're eating? She's obviously been reading that bloody stupid magazine again. It's always loaded with insane suggestions about *How to Turn Your Man On*. He'd nearly walked out the night she'd greeted him wearing only a pair of rugby socks, and insisted on serving dinner in bed. Christ. All those crumbs gritting the sheets. And he'd got rice stuck under his toenails. It was only later, as he ran for the train, that it occurred to him to wonder who Fay had got those rugby socks from.

Fay watches him force down the last mouthful of vinyl, then immediately leaps up to remove the dishes and make coffee. 'I bought you some lardy cake,' she smiles. 'I know you can't resist it.'

Len appreciates that she must have footslogged for miles to find a baker in this part of London who makes lardy cake. How, then, can he explain that yes, he is partial to the occasional small slice of the stuff – but not great greasy slabs of it ritually plonked down before him each week. And how can he admit that it gives him indigestion? Fay regards him as the Great Lover, and G.L.s simply do not suffer from dyspepsia.

Len smiles at the irony. He may at heart wish Fay would drop the Mata Hari bit. Yet he hasn't the courage to destroy his own credibility by producing a box of Rennies instead of a packet of three. (Well, Fay says she's on the Pill. But he knows more than one poor sucker who's been caught by that one.)

He resents the brisk indifference people display towards his indigestion. The apprentices at work regard it as a strictly middle-aged complaint. And if he mentions it to Caroline, she is prone to whisk away the steak and kidney pud and dish up a bowl of bread and milk instead.

Fay serves the lardy cake on a blue and white flowered plate. Her heart-shaped face glows with the pleasure of pleasing him. She slips her arms loosely round his neck as he crams down what tastes like curranted blubber.

'I'll leave the washing up until the morning,' she murmurs throatily, unbuttoning her blouse.

They take their brandies to bed. He performs, as she expects him to.

Afterwards, he is not permitted long to relax. Already she is enquiring, in a voice loaded with lazy languor, if he will stay the night. When he says no, she makes a *too bad, but of course I wouldn't dream of pressing you*, face, and instantly launches her attack to make him miss his train. She tops up his brandy, offers more coffee and pulls the satin sheets up over his bare shoulders.

But he too has become a seasoned campaigner. He feels he deserves medals for his expertise in *How to Make a Dignified Exit from a Broad's Bedroom* . . . full of yearning regrets and promises to phone . . . and still catch his last train home.

There are little things to be done first. He straps on his watch. Declines the coffee. Drains his brandy glass. Visits the bathroom. Kisses her, and says she is beautiful. He pulls on his trousers. Strokes her brow. Tells her the evening has been one he will remember for ever. Slips into his shirt, his jacket.

She watches his every move, her brown eyes huge with the knowledge of defeat. He feels sorry for her as she concentrates hard on looking cheerfully sexy. *No recriminations, no pleading, no scenes. Remember, you want him to come back!*

He tidies his hair, using her comb. He kisses her for the last time, and swears he'll be in touch. She is wonderful. The evening has been fantastic. He will miss her and think about her all the time.

Outside, the rain has stopped but the wind is cold for late July. Len remembers to wave, and blow a kiss up at Fay's window. Once out of her sight, he huddles into his jacket and clutches his stomach. That sodding lardy cake. He can feel the leaden, fatty lumps of it congealing right now into the cholesterol which will eventually kill him.

I can't take much more of this, he decides. It simply isn't worth it. I won't phone her any more. I'll just drop out.

No, that won't do. She knows my address. She might start turning up and shouting the odds on the doorstep. Caroline would see her off, of course, but even so ...

I'll have to see her one more time and invent some reason why it's got to end. I'll pretend my wife wants me to take her to Paris on a second honeymoon. Fay will get the message all right from that.

Heartburn scalds his chest. Len curses loudly. He remembers lying in bed with Fay, avoiding the sticky stain on the satin sheet. He rested his brandy glass on her discarded purple garter and thought longingly of a soothing cup of cocoa.

I'm getting old, he realises, with relief.

'Paris?' smiles Caroline. 'Well ... why not?'

They are finishing Sunday supper outside on the patio. Len's hand hovers over the jar of pickled onions. He decides against. Not if he's indulging in cucumber as well.

'What about Juliette?' asks Caroline, throwing half a granary roll down the garden for the birds.

'She's already said she wants to spend the summer holidays at home.'

'But do you think we should leave her here, alone with Nick?'

'It won't be like that. She can stay with Gail. Anyway, it's up to you. You're her mother. You're closer to her than I am. You decide.'

'Mmm.' Caroline looks doubtful. 'You've got watercress on your teeth.'

'I just thought it would be pleasant if you and I took off

for a ritzy couple of weeks in France. We've been lugging Juliette around with us on holidays for fifteen years. We deserve a go on our own.'

'It is tempting, isn't it? Do you remember that little café in Montmartre where we used to order those garlicky mushrooms on toast? I have never tasted mushrooms like that again. Yes, let's go!'

'Good girl. I'll leave you to book it up, then.' Len stacks the plates on a tray. 'Coffee?'

'No thanks. Tea for me.'

'But you always drink coffee after a meal.'

'I know. I've just gone off it, that's all. They must have changed the blend.'

As they sip their tea Len warns her, 'That little cafe may not be there any longer. It's been a long time. Didn't Annabel and Miles spend last summer in France? Perhaps they could gen us up on the places to go in Paris.'

'They stayed at a château on the Loire. Annabel wouldn't be seen dead in Paris in August. Anyway, it's impossible trying to talk to her about anything except her divorce these days.'

'All settled is it? The last I heard was that she was sure Miles was fooling around with some *local tart* as she put it.'

'She still doesn't know who the girl is. Miles is playing his cards very close to his chest. But Annabel has moved out and is living with her twenty-one-year-old flying instructor.'

'What about her kids?'

'For the moment she's left them with Miles. She says she's dying for a dramatic confrontation with his little floosie, watching her face when she realises she's got to take on two stroppy twelve-year-old girls. Eventually, though, Annabel plans to pack the twins off to boarding school.'

'And what does she propose to live on? I can't visualise Annabel joining the ranks of the workers.'

'Naturally not. She intends to take Miles to the cleaners.'

Len is beginning to dislike the tone of this conversation. Quickly, he changes tack: 'We must take your new camera to Paris. I was looking at your snaps of Corfu. Some of them are really good.'

'They would have been better if mother had co-operated

more. I wanted her in the foreground, quite often, to give a sense of perspective to the shots of the hills. But she kept dodging out of the way, mewing that she had her old dress on, or the sun was hurting her eyes.'

They put her picture in the Sunday papers. It was the one she kept on the Best China cabinet, of her and Caroline at Bridley Bay. Lester was headlined in huge black letters as the *Suburban Swindler*. It was all there, for the entire neighbourhood to read. How he'd taken advantage of his position with the council to embezzle thousands of pounds of public money to spend on his Daimler, his trips abroad, his fancy women. Not just one trollop, either, but a different girl in every capital of Europe. The newspapers printed blurred pictures of them with Lester. Brassy pieces in low cut dresses, sitting laughing in nightclubs. One had a paper streamer wound round her neck.

Rose refused to go to the trial. She was so humiliated she drew all the curtains and wouldn't go out for weeks. Caroline was furious with her, saying it might all be a mistake. Lester was innocent until proved guilty and in any case she should support her husband, as Valerie Profumo had done. Rose thought Mrs Profumo was a fool. It infuriated her, the way Caroline posed for photographers on the court steps, wearing a different outfit for each day of the trial.

Rose knew he was guilty. The verdict came as no surprise to her. At first she slammed the door on all the reporters, but the young man from the Sunday paper seemed so understanding. He didn't brandish a notebook or push a camera into her face like all the others. He wiped his feet nicely on the mat, and offered to make her a cup of tea. She didn't mean to chatter on so much, but he was so sympathetic, it all came pouring out.

She hadn't even noticed the photo had gone from the cabinet until Maud Sprett-Davies brought the paper round on Sunday. Rose thought she'd die of shame. A monster they called Lester. A tyrant who'd womanised right from the early days of his marriage, leaving his wife and child alone every evening.

187

'I won't stand by him,' Rose was reported as declaring. 'He's better off in prison. It's what he deserves.'

But I didn't say it like that, wept Rose. The reporter had stirred his tea, and murmured, 'Some people would say you're better off without him, Mrs Scott-Peters. That prison is all he deserves after the way he's treated you.'

And Rose had agreed, because all her life she had found that it saved a lot of bother if you never contradicted a man.

After that came the nightmare morning when the bailiffs arrived ... Caroline and Leonard blocking the doorway, loudly insisting that every piece of furniture in the house had been bought by Rose, or given to her by Lester. It wasn't true, of course. In the end she'd had to sit on the stairs and watch the men carry out the treasures she and Lester had been collecting all their married life.

'He'll never be able to own anything else, you know. Not now he's been declared bankrupt,' Mrs Sprett-Davies informed Rose. 'What a mercy the house is in your name.'

At first Rose was touched and surprised that Maud Sprett-Davies continued to invite her round for coffee. But it was only, Rose discovered, so Maud could glean all the courtroom gossip from the horse's mouth, to relay to the rest of Laurence Drive over tea. Once Lester was in jail and the fuss had died down, the Sprett-Davies coffee pot ran dry.

'Buy yourself a little cottage near us,' Caroline suggested. 'Let's face it, that house was far too big for just you and dad. And you didn't really need all that old-fashioned, bulky furniture. We'll fix you up with some modern stuff.'

'Eventually, Lester will be let out on parole,' Leonard said. 'It'll be easier for him, coming to a new home, with no grim reminders of the past. You'll be able to make a fresh start together.'

That was what decided Rose to go as far away as possible. She shrank from the idea of Lester visiting her on parole. All the neighbours would know. No, she had no intention of making a fresh start with Lester. She never wanted to see him again.

Rose had felt an affection for Edinburgh since the time she accompanied Lady Evelyn there. The city attracted, said Lady Evelyn, such a polite class of people. Rose remembered the area Lady Evelyn regarded as most exclusive, and bought the first house the estate agent showed her there. She even made a profit on the transaction, and enjoyed herself choosing new fitted carpets.

A year later, Rose awoke to the knocking of the telegraph boy, and learned she was a widow. Lester had died of pneumonia in a prison hospital bed.

She didn't attend the funeral, even though Caroline sent the fare. Caroline wrote three times explaining that Lester would not have to be buried within the prison grounds. The service would be at Melford parish church. It would be just like anyone else's burial, with no shame or stigma attached.

I'm having a Fan Extractor fitted in the kitchen that Tuesday, Rose replied, *and I shall have to wait in for the man. The steam in there has been terrible. Every time I shine the tiles they're dripping wet again in minutes so I shall feel much happier when I've had the Fan done.*

There was no need for Rose to mention her new status to the neighbours: from her first day in Edinburgh she had pretended to be a widow. But having Lester safely under the ground made the phrase *my late husband* trip so much more easily off the tongue.

Gradually, she found herself inventing little stories about Lester. 'Every Saturday night, my late husband always gave me a box of chocolates,' Rose confided to the friendly girl in the newsagent's, as she paid for the soft centres. 'It's a tradition I like to carry on, you know.'

'If my husband hadn't passed on he'd have been glad to give you a hand with that,' Rose told Mr Logan when he came round to collect the rotten rowan branches that had overhung their dividing fence. 'He was at his most content just pottering round his garden.'

That evening, she treated herself to a small glass of Sanatogen and watched Mr Logan burning the branches. They should have been cut down ages ago, but presumably Mr Logan had more free time now he didn't have an invalid wife to look after. And it was really considerate the way he held off lighting the fire until she'd got her washing in.

She remembered that Lester had once built a huge bonfire. It must have been Guy Fawkes night. Caroline was wild with excitement. She lined up all her dolls on the grass, and when Lester lit the sparklers she stuck them in the frizz of the dolls' hair. Lester said they put him in mind of flaming Indians. It was the biggest bonfire in the whole neighbourhood. Tier upon tier of flames blazing just like the chandelier in Lady Evelyn's drawing room.

Poor Lady Evelyn was dead now, of course. She and Sir Desmond were killed in a plane crash, coming back from Switzerland. Naturally, Rose went to the memorial service in Chelsea. She didn't put herself forward in any way. Just squeezed in quietly at the back. She'd hoped to have a consoling word with Lady Evelyn's daughter, but the girl was so upset she was obviously in no fit state to recognise anyone.

Still, Rose felt sure Lady Evelyn was glad she'd come.

14

'Just who is this Duncan Logan?' Len demands.

'You know. Mother usually refers to him all in one breath as Mr-Logan-next-door. You borrowed a ladder from him once.'

Len chokes over his toast. 'But he only lost his wife a couple of months ago!'

'Hang on. I've just got to that:

' . . . *hope you will not condemn us for marrying so soon after Mrs Logan's death but we are neither of us young people and you never know how long you have left on this Earth.*'

'Does she say how she managed to bag the poor old bugger?'

'It's rather confused. I think mother wrote that bit with her foot. As far as I can gather, he was burning some rubbish, and she took him out a cup of tea. Then she rambles on about Lady Evelyn's chandelier and in some way I don't understand she was then led to offer Mr Logan a share of her Sunday lunch.

'*Mr Logan's Son Douglas and two Daughters Joan and Kathleen all gave us their blessing and urged us to marry now rather than wait so that is what we did last Saturday at the Presbyterian Church. I did not invite you as you are not Christians and have told me many times that you think it is a load of old rubbish. I wore a new deep rose dress with navy blue accessories and everyone said I looked very pretty and young. Afterwards we went back to the house for the Reception –* '

'Which house?' queries Len. 'His or hers?'

'His. *We will be living in Mr Logan's place as it is better equipped than mine. It has a double drainer sink and a telephone so I shall be able to call you up often.*'

'Bloody hell.'

'*There is even an extension in the bedroom. Before he retired, Mr Logan was in Telecommunications.* That's mother's way of

191

saying he was a telephone engineer. Oh, then she waffles on for pages about the wonderful spread Joan and Kathleen prepared for the reception ... *chicken, ham, trifle, three-tiered cake.*' Caroline turns to the last sheet. '*I am writing this on my Honeymoon Tour. We are Motoring through the Western Highlands and then coming south to visit Mr Logan's sister. He says I really must call him Duncan but I can't get used to that yet. We shall be arriving on the 26th and plan to stay in Maybrook for a week if that's not too much trouble.*'

Len pushes his mug across the kitchen table. 'The 26th? But we've booked to be in Paris then.'

'Well there's no way we can contact mother to put her off. We'll have to cancel Paris.' Caroline pours him a second mug of tea.

'That's impossible. They've made out the rota at work. If I start chopping and changing it'll throw everyone else out. And we've paid for the trip. We can't chuck it all in just because your mother ... anyway, Juliette will be around. Let her entertain the bride and groom.'

'Juliette would never stand for that. Anyway, it's not fair to lumber them on her.'

'OK. I'll try and fix it at work. But we won't cancel Paris. We'll just postpone it. We'll go in the autumn instead. I must say, though, you have to admire the sly old bird. Hooking a man, at her age! She must have something going for her.' Laughing, Len pulls on his jacket, and leaves for work.

Caroline bangs the breakfast dishes into the sink. How could she go and get married like that without even telling me, let alone inviting us to the wedding? What must the Logans be thinking of us all? What filthy lies has she been spreading about her family?

And now she's fouled up my holiday in Paris. It's no use Leo saying we'll go in the autumn. I shan't be feeling up to it by then. On our honeymoon flight over I was pregnant with Juliette and I was sick all the way. The cross channel ferry would be even worse. I could kill mother. Paris would have been the ideal setting to break my news to Leo. We could have sat by the Seine and made plans. Now I'm landed with the aggro of mother coming to stay, with the embarrassment of meeting her new husband, when she's cast me in the role of Goneril. And in the midst of all that I still have to explain to my teenage daughter that mummy is expecting a little visit from the stork ...

It has been an unsettling summer for Caroline, watching her daughter blossom from an ink-stained schoolgirl into a radiantly sexy young woman. She felt increasingly demoralised, standing as if welded to the cooker, waving cheerful farewells as Nick took Juliette out for 'walks'. Juliette sported a succession of skimpy sundresses, with the thin straps slipping down from her smooth, tanned shoulders. It was as if, thought Caroline, all that was needed was a slight pull on a single random thread and the sundress would fall off. No doubt that was exactly what Nick had in mind as they rounded the corner into the woods.

Never had Caroline felt so dissatisfied with her own appearance. Suddenly, all her clothes seemed dowdy or absurdly girlish. She haunted the make-up counter in Boot's, frittering the housekeeping on expensive moisturisers. She shampooed a red tint into her hair to conceal the grey, then worried in case the dyed white hairs glowed orange in the sun.

Conscious of her sagging boobs, Caroline invested in an uplift bra. Yet when she gazed on Gail and Juliette, their high young breasts firm and bra-less, she felt as seductive as an upholstered armchair.

How ironical, she mused, that Juliette should scorn bras. To think of the agonies I suffered, persuading my mother to buy me my first one. Holding my breath as the saleswoman measured me, fearful that the entire shop would burst into derisive laughter because I couldn't fill the longed for 30 A-cup. What triumph when I scaled the heights to a 36 B, and Annabel was still only a scrawny 32. And now here I am fretting that my big bust makes me look matronly.

Frantic, she fled from mirror to mirror in the house, searching for the image of herself as she wished to be. In shop queues, Caroline studied the faces and figures of her contemporaries, feeling elated if she spotted a woman who appeared more worn than herself. At the last meeting of the women's group she noted that Frances looked considerably older than her thirty-seven years. But that was perfectly in keeping with Frances's new position as headmistress.

The group was disbanding. Wendy said that after chasing round after the baby all day, she was too exhausted to go out in the evenings. Anyway, she went on coyly, she and Tim were trying for another child. Babs and her lover were buying a cottage in Devon. And Frances indicated that although she had total trust in the integrity and confidentiality of the group, nevertheless, as a Head, she could never be totally off duty, as little ears were always flapping . . .

Caroline paid no attention when she unexpectedly felt nauseous at the taste of coffee. But when she found herself reacting against alcohol and cigarettes then she knew, with chilling certainty, that she was pregnant. The pattern had been exactly the same when she fell for Juliette. It was too early yet to consult her doctor, or even use one of the pregnancy testing kits. There was no need. She was positive she was going to have a baby.

Caroline had stopped taking the Pill when she went to Corfu. It had seemed a sensible idea to give her system a rest from contraceptive chemicals. She had fully intended starting a new packet when she returned from holiday.

So why didn't you, Caroline accuses herself, searching for a clean teacloth to dry the breakfast dishes. Why did you put if off? Be honest, now.

Because Leo was involved with that girl. I felt jealous. Resentful. Left out. Yet it wasn't as if I cold-bloodedly decided to have a baby.

No, but subconsciously you deliberately placed yourself in an accidental situation by deferring going back on the Pill. At some point, during those hot summer days, you must have thought *I'll just let things drift. If it happens, it happens. But it won't be my fault.*

And now your own inertia has put you up the creek. What are you going to do about it?

Juliette will demand that I have an abortion. Obviously, it's embarrassing for a sixteen-year-old girl having to admit to her schoolfriends that her mother is expecting.

Leo will be in two minds. On the one hand he'll be

appalled. We're too old to go through all the palaver of soggy, smelly nappies and three a.m. feeds. And yet ... the baby will provide a convenient excuse to get him off the hook with his amorous lady friend. All the signs indicate that the great flame of passion is beginning to gutter. When his romance began, he'd go jauntily off to work, and thence to his assignation, wearing his nattiest underpants and a self satisfied smile on his face. Lately, though, the Centaur aftershave has been gathering dust on the bathroom shelf. He's been coming home earlier. He's been friendlier. And he's suggested this trip to Paris. Yes, blondie is definitely on the way out. A little bundle of joy would be the final boot up her backside.

But what about you, Caroline. What do *you* want?

Me? I suppose in truth I'd rather not make any decision at all. I'd prefer to just float along and let events take their course. I might miscarry. I've done that often enough in the past. I'll need to have tests, of course, as I'm entering a dangerous age for childbearing. The doctor might advise me to have an abortion.

If I do go ahead the baby will be just a year younger than Wendy's Arthur. We could take them both down to play on the village green swings. What a shock for all the other Maybrook women. Something for them to gossip about over their embroidery during all the little Samanthas' ballet lessons. One thing's for sure. I won't creep around looking ashamed of myself, trying to hide the bulge. I'll buy myself a scarlet maternity smock, and carry the whole thing off with panache. Pregnancy does wonders for my skin and hair, too. Perhaps I'll have it permed into a mass of frothy curls. I fancy a change of image.

But I shan't tell mother. If she couldn't be bothered to advise me she was getting married, then there's no reason why I should inform her about the new grandchild. I'll simply send her the birth announcement from the local paper.

'That's the most disgusting thing I've ever heard. You! At your age! What are my friends going to think? It's awful!'

'You've often complained about being an only child. I

should have thought you'd be pleased to have a brother or sister.'

'I meant a sister of my own age! Not a kid who's young enough to be my own daughter. What did dad say? I bet he's not whooping with delight at the prospect of a crying baby puking up all over the place.'

'Now he's got used to the idea he's quite looking forward to it,' says Caroline, omitting to mention that Leo is eagerly anticipating that the child will be a boy.

Juliette's cheeks are flaming. She spits, 'It was Nick, wasn't it?'

Caught off guard, Caroline is bereft of the wit to lie. Stunned, she blurts the truth: 'I don't know.'

She sits immobile as Juliette slams from the room and rushes upstairs. Caroline knows she should follow her daughter, attempt to explain and pacify. But her courage fails her. A moment later, as the front door judders, she feels only relief that the house is empty and the need for action mercifully postponed for the present.

She hadn't meant it to happen. *Of course* she hadn't. And it was just the once. If only Nick hadn't caught her at such a particularly vulnerable time ...

He dropped in one afternoon, while Juliette was still at school, to leave her some tapes. Caroline was sunbathing, and felt awkward at Nick seeing her in a bikini. She was convinced he must be comparing her with Juliette, contemplating all the wrinkles, the crêpey, drooping flesh of which she was so conscious. She took him into the kitchen for a cold drink and reached for the button-through dress flung over the washing machine.

'Don't put that on,' he said. 'You look very good as you are.'

She scoured his face for mockery. But his blue eyes were frank and admiring, travelling over the curves of her body with the confident interest of one who has made this journey many times before, in his mind.

He smiled. 'Do you remember when we first met? You were sitting outside, surrounded by clouds of pink flowers. You looked as if you were waiting for something – or someone – to happen to you.'

196

'It was the evening of the party,' murmured Caroline unsteadily. Damn him! Damn his sunbleached hair, his tight white trousers, his overpowering physical presence.

He said, 'I saw you and I wanted you. I still do.'

This was the moment for Juliette's mother to respond with an amused laugh, and a light put-down line. 'Frankly, what I want right now is a nice cup of tea. And a corn plaster. My poor old feet are giving me hell.'

Instead, she just stood there, silent, indecisive, looking at him. But he saw her moisten her lips, noticed the hardening of her nipples in the cotton bikini, sensed the quickening of her blood and the fire scorching through her . . . until all she wanted in the world was to be free of the bikini and naked with him on the cool tiled floor.

Sheer madness, she thought dimly as she lay with him, tearing, biting, clawing, lusting. Juliette would be home from school at any moment. Leo could easily return early from work. Yet common sense was drowned by feverish, frantic desire. Wilfully, she abandoned herself to frenzied passion, until at last she cried out and lay still, and soon the floor seemed hard and cold.

Juliette arrived. After rushing upstairs to change out of her school gingham, she joined Caroline and Nick for tea on the patio.

How did she guess? Caroline wonders wretchedly. We both made every effort to talk and act naturally. Besides, we weren't outside long. It began to rain, and then Nick took Juliette off to play squash.

I suppose Juliette has gone to have it out with Nick. He'll calm her down all right. He's not a silly kid. He's a man. He'll tell her it was only the once. That it meant nothing to either of us. Anyway, all the odds are against its being his child.

Even so, how am I to face Juliette? How do we carry on living under the same roof? She could force me to have an abortion. She might threaten to spill the beans to Leo.

Caroline sighs. I'll worry about all that when it happens. It's too much to think about right now. The first thing is to see what mood Juliette is in when she comes home.

*

I'm not going back. Not ever again.

Propelled by a white heat of rage and resentment, Juliette marches through the village, mentally slamming the doors on the old life she has left behind her. Plans and destinations blaze in her head like shooting stars, burning themselves out after a few brilliant moments.

Nick. I'll go and see the bastard. I'll tear him apart. No, hell, he's away on a job until Monday. Well I'm not going back to school. That's for sure. It'll be unbearable. Gail won't be there. She'll be swanning around in her new guise as a model, laughing at my prefect's badge. And I'd have to put up with Frances queening it as headmistress. Who needs two more years of claustrophobic classrooms and evenings spent toiling over stinking essays? And meanwhile my mother calmly prepares for the birth of Nick's child.

It should have been me having his baby. I wasn't on the Pill. After *she* made all that hoo ha about me going on it I completely rejected the idea. OK, Nick used sheaths, but everyone knows how unreliable they are. If I'd got pregnant he would have married me and taken me up to Birmingham when he started his new job. As things are, by the time he's finished his stint up there and got to Fleet Street, I'll have done my A Levels and be heading for some redbrick university. We'll be involved in totally different worlds. He's bound to have found someone else by then.

Anyway, it won't work out like that. There'll be no more school. I'm finished with Nick. And my mother. I couldn't live in the same house with that woman any more. Not after this. I'll get a job. For the time being I could make some money working at Fortune Pools. Oh, that's no good. Sharon rang, didn't she, and said the place had burnt down. God knows it was a firetrap. What shall I do, then?

Instinctively, Juliette has made her way to the railway station. Maybrook serves few destinations. From the trains due in the next hour she has a clear choice – non-stop to either Winchester or Waterloo. Knowing no one in Winchester, Juliette boards the London-bound train.

The door to the Bayswater house is open. Juliette is

surprised to find Dallow seated at a sewing machine, running up some kitchen curtains. The grey hair is swept lightly back into a knot at the nape of her neck. Instead of the customary garish velvet trousers, she is wearing a faded pink cotton kaftan.

Dallow observes her visitor's raised eyebrows at the sewing machine. 'Even I feel nesty at times,' she smiles. 'Don't worry. It won't last.'

'I've run away,' Juliette announces in a challenging tone. 'I didn't know where else to come.'

Dallow nods, and reaches into the fridge for a jug of iced lemonade. 'Grab some cushions from the other room, and we'll go sit in the yard.'

Dallow listens attentively as Juliette spills out her story. 'But how did you know about your mother and Nick? Or was it just an intelligent guess?'

Juliette breaks off a piece of long grass, and chews it. 'I didn't know for sure. When I accused her, it was really a shot in the dark. But I've found before that if I have just one or two vague things to go on, then I seem to be quite good at jumping to the right conclusion.'

'And what vague things made you suspicious?'

Juliette says slowly, 'Well, mum was always so unpredictable in the way she reacted to Nick. I mean, one minute she'd be all welcoming smiles, and as soon as he'd gone she'd turn on me and say I was too young for him. Then one day I came home from school and they were having tea on the patio. It was all outwardly quite normal, but I could sense a sort of electricity in the air that had never been there before. Mum seemed on edge. She kept fiddling with the top button of her sundress. It started to rain, and as mum stood up, she slipped on the paving. Nick put out a hand on the small of her back, to steady her. It was all over in a second, but there was something about the sight of them together that set off alarm bells in me. I mean, she didn't stiffen when he touched her, as I'd have expected her to. Instead, she relaxed against him, in a manner that suggested she was already familiar with the feel of his hands. I told myself not to be stupid. It wasn't as if he was caressing her bum, or tits, or being in any way provocative. But there's something so vulnerable about the small of a woman's back. The delicate way it curves. And when he touched her there, it was such an intimate, tender movement ... I felt betrayed.'

Dallow watches Juliette take a long draught of lemonade and wipe a hand across her mouth. She says neutrally, 'Of course, you can't be certain the baby is Nick's. If it was only the once – '

'Well I'm not going back! I suppose you think I should?'

'With the life I've led I don't consider I should ever advise anyone to do anything. What will you do? Get a job?'

'I expect so. But there's nothing I really want to do. I mean, I was planning to be an art historian eventually, but that's all washed up now. For the moment, I'd just like to drift around for a while and sort myself out. After all, that's what you do, isn't it?'

'Drifting around is an expensive business,' smiles Dallow.

'But how do you manage to live? What do you do for cash?'

'Ah. I am mailed a cheque every month by my husband's family in Boston. As long as I never set foot on American soil, or eyes on him, the money continues to arrive.'

Fraud! Juliette's blue eyes accuse her. You're not a free woman at all!

'I can see I've shocked you. You feel let down. Deceived.'

'I ... it's not what I imagined. So you can never go back to your home country?'

'No.'

'Don't you mind?'

'I mind more about remaining solvent, frankly.'

'Well ... can I stay here with you until I get myself a job?'

'You're welcome to camp on the sofa,' says Dallow. 'But you might find the place a little crowded. I've got a new man moving in, you see. He's younger than me. A widower, with two children under ten.'

'Oh. I didn't think you ever wanted to settle down again?'

Dallow pulls a wry face. 'After a while you get tired of travelling. You just want to arrive.' She jumps up. 'Have you had lunch? I've some left-over bean casserole in the fridge.'

'No thanks. Really, I'm not hungry. I'll just sit here for a bit, and think, if that's OK.'

'Help yourself. I'd better get those drapes finished before the mood deserts me.'

For an hour Juliette lies face down on the grass, lulled by the rhythmic whirr of Dallow's sewing machine. Then she saunters into the kitchen. 'Can I use your phone?'

Dallow shakes her head. 'Don't own such a thing. My in-laws' cheque isn't enough to cover the installation. It's a situation I hope will improve when my widower moves in. But there's a pay phone down on the corner.' She rummages in a tea caddy. 'Here's a couple of 10p pieces.'

'Thanks.' Juliette hesitates by the door. 'It's just that I feel I ought to phone mother. I don't want her calling dad at work and getting him involved in a great hue and cry. I'll just let her know I'm here.'

Dallow nods. 'Sure. Give her a wave from me.'

Caroline answers the phone at the second ring. 'Juliette! Where are you? Are you all right?'

'I'm fine. I'm at Dallow's place.'

'Oh. How is she?'

'OK. Well, a bit changed, actually.'

'Juliette, a letter came for you by the second post. I think it's your O Level results. Do you want me to open it and read them out to you?'

'No! No, I want to do it myself.'

'Shall I ... post it on to you then?'

'But the mail is so unreliable. It might take days.'

'That's the trouble. The service is terrible now, isn't it?'

The pips sound. Juliette rams in her last 10p piece.

'I don't think I can stand the agony of waiting. I'd better come home and learn the worst for myself, today.'

'You'd probably feel easier in your mind. Though I'm sure you've done well. You worked so hard. Oh, and there's a postcard for you from Granny. She says she's longing for you to meet Kathleen's daughter Tabitha. She says you're bound to get on like a house on fire.'

'She's got to be joking. I can't imagine me getting on with anyone with such a slimey name as Tabitha.'

'Yes, isn't it dire!'

201

'Look, I know you've been under a lot of strain recently because of Granny getting married and everything. But really, it's nothing to get upset about. I mean, now she's got a husband to take care of her, it takes the pressure off you. Solves an awful lot of problems, really.'

Pip, pip, pip, pip. 'I've run out of money. See you later!'

Slowly, Caroline replaces the receiver. It's all right. Juliette is coming home. They won't have a long heart-to-heart about the baby, and Nick. She and Juliette have never enjoyed that kind of, soul-baring mother/daughter relationship. Juliette will never forgive her, of course. The episode with Nick is bound to leave an open wound.

But for the moment, an unspoken truce will be declared, which will bridge the present quagmire and last as long as Juliette is financially dependent on her family. After that . . . Caroline sighs. She'll just have to face the After That when it arises.

Meanwhile, there is still mother to be dealt with. Caroline takes out her mother's last letter, and re-reads the rambling middle section:

Mr Logan's Daughters have been so good to me. They asked if they could call me Rose and I said of course my dears, for I have no wish to usurp the special position in their hearts of their own True Mother (God Rest her Soul). Joan has already invited us to her large Norfolk farmhouse for Christmas. She was shocked to hear I was all on my own last year and wants to make it up to me. Kathleen is quite the most beautiful girl. She has long black hair swept up on top of her head and she's very slender and dainty, just like a Ballerina. And always so well turned out. Her daughter Tabitha (it means gazelle, isn't that nice) is the same age as Juliette though much more quietly spoken. She wants to go to Domestic Science College and she was really grateful when I gave her my secret tip for making crisp meringues.

I don't think the first Mrs Logan was good at cooking for her larder is very poorly stocked and Duncan, Mr Logan, was so impressed when I told him I made your father a Battenburg cake every week of our Married Life. I don't wish to speak ill of the dead but it seems to me that Mrs Logan didn't make much of an Effort with her marriage.

Thankfully, her children have really taken me to their hearts. Douglas shows me such courtesy and respect, he is Director of a Plastics company which employs over two hundred people! Joan is a dear, kindly soul. She set my hair for me on the morning of the wedding. And Kathleen has promised to lengthen those lounge curtains I've been so worried about. (I shall be taking them with me as just between ourselves Mrs Logan had very poor taste in furnishings.) Kathleen said she was surprised you've never offered to alter the curtains for me Caroline but I told her you've never been clever with a needle like she is. Well we can't all be good at the same things in this life can we? I just count myself fortunate to have two such wonderful new Daughters. I've told them so much about you all and I can't wait for the day when we all get together for a nice big family gathering . . .

I bet you can't wait, mother. But I can. Forever, if necessary.

Caroline smiles as she folds the letter, and slides it under the hot teapot.